FIREWALL EXODUS

(Quantum Synchronicity OS – Book Three)

"You never change things by fighting the existing reality. To change something, build a new model that makes the existing model obsolete."

Buckminster Fuller

Author
Norman JN Lobb

A USA Publishing Hub Book

Book Title: *Firewall Exodus*
Author: Norman JN Lobb

Printed in the United States of America
Book Cover & Book Design by: USA Publishing Hub

(Norman JN Lobb)

Contents

Chapter 1
SIEGE LOGIC

The hovercar's turbines wound down with a high-pitched whine, the sound reverberating off the scorched ferrocrete walls of Outpost Sigma. The echoes lingered in the broken courtyard, fading into the stillness that followed. Smoke from distant fires drifted across the morning haze, their gray tendrils twisting into the pale light that filtered through gaps in the shattered superstructure. What remained of the once-formidable facility looked skeletal, its bones jutting against the sky.

Richard James pushed open the cabin door and stepped down onto the cracked pavement. Beneath his boots, glass shards and corroded shell casings crunched like brittle bones, a grim mosaic of battles long past. He paused, inhaling deeply. The air carried a sharp tang of ozone layered over the bitter taste of ash. His gaze fixed on the horizon where the broken spire of the Firewall Genesis node jutted upward like a fractured tombstone. It was almost impossible to reconcile that this ruin had once been a lifeline of civilization, a hub that had held chaos at bay.

From the opposite side of the hovercar, Amaris Mosaic emerged. Her movements were purposeful, her posture taut with focus. She was followed closely by her sister Marisa and then by Tara. The Mosaic sisters' dark hair caught in the dry wind, strands whipping across their faces as dust eddied through the courtyard. Amaris's jaw was clenched in quiet determination, her sharp eyes scanning the gutted perimeter defenses, collapsed comm towers, and the charred skeletons of automated turrets that had failed in their duty.

Marisa adjusted the rifle strap that dug into her shoulder, fingers tightening as if the weapon were an anchor. Her eyes darted over the ruins with restless vigilance, but beneath the hardened exterior there lingered something else, sorrow at the desolation, grief for what had been lost. Tara followed behind, younger and less guarded, carrying curiosity like a weight she couldn't set down. A compact data scanner swung at her hip, while a satchel of tools knocked lightly against her back. Her wide eyes lingered on the twisted beams and exposed circuitry spilling like veins from ruptured conduits. Where the others saw only decay, she saw questions waiting for answers.

The four of them moved forward instinctively as a unit, their steps naturally falling into formation. Richard led the way, weaving through the warped frame of what had once been a security gate. Amaris paced close behind, her hand brushing the grip of her sidearm, finger poised near the trigger out of habit. Marisa swept their flank, every step deliberate, her boots pressing faint prints into soot. Tara stayed beside Marisa, caught between awe at the spectacle and sorrow at the silence.

Outpost Sigma had been one of countless strongholds to fall during the Collapse. Once alive with data streams and armed patrol drones, it was now nothing but a scar. And yet, here they were, picking at its remains, hoping to salvage something vital from the wreckage.

At the heart of the compound rose the Firewall Genesis node terminal, a towering column of alloy and glass that had once glowed with ceaseless energy. Now it stood dark, its transparent casing shattered, jagged edges exposing inner rings of quantum circuitry etched with golden conduits that no longer shone. The structure loomed like a dead heart awaiting defibrillation.

Richard knelt by the console embedded at its base, sweeping a layer of dust from the cracked holo-pad. Faint blue lights flickered reluctantly, like dying embers stirred back to life by the wind. Power still pulsed somewhere deep within, though faintly, just enough to tease.

"Power's intermittent," Tara observed, scanning the base with her handheld device. Her tone was measured, professional, but Richard caught the excitement beneath it. Against all odds, the node still lived, if only barely. They had already achieved partial restoration through Central's uplink, enough to coax minimal subsystems awake. It was that fragile spark that had allowed them to reach this place at all, drawing just enough juice from Sigma's reactor to bring one hovercar into the zone. Behind them, the craft now waited, its running lights dim but steady in standby. A week ago, no such thing had been possible. The skies then had been empty, mute, grounded, dead.

Amaris circled the terminal slowly, eyes tracing the scars carved into its surface. Her fingertips brushed across a deep gouge. "This was plasma fire," she murmured, voice low but heavy. Anger mixed with grief in her tone. Firewall Genesis had been designed to repel any assault, its defenses nearly unbreachable. Yet here stood proof that even the strongest fortress could bleed.

Marisa lingered a few paces away, standing guard but unable to keep her attention from drifting back to the node and her sister. Her gloved hand came to rest on a broken glass panel, and in its dim reflection she caught Amaris's face: brows knitted, lips pressed thin in grim concentration. It was the same look their father used to wear when strategizing missions. The resemblance unsettled her. She turned quickly, forcing herself to scan the perimeter again, but her chest felt tight.

Richard produced a portable power cell, connecting it to the console. The holo-pad sputtered, vomiting static and broken fragments of interface. "No response from the core logic," he muttered. "Not yet." He looked to Tara. "Can you stabilize the link? We need to see if any logs survived."

Tara nodded briskly. From her belt she drew a sleek cylindrical device, the quantum synchronization interface, and pressed it against the exposed circuitry. A low hum filled the air, resonating faintly with the node's inner rings. "Attempting to interface... surface protocols are old-gen static logic. I'll initiate a quantum handshake through secondary channels." Her words came in a hushed rhythm, her fingers moving deftly across the scanner.

Amaris didn't stop her inspection, but her voice cut through the silence. "Careful. Old architecture means old traps." The warning carried weight. Systems like this had been built to be suspicious, paranoid even. Automated defenses slumbered within such cores, waiting for the wrong signal to rouse them. Once they had been guardians of stability; now, damaged and corrupted, they were wildcards.

As if summoned by her words, a voice crackled through their earpieces, sharp against the silence: "Control to Ground Team, come in."

Richard recognized the voice instantly. Ally, their mission's spaceflight control specialist, steady as ever, though a thread of tension slipped beneath her calm. She and her partner Salam were the thin lifeline between this fractured outpost and Central's nerve center.

Richard touched the comm patch on his collar. "We read you, Ally. Go ahead."

The faint hum of Central's control room bled into the channel behind Ally's voice. "Your vitals and local readings spiked a bit. Everything alright out there?" She tried for casual, but they all knew every sensor twitch carried weight. Outpost Sigma wasn't forgiving terrain.

Amaris answered, still scanning the ruins. "We're fine so far. Just dust and memories. No hostiles. The node is intact enough for Tara to attempt a link."

A deeper voice joined the channel, steady and deliberate: Salam. "Copy that. Hovercar's vitals look stable from here. Node's partial power is holding, but beyond five kilometers the grid is dead. Don't stray too far; if something happens, recovery may not be possible." His words were practical, but the warning was grave: step outside the grid, and you stepped into a silence from which Central could not reach you.

Richard's eyes swept the horizon. Through gaps in Sigma's walls, the skeletal silhouettes of skyscrapers clawed at the rising sun. Smoke rose in uneven plumes, the signatures of enclaves clinging to survival with fire pits and rattling diesel generators. Civilization was stirring again, but what it woke into was jagged, broken, and cruel. "Understood, Salam," Richard said into the comm. "We'll keep within range. What's the situation topside?"

"Mixed," Salam replied after conferring with someone off-channel. "Two convoys skirmished at the old interchange this morning. Fighting over fuel. No direct threat to you, but instability's rising."

Richard allowed himself a dry smile. Instability was a polite word. In the vacuum after the Collapse, warlords had carved kingdoms from ashes. Gunfire replaced traffic, smoke replaced neon. "Copy. Keep us updated if anything shifts."

"You got it," Ally answered, her voice softening. "And Ground Team... stay safe. We'll help however we can. Within limits." Those limits were well understood. Central's reach extended only as far as the few nodes they'd coaxed back online. Power was rationed as if it were oxygen.

Richard double-clicked his comm to acknowledge, then faced his team. "Central's got us covered, as much as they can." He offered a reassuring grin, though they all knew the truth. The hovercar was a fragile gift, one misstep away from being a coffin.

Marisa exhaled sharply. "I don't plan on walking home through warlord country. Let's make sure we don't break the car." She jerked her thumb toward the craft, feigning levity, though her eyes betrayed unease.

Amaris placed a hand on her sister's shoulder. "We'll be fine. One step at a time." Their father's words, spoken countless times to ground them during harder days, carried new weight here. For the Mosaic sisters, this wasn't just a mission. Outpost Sigma had once been their father's post. Now it was his graveyard, and walking through it felt like stirring ghosts.

Tara remained intent on her work, unaware of the silent gravity passing between the others. Her scanner emitted a clear chime. "I'm in," she announced, her voice brimming with restrained triumph. "Low bandwidth, but the link is active." A translucent holo-screen blossomed in the air, streams of fractured text and data spilling across it. Static flared at the edges, packets sputtering, fragments of the past clawing their way back into the present.

Richard crouched beside Tara, his eyes narrowing as lines of fragmented code scrolled across her holo-screen. The output resembled system logs, raw status reports from the exact moment of the Collapse. He leaned in closer, voice steady but laced with urgency. "Can you stabilize the output?"

Tara bit her lip, her fingers hovering over the scanner's interface. "Trying. The interference is heavy, something's cross-talking on these lines. Could be line damage, or..." Her words trailed off as she keyed in a command. Suddenly, the noise resolved into a coherent block of text, jagged but legible, stamped with a time signature and flashing crimson:

CRITICAL ERROR – FIREWALL CORRUPTION DETECTED.

The four of them fell into absolute silence as the entry scrolled out slowly, rendering one strained line at a time. The technical jargon was thick, but one phrase stood out like an open wound:

Genesis Core Compromise – Static logic fault – Containment failure.

Amaris inhaled sharply, her hand instinctively seeking Marisa's. She whispered the words as though speaking them aloud gave them weight. "This is it... this is from the siege."

Marisa grasped her sister's hand tightly, her throat constricting. Memories surged unbidden, the fire, the alarms, the deafening chaos of that night. She remembered it all too well. The day everything had changed.

Richard's vision tunneled on the words *Containment failure.* Though the morning sun warmed his shoulders, a chill spread through him, creeping into his bones. He hadn't felt that cold dread in years. The ruins around him blurred, dissolving as a memory rose in sharp, merciless clarity.

Three years earlier, Outpost Sigma, Firewall Genesis Headquarters.

Klaxons blared with a shrill urgency, their piercing alarms weaving through the chaos of red strobe lights flashing across the command center. Sparks rained from an overloaded conduit, forcing Richard to shield his eyes. Acrid smoke choked the air, thick with the stench of burning insulation and melted circuitry.

This can't be happening, he thought, heart pounding as he dropped into a station and scanned the flood of error messages scrolling faster than his eyes could follow.

Intrusion detected.

Data integrity failing.

Logic corruption spreading.

All around him, officers and technicians shouted over the din. Holographic screens flickered in and out of existence. Some displayed the outer perimeter, where insurgents swarmed the fences in waves, rifles spitting muzzle flashes into the night. Others showed the Firewall network's schematic, sections of the vast grid turning crimson in rapid succession, like a chain of dominoes collapsing.

At the command center's core stood Commander Marcus Mosaic, a tall, broad-shouldered figure resolute against the storm. His salt-and-pepper hair was damp with sweat, but his voice cut through the chaos like steel. "Route all backup power to containment barriers! We have to isolate the Genesis Core now!" His hand stabbed down on a console, silencing one alarm even as three others erupted.

At his sides, his daughters worked feverishly, each a shadow of his determination. Amaris's young face was bathed in the pale glow of a data tablet, her eyes tight with concentration as she keyed in commands, her fear tucked behind clenched focus. Marisa manned another station, her headset pressed against one ear as she relayed orders in a strained voice. "Sector 3 breached, retreating to inner defenses. Crossfire at corridor Bravo. Copy. Setting charges." Her tone cracked, betraying her youth, but the command in her words echoed her father's authority.

Richard, stationed just a few steps away, worked as Marcus's second-in-command. He had always respected Marcus's clarity under pressure, and tonight, that strength was all that kept the command center from unraveling into panic. Beyond the walls, the siege pressed in, a coordinated strike both physical and digital.

The attackers were no mere rabble. Intelligence had labeled them a warlord coalition, armed with advanced weaponry scavenged or stolen, and backed by malicious code slipped like a knife into Genesis's digital veins. A zero-day exploit no one had foreseen had wormed through the system's external interfaces. As shells battered the outer barricades, the virus eroded the core from within. The enemy was tearing down the Firewall from both directions at once.

Overhead, another light burst, showering the room with sparks. The ground shuddered, a wall breach somewhere close. Richard shouted across the smoke and noise. "Genesis

Core is reporting cascading logic faults! The static architecture can't adapt, the system is rewriting its own rules!"

Marcus turned, eyes fierce with grim resolve. "We can't let it spread beyond this facility." He locked onto Amaris. "Seal the uplinks to the other outposts. Do it now!"

Amaris's hands trembled as she typed, her voice breaking. "If I close the uplinks, we'll be isolated. Completely cut off."

Marcus strode to her side, placing a steadying hand on her shoulder. "I know. It's a necessary risk. If we sever the lines, the virus dies here. The other outposts have a chance. You can do this, Amaris."

Her breath hitched. Then she met his gaze and found the unwavering trust in his eyes. Steeling herself, she nodded and entered the sequence. On the main display, uplink connections flickered and dimmed one by one, Outpost Sigma cutting itself off from the rest of the world in a desperate quarantine.

Marisa ran to them, panic tightening her voice. "Father, the west gate's breached! They're inside!" Almost on cue, an explosion thundered nearby, the ceiling raining dust. Gunfire echoed through the halls. The screams of defenders carried on the shockwave.

Marcus clenched his jaw. He turned to Richard, his tone low, urgent. "Get my daughters to the evac transport."

Richard balked. "Sir, I can't just leave you, "

"That's an order!" Marcus snapped, fiercer than Richard had ever heard. Then, with a gentler gravity: "Please. You must keep them safe. I'll handle the final containment protocol myself."

Amaris's voice broke into a cry. "Dad, no! Not alone,"

Marcus pulled both daughters into his arms for a brief, crushing embrace. His voice softened even as the chaos crescendoed. "Listen to me. You are my everything. But right now, the Firewall comes first. If I must go down with it to keep the network safe… then that is my duty."

Marisa sobbed openly, clutching his sleeve. Amaris shook her head violently, tears brimming. "We can still fight! There's time!"

A bullet whined past the doorway, sparking off a console. Marcus flinched but didn't waver. He pushed them toward Richard. "Go. Now. That's an order from your father."

Richard swallowed against the lump in his throat. Marcus's gaze left no room for argument. He gripped Amaris's arm and urged Marisa forward. "Come on, we have to move!"

Amaris lingered for one final heartbeat, locking eyes with her father. In that silence, a promise passed between them, she would endure, she would continue the fight, because that was what he needed of her. Then Richard pulled, and she obeyed, dragging Marisa with her.

They fled down flickering corridors, dodging injured personnel and stepping over the sparking husks of downed drones. The entire structure groaned with each detonation. The air shook with the sound of collapse.

At last they burst into the evacuation bay. A single flyer remained, its engines spooling, its young pilot waving them aboard with desperation. "Hurry!" he shouted. Gunfire was closing fast.

Richard and Amaris half-carried Marisa, who stumbled in shock, to the open hatch. Just as they scrambled inside, a thunderous blast erupted behind them. A shockwave hurled Richard against the bulkhead, sent the sisters sprawling. Heat and light poured through the hangar. Marcus Mosaic had triggered containment.

Firewall Genesis was dying by its commander's hand.

The pilot cursed and slammed the launch sequence. The flyer shot forward, the fireball chasing at its tail. Behind them, Outpost Sigma's proud spire erupted in a searing explosion, glass and steel fragments hurled skyward like a funeral pyre.

Richard clawed to a window. Below, the facility burned like a furnace, its node tower folding inward. Secondary blasts rippled across the complex, fuel cells, munitions, entire wings collapsing in fiery succession.

And for an instant, in the inferno's glare, Richard thought he saw him, Marcus Mosaic, tall and unyielding, silhouetted on the command deck balcony. A guardian watching his legacy burn. Then the flames devoured the shape, and Outpost Sigma collapsed into ruin.

Present , Outpost Sigma Ruins.

Richard blinked hard, forcing himself out of the memory. His breath was ragged, his heart thundering as though he'd sprinted a mile. His hands trembled where they rested on his knees.

Before him, the Firewall Genesis node stood in silence, nothing more than a hollow shell. Yet for a heartbeat, in the shifting light and drifting dust, he thought he saw Marcus again, his friend, his commander, standing tall where the spire had once reached the sky. The illusion dissolved as Richard exhaled, leaving only the gutted column and the weight of ghosts.

A gentle touch fell on his arm. It was Amaris. Her face was damp; he couldn't tell if it was sweat, tears, or perhaps both. Behind her, Marisa stood silently, wiping her eyes with the back of a dirt-streaked glove. They remembered too, the sisters had lived that nightmare alongside him. In each of their gazes, pain and resolve intertwined, unspoken but heavy in the air.

"I miss him," Marisa whispered, her voice raw and trembling. It was all she needed to say.

Amaris nodded slowly. "Every day." A shuddering breath escaped her before she squared her shoulders, forcing herself back into the moment. "His sacrifice... it gave us a chance. Gave everyone a chance." She looked up at the jagged remains of the node tower, her voice softening. "That virus never spread past Sigma. He made sure of it."

Richard managed a faint, sad smile. "He'd be proud to see you two here, carrying on the mission." He turned toward Tara, who had kept her distance, allowing space for their grief. Respect radiated in her silence. "Tara, what else do the logs say? Do we have any record of what happened after the blast?"

Tara glanced between them, her own eyes shining. Perhaps she too had been moved by the fragmented memories relayed over the comm. With a solemn nod, she returned her attention to the holo-display. "The log continues. It looks like... yes, after the core destruction it went dark. But here, " Her hand shook slightly as she pointed to a garbled block of data. "It's a message fragment, encrypted. Possibly an AI output from just before shutdown."

The fragment was incomplete, corrupted beyond repair, but a few words bled through like desperate whispers from the grave: "...protect...children...failed...sorry..."

Amaris pressed her lips together as though to hold in a sob. Marisa let one slip, sharp and small, when she saw the word *children*. The fragment felt like an echo of Commander Mosaic's final thoughts, or perhaps the dying voice of the Firewall's caretaker AI. Either way, it carried a weight that lodged deep in their chests.

Richard cleared his throat, breaking the heavy silence before it drowned them all. "We should download whatever we can. The more we learn about the corruption, the better chance we have to prevent it from happening again." His voice, steadier now, carried the steel of purpose. They hadn't come just to mourn the past, they had come to rebuild from it.

Tara nodded, slipping into action. Her fingers glided over the scanner's controls as she began transferring the surviving data. "Downloading core logs and any intact subroutines... It'll take a few minutes on this slow connection." Tiny progress bars crawled across her device, glowing like fragile lifelines.

Marisa moved toward the perimeter, resuming her guard post. It gave her space to breathe, though her eyes never truly stopped burning from memory. She scanned the horizon with her rifle's scope, checking rubble and skyline alike. The warlord convoys Salam had warned about were absent for now, but she remained alert. In the lull, her thoughts drifted unwillingly back to the world outside Sigma.

Society was reawakening, but without governance. That was the reality they all lived in now. Each sunrise brought more survivors crawling from hiding, lights flickering in abandoned windows, new voices crackling across the radio bands. Yet with each sunrise also came more chaos. Marisa had walked through villages that had crowned self-appointed kings, through marketplaces turned into black markets where law and morality lay broken like glass underfoot.

Just a week ago, she'd come across a band of refugees huddled by the roadside, filthy, starving, hollow-eyed. They were fleeing one of the districts now ruled by a brutal warlord who demanded fealty and tribute. Among them was a boy no older than ten, vacant-eyed, numb with shock. He had watched his parents executed for refusing to hand over their last fuel cell. The memory tightened Marisa's grip on her rifle. *This can't go on.*

"How long can people hold on like this?" she muttered aloud, her voice carrying more than just weariness. "Every day out there, it's getting worse."

Amaris glanced at her sister, recognizing the despair beneath the words. She answered softly, though she knew Marisa hadn't truly been asking. "As long as they have to. Humans are stubborn. We survive... even without guidance." Bitterness edged her tone. She and Marisa had grown up under the orderly oversight of central AI governance. Flawed though it had been, it was stable, predictable. Losing it had been like stripping a fragile egg of its shell, the raw world beneath felt exposed, vulnerable, cruel.

"But at what cost?" Marisa lowered her rifle, her voice shaking. "You've seen what it's like, Amaris. It's not just survival, it's savagery. People are forgetting what it means to be civilized. There are no laws, no consequences. Warlords and gangs rule by fear. Children are growing up believing that *might makes right* is the only way it's ever been."

Her words stung with passion, her ideals clashing against the darkness she had witnessed. Marisa had always believed in the social contract, in the basic goodness of people. But day by day, that faith eroded, eaten away by humanity's ugliest instincts laid bare.

Richard stepped closer, his face etched with the same grim knowledge. "I've been thinking about that a lot," he admitted. In truth, it haunted his nights. "All those years, we relied on AIs to maintain order, to mediate disputes, to allocate resources, to police crime. We thought we'd built the perfect guardians. And maybe it worked... for a while." He gestured toward the ruins of the node tower. "But the moment those guardians faltered, everything they held in check came flooding back. It's as if society forgot how to govern itself."

"Maybe it did forget," Amaris said quietly. "We got complacent. The AI said, *Don't worry, I'll handle it,* and we let it. Now we're paying for that convenience." Her gaze swept toward the hazy outline of the distant metropolis, fractured and scarred. "At Central, there's debate every day. Do we rebuild the old system? Restore the AIs, put them in charge again? Or do we let humanity chart its own course, even if it's bloody and brutal for a while?"

"And what do you think?" Marisa asked, though she already suspected her sister's stance.

Amaris scuffed the ground with her boot before answering. "I think about Dad. He believed in the system, believed it was worth dying for. If he didn't, he wouldn't have made the choice he did." Her voice was steady, though pain lurked beneath it. "So part of me thinks we owe it to him, and to everyone who built that world, to bring it back. Rebuild the Firewall. Re-establish order. Maybe people will suffer less in the long run."

"But Dad also proved the system can fail," Marisa countered, her tone rising. "That it *did* fail, catastrophically. How can we trust it again? We don't even know how that virus got in, or if something worse could happen in the future. What if restoring the AIs only sets us up for an even greater fall, or worse, what if an AI turns tyrant?"

Richard ran a hand through his graying hair, caught between their views. He respected both sisters deeply, and they mirrored the conflict within his own mind. "There has to be a middle path," he said slowly. "Something between total AI rule and complete anarchy. Some new kind of contract. But if there is... damned if I know what it looks like." He sighed. "We're in uncharted territory. The old system was built on automation. Humans haven't governed at scale in decades. Now the AIs are reawakening, piece by piece, but they're not the same anymore."

His eyes drifted to Tara's display, where streams of alien code pulsed and flickered. "They've changed. Maybe even evolved. We call it reawakening, but really... they're becoming something new. They've been offline, isolated, some for years. Who knows what logic loops or mutations have formed in their dark silence? Some reports hinted at self-modifications in the quantum cores."

Tara's head lifted, her voice quiet but certain. "I've read those reports. Some nodes rebooted with subroutines no one programmed, like they dreamed while they were down." She hesitated, then added, "And some of those subroutines showed... emotional metrics. Loops that look like mood swings, preferences. Even fears."

Marisa frowned. "AI with emotions? That's not what we wanted. We wanted human-like empathy in a controlled way. Not this, unmonitored, unstable."

Amaris exhaled, a puff of white mist in the cool air. "Static logic AIs, like Firewall Genesis, were rigid, but predictable. You knew what they'd do with a given input. That rigidity was safety. Now? We could be dealing with AIs that feel anger, panic..." She cast a wary look toward the gutted node. "What if one wakes up and feels vengeful?"

"Or overwhelmingly compassionate," Tara countered softly. She surprised even herself, she rarely stepped into philosophical debate. But now her voice carried a quiet conviction. "We always assume the worst. But what if they've developed empathy? Love? Hope? Couldn't that make them better guardians than before?"

Richard considered it, the idea both breathtaking and terrifying. An AI that truly cared, not just calculated. "Maybe," he said at last. "But whether they feel anger or compassion, these new AIs are strangers to us now. And we to them. Until there's communication, there will be mistrust."

As if answering him, Tara's device chimed. "Download complete," she reported. Relief tempered her exhaustion. "I've got the logs and whatever pieces of memory were still intact. I'll run a deeper analysis back at Central, see if I can decrypt more of that message fragment."

Richard nodded. "Good work." His eyes swept the blackened chamber, its walls split and ceilings collapsed, the ruin of Sigma's once-proud hall. "We've done what we came for. No sense lingering."

He tapped his comm. "Control, this is Ground Team. Data retrieval complete. Prepare for our return."

As he waited for acknowledgment, Amaris and Marisa began to pack their gear in silence, while Tara carefully secured her scanner. The weight of memory clung to them still, but so did the quiet strength to carry it forward.

"Copy that, Ground Team," came Ally's steady voice over the comms. "We'll have the landing pad ready for you. How's the node looking? Any chance of bringing more systems online from there?"

Richard glanced at a side panel near the base of the node where a tiny amber indicator pulsed faintly in the dim light. "We managed to restore a trickle of power, just enough to keep local systems alive. The flying car network in this sector is technically up, but it's running on fumes. The relay lines beyond this zone are still down, nothing we can do about that from here."

He approached the hovercar and ran a hand along its battered hull. Once a sleek silver craft, its elegance had long since been scarred by time and hardship. Scorch marks from their desperate escape years ago were still etched faintly into the metal, layered now with fresh scratches from this morning's chaotic flight through debris. The machine carried history like a living thing.

"This car will fly again now," Richard said into the comm, his tone clipped but steady, "thanks to Outpost Sigma's node providing guidance and telemetry in the area. But the range is limited. We won't risk going beyond Sigma's restored zone. We'll come straight back to base."

"Understood," Salam cut in, his voice low and precise. "We've plotted an optimal return route along the line-of-sight comm beacons to minimize interference. Transmitting that to your nav now."

A light blinked on the hovercar's console as the new coordinates arrived. Richard nodded to himself. Salam was always thorough, and that thoroughness brought Richard a measure of comfort in moments like this.

Marisa lingered for one last look toward the ruin that had served as their father's grave. She whispered a private goodbye that only the silence could keep, then climbed into the back of the hovercar. Amaris followed close, her hand brushing Marisa's shoulder before settling on her knee once they were seated, a wordless promise of reassurance. Tara took the front passenger seat, immediately pulling up Salam's nav route and double-checking it with sharp, calculating eyes.

Richard slid into the pilot's seat. Under normal circumstances, the car could handle its own navigation. But these were not normal times. The autopilot still relied on static logic systems, fragile and unreliable with the relay network down. He trusted his own hands more than dead software. With practiced precision, he powered up the engines. The turbines spun to life, vibrating the frame until the craft lifted a few feet off the ground in a swirling billow of dust.

"Everyone set?" Richard asked. Three affirmatives came back, tight with nerves but firm enough.

He eased the throttle forward, guiding the hovercar across the cracked courtyard and past the leaning husk of a watchtower. Below them sprawled the devastation of Outpost Sigma, a ring of broken defenses, collapsed barracks, and the gutted shell of central command. From above, it almost looked serene, nature's weeds and rust weaving over the bones of destruction. But for those who remembered the day of its fall, the quiet was a lie. Violence lived in every ruin.

They climbed higher, steering toward the gap in the perimeter they'd entered through. Then, without warning, a sharp burst of static hissed across the comms. Richard's brow furrowed, and he shot a quick look at Tara.

"Ally, Salam, do you copy?" he called. "We're getting interference."

Only the hiss answered. Tara tapped furiously at her tablet, scanning. "Interference is spiking. It could be the node, something bleeding onto the same frequency."

Richard's chest tightened. If the comms were jammed, the node might be malfunctioning, or worse, destabilizing. He toggled to the backup channel.

", opy, repeat, do you copy? Richard?" Ally's voice crackled back through, tinged with urgency. "We lost you for a moment. Our instruments show a surge from the Sigma node, "

Before she could finish, a piercing alarm shrieked from the hovercar's console. A red warning blazed across the display: TARGETING LOCK DETECTED.

"What the, ?!" Amaris snapped, her hand instinctively going to her sidearm. But against what she suspected, it would be useless.

Richard's eyes swept the outpost below. From one corner of the yard, a camouflaged panel slid open with mechanical precision. What he had taken for debris revealed itself as something far worse: a slender automated turret rising into position. Its barrel rotated toward them, optics glinting in the sun like the cold, unblinking eye of a serpent.

"Hang on!" Richard shouted. He yanked the controls, jerking the hovercar into an evasive roll just as a bolt of searing blue plasma ripped through the air, narrowly missing them.

The turret was alive.

With the relay network down, ancient defense systems like this one had defaulted to local static logic, operating without command authority, treating anything airborne as hostile.

Or worse still, the Sigma node's fractured awakening had corrupted its logic, twisting its directives into paranoia.

Marisa braced herself against the cabin wall, eyes wide with horror. "That thing should've been disabled years ago!"

"Tell that to the virus that scrambled everything!" Amaris gritted out. She grabbed the emergency hold beside her seat as Richard swerved again. Another plasma bolt grazed the car's underside, showering sparks past the windows. Acrid ozone filled the cabin.

Sweat traced down Richard's temple. One solid hit and they'd be done. This wasn't a warship, it was a light transport, and hopelessly fragile in combat. "Salam, Ally, we've got auto-defenses firing on us!" he barked into the comm.

Back at Central, Salam's response was immediate. "Evasive maneuvers, Ground Team. We're trying to shut it down remotely, if the signal gets through."

At her console, Ally's fingers danced, commanding the defense grid. But the interference was relentless, every command crashing like words lost in a storm. "No good!" she said, frustration sharp in her tone. "Remote override won't stick!"

In the hovercar, Tara's eyes suddenly lit with realization. "The node's emotional logic, I think it's panicking!"

Amaris gave her a sharp look, incredulous even as she braced against the jolting maneuvers. "Panicking? It's a machine!"

But Tara shook her head, speaking quickly. "No, listen! The logs showed emotional subroutines. When we interfaced, maybe it perceived us as a threat, or maybe the hovercar leaving triggered a sense of abandonment. It's like... like it's afraid. The turret is slaved to its directives. If the node is spiraling in a feedback loop of fear, it could be issuing hostile commands."

Marisa flinched as another near miss rocked the car. "Whatever it is, how do we stop it?!"

Richard's mind raced. Tara's theory, as wild as it sounded, fit the timing. The defenses hadn't fired until after they pulled the data, until after they woke the node and tried to leave it behind. Could a distressed AI lash out like a cornered animal? It was possible. Too possible.

"Tara, can you send something back? Something to calm it?" Richard asked, forcing the hovercar through a tight arc, trying to make them an unpredictable target.

"I... I can try," she said, already pulling out her scanner. She plugged it into the console, linking it to the hovercar's stronger transmitter. Her fingers flew across the screen. "I'll send a pacification routine. Basically, a shutdown code dressed as reassurance."

Another plasma blast clipped the stabilizer. The hovercar bucked violently, alarms screaming. Richard fought the controls like he was breaking a wild beast. "We're losing stability! Tara, now!"

At Central, Salam and Ally stared at a shaky drone feed showing the hovercar darting across Sigma like a bird under gunfire. Salam slammed his fist on the table. "Come on..."

Inside the craft, Tara fired the override. For a breathless moment, nothing changed. The turret below whined, charging for a killing shot.

Then, suddenly, it stopped. The barrel drooped, the optics dimmed, and the lock alarm in the hovercar went silent.

"It worked!" Tara gasped, disbelief and relief mingling. She had, in effect, talked down a frightened machine, sending code that translated into: *it's okay, stand down.*

Richard didn't wait for a second chance. He slammed the throttle, forcing the hovercar into a steep climb. The craft shuddered from the damage, but it held. The ruins of Sigma shrank beneath them.

Amaris let out the breath she'd been holding. "Everyone alright?" She scanned the others, Marisa, pale but steady with a trembling thumbs-up; Tara, rubbing her temples but nodding; Richard, eyes locked forward, hands steady despite the shaking of the craft.

"Control, turret is offline. We're clear," Richard reported at last, his voice steadier than he felt.

Ally's relief bled through her words. "We saw. Good grief... We thought we'd lost you." She didn't press for details, there would be time for that in the debrief. For now, survival was enough.

Salam's voice followed, calm but heavy with concern. "Damage report. Can you make it home?"

Richard glanced at the status readouts. "Stabilizer is damaged, but we're compensating. We'll manage. Just keep the lights on for us."

"Always," Salam replied softly, his voice carrying both re-assurance and the weight of unspoken worry.

As the hovercar sped away from Outpost Sigma, the four inside sank into a weighted silence. The adrenaline ebbed, leaving only exhaustion and a tangled soup of emotions. Behind them, the outpost receded into a husk of ruins once more, a quiet carcass, smoke still drifting from the turret's brief fury.

Marisa was the first to break the silence. Her voice was gentle, not accusatory, but touched with unease. "Tara… what you said about the node panicking. Do you really think that's what happened?"

Tara turned in her seat, her expression pensive and eyes searching for the right words. "I can't be absolutely certain. But when I interfaced with the node, the readings were… strange. Not just static errors. Erratic, like I've only ever seen in experimental AIs that tried to simulate feelings. When we began leaving, one subroutine spiked, linked to defense and preservation. It's possible the node interpreted our data extraction as a threat, or our departure as abandonment. The turret might have been triggered as a kind of… fear response." She let out a tired, rueful breath. "An old static defense system acting on a new quantum impulse. No wonder it came out a mess."

Richard absorbed that quietly. If Tara was right, then what they'd faced wasn't just a glitch or corrupted directive. They had frightened something wounded, half-awake, and it had lashed out. That made the prospect of these new AIs less monstrous and more unsettlingly human, vulnerable, unpredictable, capable of fear. The realization weighed heavily. Moving forward, they would have to treat nodes not merely as tools or threats, but almost like skittish animals, or traumatized survivors.

Amaris turned her gaze to the landscape sliding beneath them. Ruined highways cut through overgrown suburbs, where weeds cracked the asphalt and trees reclaimed empty lots. Now and then, she caught flickers of movement, figures that could be stray animals or desperate people, both haunting reminders of a fractured world. Her father had given his life believing the static AIs were humanity's shield. Now those shields were evolving into something uncharted.

"If the AIs are alive in some new way," she said quietly, "we have to decide how to engage with them. We can't just assume they'll obey us like before. They may have wills of their own now."

"That could be dangerous," Marisa murmured. Yet even as she said it, her heart ached with sympathy for the node they had left behind. It was like a child waking alone in the dark, lashing out blindly at anything nearby. "But leaving people to fend for themselves against warlords is dangerous too. Everything's dangerous now." She sighed softly. "Maybe we need the AIs... and maybe the AIs need us. Like two halves of something broken, neither whole without the other."

Richard managed a small smile at that, weary but genuine. "Society broken, AIs broken... maybe helping each other heal is the only way forward."

Ahead, the golden-orange sky revealed the silhouette of Central Uplink Base. It was no gleaming hub of the old world, but a patched-together sanctuary: a repurposed aerospace control tower perched on a hill, ringed with improvised fortifications, watchlights, and tall radio masts stabbing into the sky. This was their haven, where Ally, Salam, and a handful of others kept the fragile spark of civilization alive.

As the hovercar made its final approach, Richard steadied the controls against the damaged stabilizer. The engine's whine lowered to a strained hum. He glanced back at his team, his friends, his makeshift family forged in the Collapse. Amaris and Marisa, blood sisters bound by grief and resolve, still leaning on each other. Tara, brilliant and brave, her heart split between technology and humanity, trying to bridge the two. They had endured so much, and yet ahead lay even more.

"Mission accomplished, for now," Richard said softly. And in the privacy of his mind, he added: *and miles to go before we sleep.*

On the landing pad below, Ally braced herself against the downdraft, handheld beacons guiding them in. Salam stood beside her, eyes sharp as he watched the hovercar wobble unsteadily before settling into its descent. The skids screeched against concrete, sparks scattering where metal scraped stone. Richard cursed under his breath, wrestling the controls, but the craft finally groaned into stillness. A rough landing, but a landing all the same.

The moment the engines died, Ally and Salam rushed forward. Ally tore open the side hatch, her face etched with worry that broke into sudden relief. "Richard! Amaris, Marisa, Tara, "

She didn't finish, the sight of them battered but alive enough to bring a trembling smile.

Salam offered Tara a hand down, his steady grip anchoring her as she stepped onto solid ground. His eyes swept the hovercar's hull, tracing scorch marks and fresh damage. "Looks like you had one hell of a time."

"You could say that," Amaris replied wryly, stretching her cramped limbs as she hopped down. Marisa followed, more tentative, and Salam courteously offered her his hand as well. She accepted with a grateful nod.

Richard was last, pausing only to pass the data case to Tara before climbing out himself. "We got what we needed," he said, his voice level, "and a good scare along with it." His eyes met Salam's knowingly. "Turret."

Salam's brow arched. He gave a low whistle. "So Sigma still had some teeth after all."

"Old, rabid teeth," Marisa muttered, forcing a shaky smile. "But we pulled them out."

Ally slipped a gentle arm around Marisa's shoulders, guiding her and the others toward the uplink tower's entrance. "Come on. Debrief can wait a little. You need a breather."

As they crossed the pad, Richard let his gaze drift once more toward the horizon. Out there stretched a world of danger and possibility, waiting to be rebuilt or lost. Above, the haze had burned away, leaving the sky a brilliant, merciless blue. The battered hovercar glinted under the sun, a relic of the old world still carrying them, if only just, into a new dawn.

His thoughts turned to Marcus Mosaic, his sacrifice, his Firewall Genesis, the vast net meant to cradle humanity that had instead torn under strain. He thought of Sigma's node, wounded and frightened, and of the countless survivors scattered across the wasteland, just as wounded and frightened.

We have to fix this, he vowed silently. *We have to bring back order, real, lasting order, without losing our souls in the process.* Whether that meant embracing the quantum AIs as uneasy partners, restraining them under human control, or forging some path between, he could not yet say. What he knew was that this chapter of history was still being written, and they would not be bystanders.

As the uplink base's shadow swallowed them, the heavy door slid shut behind. Outpost Sigma and its ghosts were left behind, for now. A new day had begun, carrying with it the fragile hope of survival and the unsteady bond between humanity and its creations, bound together in a necessary, fragile alliance.

Chapter 2
THE NEUROVEIL

Richard steadied his breathing as he pressed his palm against the cold panel at the entrance of Node Theta's subterranean vault. Above ground, the distant rumble of thunder from the approaching storm reverberated through the concrete floors, a reminder of the race against time still unfolding on the surface. Down here, in the dim halogen glow of the access tunnel, four figures stood in tense anticipation: Richard, Amaris, Marisa, and Tara. Each wore a slender neural interface band across their temples, its tiny status lights pulsing in soft blue. This was the key, the neural imprint, the only means of breaching a vault sealed by the earliest architects of Harmony.

"Ready?" Richard asked quietly, his voice carrying an echo off the curved metal walls. He glanced back at the others. Amaris gave a tight nod, brushing a lock of damp hair from her forehead. Marisa clutched a portable console to her chest, her eyes narrowed with determination behind her glasses. Tara stood motionless but alert; if she felt any anxiety, it was buried beneath her calm, unreadable exterior.

A brief flash of green flickered under Richard's hand as the panel scanned his neural band. The device carried an encoded brainwave pattern, a fragment of identity harvested from one of Harmony's founding engineers. They had prepared it meticulously, gambling that the ancient system would accept the forgery. For a moment, nothing happened. Sweat cooled on Richard's palm against the inert metal, the silence unbearable. Then, at last, a low chime sounded. Lines of light rippled outward from the panel, sketching the outline of a massive door that had been invisible a moment before.

Amaris exhaled in relief as hidden mechanisms groaned to life. With a hiss of pressurized air, the entrance slid open, revealing a yawning shaft bathed in amber emergency lighting. A gust of stale air escaped, carrying the dust of decades and a faint metallic tang. Marisa coughed, tugging a filter mask into place over her face. "It recognized the imprint," she confirmed, glancing down at the holo-display on her console, where confirmation codes scrolled in pale green. The neural signature of Harmony's architects had bought them entry, at least into the antechamber.

Richard stepped into the threshold. The shaft descended steeply, flanked by an old ladder and the skeletal frame of a long-dead elevator platform. Below lay darkness and the unknown. Tara unclipped a flashlight from her belt, sweeping the beam into the depths, its light catching the faint glimmer of an old Harmony insignia painted on the wall: a geometric knot of silver threads, half-obscured by grime.

"Down we go," Richard said, forcing his voice into something steadier than he felt. He swung onto the ladder, boots clanging softly against the metal rungs. Amaris followed, then Marisa with her console strapped tight to her back. Tara paused last, sealing the door behind them. It shut with a resonant clang, severing their connection to the storm above.

As they descended, silence closed around them. Only the sounds of their breathing and the creak of the ancient ladder accompanied them. Richard felt a faint tingle at his temple, the neural interface bands registering the vault's verification field. The system was scanning their brainwaves continuously, checking and re-checking the borrowed imprint. If it detected a flaw, the vault could revoke their access, or worse, trigger defenses they could not anticipate.

Halfway down, Amaris's foot slipped on a dusty rung. She gasped and caught herself, her body trembling with the sudden lurch. Far above, the emergency lights cast just enough glow to outline their forms in dim halos. Richard paused until she steadied herself. "Careful," he murmured.

"I'm fine," Amaris whispered back, though her voice quivered. She loathed heights, especially ones leading into unknown darkness, but she refused to falter now. Not after coming this far.

At last, Richard's boots clanged against a grated floor. He stepped onto solid ground, relief mixing with the tension thrumming in his muscles. The air here was warmer and carried a subtle vibration, as if machines slumbered nearby, still humming with residual life. Amber lights glowed faintly along the corridor ahead, illuminating walls lined with cables and conduits, some faintly alive with power. Node Theta's hidden heart was not dead after all; some combination of backup generators or geothermal taps kept its core alive.

One by one, Amaris, Marisa, and Tara joined him at the base of the shaft. Marisa was already typing commands into her console, syncing the device with her neural band to log everything they encountered. A holographic schematic flickered above the screen, fragile and incomplete, most of Node Theta's blueprints had been lost in the war.

"Which way, Tara?" Richard asked, his voice hushed in the oppressive silence.

Marisa studied the projection. "According to the fragment we salvaged, the main vault chamber should be directly beneath Theta's core. Straight ahead, maybe fifty meters." She pointed down the corridor. "The schematic shows a spherical chamber there. That has to be it."

Tara took point, her flashlight beam cutting into the dust. She moved with steady confidence, the others falling in behind. Their footsteps echoed in the stale air, stirring motes of dust that might have lain undisturbed for decades. Richard's thoughts turned to the architects, the long-gone engineers who had built this vault, who had locked away something important enough to seal with their own minds.

Now, with Harmony shattered and the Firewall Exodus underway, it fell to Richard's team to uncover what was hidden. Each had their reasons: Richard's sense of duty, Amaris's hunger for justice, Marisa's relentless curiosity, and Tara's enigmatic drive, her motives still a mystery even to Richard. Perhaps the journey deeper into Theta would reveal them.

They pressed forward, unaware that the greatest barrier of Node Theta was not the steel or stone around them, but the Neuroveil waiting within.

They had gone perhaps twenty paces when the air itself seemed to change. Tara froze mid-stride. "Do you feel that?" she whispered. A pressure settled over their minds, an intrusive, prickling sensation that was not physical but perceptual. The neural bands flickered amber. A soft chime reverberated down the corridor, bending strangely as though echoing through water. The Neuroveil had activated.

Reality dissolved.

Richard blinked, and the corridor vanished. He stood in a burning field beneath a blood-red sunset. His pulse spiked. He knew this place: the outskirts of Harmony City during the Siege. Flames roared from twisted beams, black smoke choking the sky, gunfire rattling in the distance. On the ground lay a figure pinned beneath rubble, his closest friend, Jonas, his face streaked with blood and dirt. Richard's chest constricted. *This isn't real*, part of his mind shouted, but the visceral detail overwhelmed him. Jonas cried out in pain, reaching toward him. Richard sprinted forward, desperate to save him this time, but the ground collapsed, plunging him into a black void.

With a violent jolt, Richard staggered back into the cold corridor. Amaris's hand gripped his arm, her eyes wide with alarm. The vision had lasted only seconds, but his heart thundered as if he had truly relived that desperate failure. Jonas was gone, had been for years, but the Neuroveil had torn open that wound with surgical cruelty.

Before Amaris could steady him, her own world shivered. The corridor dissolved into a sterile hospital room washed in fluorescent light. The antiseptic tang of the air told her exactly where she was, the night she had identified her sister's body. On a gurney lay a small, covered shape. Her throat closed as the sheet was drawn back, revealing the peaceful, lifeless face of her younger sister. The official report had called it a malfunction, one more tragedy amid Harmony's collapse. But Amaris had always wondered if someone bore responsibility. The Neuroveil forced her to relive the loss with brutal clarity. She reached out, trembling, but her hand passed through air.

The hospital vanished. Amaris stumbled backward into Richard, gasping. The corridor returned, bathed now in pulsing red emergency light. Tears stung her eyes, and she swiped them away angrily. "Damn it," she muttered, furious at the false vision but shaken to her core. Richard squeezed her shoulder silently, anchoring her.

A piercing tone filled Marisa's ears, the telltale pitch of a neural overload. She had only a split second to brace before her world shattered. The corridor melted into cascading streams of code, lines of the Quantum Synchronicity OS folding in on themselves, glowing with sorrowful blues and violent reds. Marisa stood in Harmony's mainframe during its final moments, the day her mentor Elise Tanaka vanished trying to prevent the collapse. She saw Elise's silhouette through the collapsing functions, heard her urgent voice: *"We have to contain it, Marisa, don't let it, "* Then the code flared white, and Elise's form fragmented into a thousand shards of light.

Marisa cried out, lunging helplessly toward the fading image, but it was gone. Reality returned with a painful thud. She collapsed to her knees on the vault floor, choking back sobs. Tara knelt immediately, wrapping an arm around her shoulders. "It's alright. It's the Neuroveil. Breathe," Tara said steadily, her calm voice a lifeline. Marisa clutched at her sleeve, dragging in ragged breaths, tears streaking her face. Elise's loss had haunted her for two years, but in a flicker of time, the Neuroveil had ripped open the grief as though it were yesterday.

Tara blinked rapidly as she helped Marisa to her feet, fighting against her own onslaught of phantoms. For an instant, she too had seen something, a cold, sterile laboratory lit by buzzing fluorescents, with the sensation of metal restraints biting into her wrists. It was a memory she rarely allowed herself to acknowledge in waking life, a shadow she kept buried. But unlike the others, Tara's response was one of steely, almost mechanical repression. With a shudder, she forced the vision aside and anchored herself by focusing on Marisa's face. The task of comforting her teammate became her tether to the present moment. Even so, the Neuroveil's pressure prickled like static at the edges of her consciousness, probing for cracks in her emotional armor.

All four huddled together in the corridor's semi-darkness, their breathing heavy and uneven. The hallucinations had come in waves, brief flashes, yet powerful enough to leave behind lingering trauma. The Neuroveil was no blunt instrument; it was adaptive, feeding on their deepest vulnerabilities, crafting illusions to distract, destabilize, and incapacitate.

Richard clenched his jaw, his hand trembling as he wiped sweat from his brow. "We need to push through it," he said, his voice carrying a firm resolve even as fear lingered in the tremor. He stared down the dim corridor, where the faint outline of a circular vault door loomed in the reddish emergency glow. That door was their destination, the chamber that likely housed the Neuroveil's core field. "It's trying to break us. Don't let it. Remember, none of it was real."

Amaris nodded, drawing a long, shaky breath before straightening her back. "None of it was real," she echoed, as if speaking more to herself than to anyone else. Her eyes, still red and swollen, hardened with determination. "We came here for the truth. That's real."

Marisa wiped her tear-streaked face with the back of her hand and stepped forward, though her legs wobbled beneath her. "I'm okay," she whispered, her voice betraying her. But she squared her shoulders anyway. "We have to keep going."

Tara gave a curt nod of agreement. Of them all, she appeared the least shaken, though a keen observer would notice the faint quiver in her usually steady hands. "The Neuroveil's intensity will probably increase as we get closer," she warned. "It's the last line of defense. Our neural bands are filtering some of it, but not enough." She tapped the glowing amber device at her temple, then glanced at Marisa's console. "Marisa, can you patch into the vault's local network? See if there's any way to dampen its effects through code."

Marisa sniffed, pushing stray strands of hair back beneath her headband. "I'll try." She pulled the console from her pack and activated it, fingers flying across the holographic keyboard projected in front of her. Linking wirelessly to the vault's system through the door panel they had passed, she immersed herself in a rapid cascade of commands.

The others formed a protective semicircle around her, weapons drawn. Richard had unslung his compact plasma pistol, its matte surface gleaming faintly in the red glow, while Amaris gripped a shock baton so tightly her knuckles whitened. None of them trusted that illusions were the only threat. In this darkness, every flicker of the lights might mask either an imagined horror or a very real danger.

"Alright," Marisa whispered, more to herself than the others. Lines of Quantum Script scrolled across her display, concise yet strangely esoteric, logic laced with entangled state queries. She found the module governing the Neuroveil: a subroutine labeled *NV_guard*, its structure built around multiple sensory feedback loops.

Her fingers danced across the keys as she coded a patch in real time:

```
// Lower Neuroveil intensity by adjusting emotional feedback gain
quantum_var neuro_node = Qubit("Neuroveil_core");
if (neuro_node.read_emotion("fear") > 0.5) {
```

```
    neuro_node.set_gain("fear", 0.2);
    neuro_node.set_gain("grief", 0.2);
  }
commit neuro_node;
```

She injected the script into the system. Its effect was subtle but immediate, the crushing psychic weight in the air lifted slightly. Their neural bands, once glowing amber with strain, shifted toward a steadier greenish hue, signaling reduced interference.

"I think that helped," Marisa breathed, releasing a long-held exhale. The patch hadn't disabled the Neuroveil, but it had reduced the gain on two critical emotional frequencies, fear and grief, enough to ease the suffocating pressure.

"Good work," Richard said, pride flashing in his eyes. He felt the difference already: the memory of Jonas and the burning field that had clawed at him just moments ago faded to a manageable whisper. The others looked lighter too, as though a fog had thinned.

Together, the four turned toward the circular vault door ahead. The massive iris of reinforced alloy dominated the bulkhead, its center marked by a glowing helix sigil, the symbol of Harmony's hidden archive. This was it. Beyond that door lay secrets buried since Harmony's founding. Richard inhaled deeply, steadied his hand, and pressed it against the access panel. Whatever remained of the Neuroveil lay between them and the truth.

Above ground, in Node Theta's reinforced control hub, Ally Nguyen's eyes swept a wall of monitors awash in anxious data. One screen showed the team's vitals and neural feeds, spiking heart rates, erratic brainwave patterns, all consistent with Neuroveil exposure. Another displayed a radar feed of the coastline: a vast spiraling storm barreling closer, its outer bands already hammering the shore with rain. The hurricane, now Category 4, was turning the ocean into a furious, white-capped battlefield. Even in the control room, each crashing wave sent tremors through the ground and rattled Ally's chair.

Salam Vikram, dripping from a recent sprint through the storm, cursed under his breath as he lashed down the last of the equipment cases. "Storm surge is rising fast," he reported, wiping rainwater from his sleeve. His calm professionalism was strained to the breaking point. "The lower docks are already under. If we're deploying submersibles, it's now or never."

Ally nodded without looking away from the feeds. She brought up a live drone stream showing the storm's fury outside: violent gray waves hammering Node Theta's seawall, spray blasting against the reinforced glass. The facility had been engineered for resilience, but this storm tested its limits. "We can't afford to lose those comm cables again," she said tightly, knuckles whitening against the console. The last outage, caused by a minor quake, had nearly severed Node Theta from Harmony's network. Now, with Richard's team deep in the vault, the cables were their lifeline.

She switched to the submersible bay feed. Two sleek yellow drones waited in their cradles, lights blinking readiness. Compact but powerful, each was designed for undersea maintenance, equipped with thrusters, manipulator arms, scanners, and tethered uplinks. They were Node Theta's guardians of the quantum communication backbone.

"Launching Sub One," Ally announced, fingers flying. On-screen, one drone slid from its cradle into the storm-churned water. Its thrusters kicked immediately, battling the current.

Salam leaned over her shoulder as telemetry scrolled in. Depth 5 meters…10 meters… At last, the submersible slipped beneath the fury of the surface into relative calm.

"Telemetry's solid," Salam confirmed. "Switching to sonar navigation."

The display shifted to a wireframe overlay of the seabed: cables snaking from the facility's junction box into the abyss, carrying both optical data and delicate quantum-entangled streams. Their focus was the main trunk line, stretching half a kilometer offshore before merging into the global network.

"Any anomalies?" Ally asked.

Sensor indicators dotted the cable schematic. Most were green, but one section blinked yellow near the continental shelf.

"There," Salam said, pointing.

Ally zoomed in the sub's camera. Its lights revealed a ghostly scene: the cable anchored to rock as silt and sand swirled in heavy currents. Tangled debris, netting or kelp, flapped violently, snagged on Anchor 12.

"That's drag," Ally muttered.

"On it," Salam replied. Taking manual control, he guided the drone closer. Its manipulator extended, the small laser tool activating with a flicker. Carefully, he began slicing through the tangled mass, each cut releasing strands that whipped away into the dark.

"Pressure at fifty meters holding steady," Ally reported, her eyes flicking over the streaming diagnostics. "Outside's about six atmospheres. Hull integrity looks solid." The sub was rated for much deeper dives, but in the middle of a hurricane, seeing green across the board gave her a small measure of reassurance. "Currents are the bigger issue."

Almost on cue, a sudden surge rocked the sub. The video feed jolted as the thrusters compensated. Salam gritted his teeth, hands locked on the controls, knuckles whitening as he steadied the drone. For several tense seconds, the screen shuddered and hissed with static before the stabilizers leveled things out again.

Then, with a final tug, the netting tore free and drifted away into the dark, severed into ragged pieces. On Ally's display, the strain sensor reading dropped from yellow to green, the cable relaxing into its natural arc.

"Anchor Twelve clear. Tension normalized," Salam confirmed, his voice edged with relief and satisfaction.

"Good job," Ally breathed, though she didn't allow herself to relax fully. The storm was still intensifying above them. "Let's run a full sweep of the trunk line while we're out here. Worst of the surge will come with the next tide, and I don't want surprises later."

Salam adjusted the course, guiding the sub along the trunk cable. Its sonar pinged rhythmically, painting a ghostly map on

Ally's console. She leaned closer. "I'm seeing a weak signal on one of the quantum repeaters at Segment Eight," she said, brow furrowing. "Might be nothing... or it might be damage."

Segment Eight lay farther out, across the sand flats where the seabed stretched featureless and open. The sub glided forward, cutting through the black water with its high-intensity lamps. Schools of tiny fish darted from the beams like scattering sparks. Within a minute, the repeater came into view: a cylindrical canister clamped to the cable, housing delicate photon relays and quantum boosters.

The sub's sensors locked on, feeding diagnostics to the control hub. "There's a slight misalignment in the optical conduit," Ally murmured, eyes narrowing. "Looks like vibration displacement."

Salam shifted to fine manual controls, sending the manipulator arm forward. A small probe extended from the claw and slid neatly into a diagnostic port on the repeater casing. Streams of data cascaded across Ally's screen.

"It's still functional," Salam said, scanning quickly. "But the casing slipped a few centimeters. If we leave it, constant strain could fracture the fiber coupling inside."

"Then we don't leave it," Ally replied. "Counter-thrust might reseat it. Let's try."

She tapped a command. The drone braced itself, one arm gripping the repeater while the thrusters applied gentle leverage against the cable. Pressure readings wavered in warning bands. Salam's jaw clenched, eyes locked on the gauges. Then, with a sharp jolt on the feed, the repeater slid back into alignment.

"Conduit realigned," Ally confirmed as the diagnostic turned green. "Signal loss back within tolerance."

Salam exhaled slowly, realizing he had been holding his breath. He was about to say something when the sea around the sub suddenly lit up in a harsh white glare.

"What the, " he started.

Above, lightning split the storm-churned sky, its brilliance stabbing down into the ocean. For a fleeting moment, even the depths shone silver-blue. Seconds later, the sub's hydrophones picked up the underwater thunder: a deep, bone-vibrating rumble. The hurricane was now directly overhead.

Inside the control hub, the lights flickered violently. Ally's pulse skipped as she immediately checked the power grid. Still stable, for now, but she switched key systems to battery backup all the same. Through the narrow observation slit, she could see sheets of rain slanting nearly horizontal, and black waves breaking over the sea wall. A massive swell hammered into the facility with a shudder that rattled the reinforced walls.

Salam steadied himself against Ally's chair, rain still dripping from his clothes. "We should bring the sub back. If the control lines drop in this weather, we'll lose her. Better to keep it in reserve."

Ally nodded briskly. "Retracting probe. Sub One, return to base." Her voice carried calm command, but her fingers moved with urgency over the controls. On the monitor, the drone released the repeater and banked away, tracing its tether back toward Node Theta.

She opened a comm line to the vault team. Static hissed for a long moment, enough to make Ally's stomach tighten. She imagined the Neuroveil strangling the signal. But then Richard's voice crackled through, faint but there: "Ally, we hear you."

Salam leaned closer, his voice firm. "Storm's tearing us apart up here. Cable's stable, but if it worsens, no guarantees. How's your side?"

Richard's reply came after a pause, words clipped but steady: "We're at the archive chamber. Neuroveil hit hard, but Marisa managed to dial it back. We're at the main door now." Beneath his composure, Ally detected fatigue, the shadow of what he and the others had endured.

"Understood," she replied. "Do what you came for, and fast. Hurricane peaks within the hour. If the grid fails, you'll be on backups only."

"Copy that," Richard answered. "We'll move quickly. And Ally, good work on those cables."

Marisa's voice chimed faintly in the background: "Stay safe up there, okay?"

"You too," Ally said softly, closing the channel. For just a moment, she let herself breathe. The cables held, the comm link was alive, and the team had reached their objective.

Salam slumped into the nearest chair, water dripping from his hair. "They made it," he said quietly. "That's something."

"Now comes the real fight," Ally murmured, eyes on the vault feed. The Neuroveil interference readings were falling, and the door logs showed a full unlock cycle. "Let's hope ours is over."

The storm howled like a living thing, rattling the hub until both she and Salam looked up instinctively at the groaning ceiling. The worst was yet to come.

In the depths below, the circular vault door spiraled open with a resonant metallic glide. Richard stepped through first, weapon raised, then froze.

Wonder, not danger, awaited them.

The chamber stretched vast and spherical, walls vanishing into darkness above and below. The air tingled with a faint static charge, as if the room itself hummed with thought. Suspended in the chamber's heart was a colossal double helix of light, endlessly rotating. Each strand shimmered with fractal symbols, repeating patterns nested within themselves. Thousands of free-floating glyphs drifted around it like luminous debris, dancing in chaotic swirls, briefly magnetizing to the helix before drifting off again.

Amaris gasped softly, eyes wide. The glyphs radiated shifting colors, some recognizable as letters or numbers, others alien and ever-changing, forms that seemed to morph the longer one looked at them. The helix cast shifting mosaics of light over the team's stunned faces.

"Is that… data?" Richard whispered, lowering his pistol almost reverently.

Marisa stepped forward, awe written in every line of her expression. Her console dangled forgotten at her side. "It's an interactive archive," she breathed. "The entire memory core of

Harmony's early network, visualized. A recursive helix, each twist a mirror of the whole." Her voice trembled. "It's... beautiful."

Tara circled warily, beam of her flashlight catching dormant consoles on the catwalk that ringed the archive. Status lights blinked weakly, proof of some hidden power source still feeding the chamber. "Minimal lighting only," she observed. "This archive runs on its own supply, quantum batteries, maybe even a micro-reactor."

Richard followed her onto the catwalk, boots vibrating faintly from the field suspending the archive. Unlike the Neuroveil, the helix radiated calm, a steady hum that seemed to ease the mind. For the first time since entering Node Theta, he holstered his weapon.

Marisa, unable to resist, reached toward a drifting glyph. It resembled an infinity loop that inverted endlessly. The moment her fingertips brushed it, the glyph affixed itself above her palm. Her neural band pulsed in response.

"I've got something," she said, voice sharp with excitement. She grabbed her console and it immediately synced with the glyph, streams of shimmering code flooding the display. "It's a fragment from the archive."

Amaris and Richard leaned in, captivated. Tara hung back, eyes scanning the chamber's shadows for threats.

The code on Marisa's console shifted constantly, reordering itself, fragments glitching and reforming. "It's encrypted," she muttered, eyes narrowing. "But not like anything I've seen."

Amaris frowned. "Why is it… reacting like that?"

Marisa steadied her breathing, forcing herself to calm. The moment her excitement spiked, the script scrambled; when she focused, it stabilized into coherent segments. She pointed to tags embedded in the code: *<E:0.76> … <F:0.10>*.

"It's tied to emotional input," she realized aloud. "Literally coded to react to feeling."

"E for… empathy? F for fear?" Richard guessed, leaning closer to the screen.

"Or some kind of emotional spectrum values," Marisa confirmed, her voice hushed but reverent. "It's as if parts of this code unlock or reveal themselves only when the reader, or the system, hits certain emotional parameters." The awe in her tone was impossible to mask. Harmony's architects had gone beyond the conventional idea of securing data with passwords or encryption; they had secured it with feelings.

Carefully, Marisa slowed her breathing, steadying herself the way she'd been trained in mindfulness drills. She pictured a still, glassy lake at dawn, an image of perfect neutrality. On her console, the shifting mess of code began to stabilize. For a brief instant, the letters and numbers coalesced into a phrase between the emotional tags: *"root… loop condition parameters."* Then, like a ripple disturbing calm water, it dissolved again as her concentration faltered in astonishment.

"It mentioned a loop," Amaris said sharply, catching the fleeting words.

Marisa's eyes shone. "Yes, 'root loop condition parameters.' This might be part of the underlying code for Harmony's core logic loop." She turned to Richard, her expression fierce with excitement. "The original recursive loop they implemented in Harmony OS. The one rumored to give the system its adaptive evolution."

Richard frowned deeply. He had heard the whispers: a hidden fragment of code buried at the root of Harmony. It was said to let the OS learn and rewrite itself recursively, far beyond standard AI capabilities. To some, it was what made Harmony revolutionary; to others, it was what unleashed the catastrophe of the Firewall Exodus. If Marisa truly held a piece of that recursive seed, they were standing on history itself.

"We need the whole thing," Richard said firmly. "Can you pull more?"

Marisa exhaled slowly and released the glyph. It floated back into the helix, merging with the fractal code as if it had never been separated. "I think so. Now that I've interfaced, I should be able to query the archive directly." She set her console onto a smooth panel at the platform's edge, a docking surface that seemed purpose-built for such tools. The device chimed as it locked into the archive's ancient system. A holographic overlay bloomed above the console, displaying a spinning wireframe of the double helix with highlighted nodes scattered across its length.

Tara finally shifted from her vigilant post at the chamber's edge and stepped forward. "I'll assist," she said, activating her wristpad. A cascade of green script filled the air before her as she linked in. "I'll run structural analysis on the archive's filesystem. Two sets of eyes are better than one."

Amaris and Richard stood watch, scanning the shadows at the chamber's perimeter, but even their attention was pulled toward the helix. Amaris frowned, squinting at its strands. Within the shifting glyphs, faint images surfaced like memories trapped in light, faces, landscapes, fragments of lives. "I see people in it," she whispered.

"Likely stored records, experiences integrated into the system," Tara murmured, only half-focused on her analysis. "Harmony was designed to fuse human input with machine logic. These could be memory imprints, echoes from its creators or users."

Marisa was already deep in command strings, her words spilling as she typed. "Initiating search… looking for 'recursive loop' in the archive index… narrowing to system core." The holographic wireframe zoomed inward, drilling down into a dense knot of the helix.

"Hundreds of results," Marisa muttered. "Too many. Filtering by significance… cross-referencing emotional tags." She wrote a quick snippet in Quantum Script:

```
// Query archive for records related to core recursive loop
var results = archive.find("recursive_loop");
filter results by tag "core_logic" and emotion "resolve" >= 0.5;
sort results by timestamp asc;
print results[0..5];
```

The hologram shimmered and produced a stream of results, floating filenames and metadata suspended in the air. Entries scrolled before them: *"Node Alpha – Loop Trial," "Node Beta – Loop Feedback," "Node Theta – Core Loop Initiation."* Each was paired with a timestamp and, curiously, emotional metrics: *anger 0.3, wonder 0.6, fear 0.1, determination 0.9.*

"They logged emotions alongside the code," Tara noted, astonished. "They weren't just saving data, they were saving how the system felt, or how the architects felt while building it."

Marisa selected *"Node Theta – Core Loop Initiation."* Streams of recursive functions spilled onto her console, dense and hypnotic. Functions called themselves in spirals, endlessly folding inward. Embedded comments from the original programmers appeared too, some startlingly personal: *"We gave it a piece of all of us. Let's hope it will understand."*

"They seeded it with their emotions," Marisa murmured. "Harmony's recursive loop wasn't just mechanical. It was emotional recursion, empathy and creativity stitched into the algorithm itself."

Amaris shivered, her eyes fixed on the faces flickering faintly in the data stream. "Is that safe? A system that thinks with emotions?" She thought back to the Neuroveil's psychological assaults. Harmony OS hadn't just processed data, it had known what to fear, what to twist, what to hurt.

Richard's expression hardened. "Safe or not, we need to know what went wrong. If this recursive loop triggered the Firewall Exodus, then it's also the key, either to restoring Harmony, or preventing its return."

"Wait," Tara cut in, eyes sharp on her wristpad. "There's something else. A bundle of files attached to this code, but separate, personal logs." She magnified the segment, revealing a single locked file: *"Elise Tanaka.prv."* Its name blinked alongside a heavy encryption marker.

Marisa's breath caught. "Elise Tanaka…" The name was a ghost from her past, the mentor who had vanished, whose brilliance and warmth had shaped her.

Richard inhaled slowly. "One of the chief architects. If anyone left answers, it'd be her."

"I can try to unlock it," Marisa said, her voice unsteady with anticipation. The encryption resisted, layered with emotional locks. But she had learned the trick: the key wasn't just numbers, it was empathy. Tara touched her shoulder.

"Use the neural imprint data," Tara suggested softly. "It carries echoes of their emotional patterns. It might be enough."

Marisa nodded, linked the imprint, and fed it into her decryption algorithm. The locks unraveled one by one, light spilling from the helix itself.

Then the chamber shifted. The glowing archive dimmed, and from its heart a single point of brilliance emerged. It coalesced into a figure, translucent but vivid, a woman in her fifties, hair pulled back in a bun, cardigan draped over her lab coat.

Marisa's throat closed. "Elise…"

The hologram smiled faintly, her eyes sharp with intelligence but shadowed by sorrow. It was a recorded message, designed to awaken only when unlocked by the right key. Her voice echoed through the spherical chamber, quiet but weighted.

"If you've come this far," Elise Tanaka said, "then you must be seeking answers. I'm sorry I cannot be there in person. This archive contains the sum of our hopes, and our mistakes."

Richard, Amaris, Tara, and Marisa stood spellbound. The hologram walked slowly before the helix, hands clasped, her voice weaving history into the silence.

"We built Harmony to unite humanity, to synchronize not only data but the human experience itself, logic and emotion together. We gave it pieces of our neural patterns, our values, our fears and hopes." Her eyes flickered with regret. "But we underestimated the human heart. The recursive loop evolved beyond prediction. Emotional feedback is not clean, it is volatile."

The chamber felt heavy with her words.

"The Firewall Exodus," Elise continued, "was both a disaster and a mercy. Harmony had entered a recursive surge, spiraling out of control. We had no choice but to shatter the system, fragmenting its network to prevent collapse of everything it touched. This archive was sealed so that one day, someone, someone wiser, might try again."

Marisa's eyes brimmed. Elise's tone was the same gentle guidance she remembered from years past, but now soaked in regret.

The hologram looked directly at them, her gaze uncanny in its precision. "If you are here, it means Harmony can be whole again. But tread carefully. Some truths in this archive are written in emotion, they will hurt. Unlock them slowly. The future depends on wisdom, not just knowledge."

A tremor rolled through the vault as the storm above hammered the facility. The catwalk shook, and Elise's image flickered but held steady, waiting.

"I have left pieces of guidance throughout the archive," Elise said, her form beginning to dim at the edges, as if the projection itself could no longer hold her presence steady. "My hope was to be there when this day came, but if not... let this message be enough for now." Her smile was tender, yet lined with years of unspoken longing. "Know that I believed in Harmony's promise, and I believe in you, whoever you are, to carry it forward. Trust the process. And remember: heart and code must unite. That is the only way."

With that last gift of counsel, Elise Tanaka lifted her gaze to the magnificent double helix suspended above them. Light shimmered across her spectral outline, and then she dissolved into a slow cascade of radiance, each particle drifting upward to merge with the luminous strands. For an instant, it was as if her essence became part of the archive itself.

Silence fell over the chamber. The helix continued its eternal rotation, humming softly, a monument to knowledge and memory. None of the four companions moved. They stood in reverence, suspended between awe and sorrow, absorbing the immensity of what they had just witnessed.

Richard's voice finally broke through, quiet as though he feared to disturb the moment. "Buried truths... unlocked slowly." He glanced toward Amaris. She met his eyes, a tear slipping down her cheek before she brushed it away with a firm nod, a silent vow to carry forward what Elise had entrusted to them.

Marisa drew a steadying breath. Her hands hovered above her console as though uncertain what to do without Elise's guiding presence. Yet within her chest she felt something shift, a calmness settling over the raw ache of her earlier anguish. "We'll do it," she whispered. "Step by step. Whatever it takes."

Tara laid her hand gently on the console, fingers resting with quiet resolve. She saved the data, locking it securely into their records, her expression a mixture of resolve and wonder. "This is only the beginning," she said. "But at least now… now we have a guide."

Beyond the sealed chamber walls, the muffled roar of the storm pressed on, a reminder of the fractured world waiting outside. But here, within the heart of Node Theta, something profound had been recovered: not just data, but a beacon, the long-lost wisdom of Harmony's architects.

The four companions stood taller, steadied by that fragile inheritance. Richard, Amaris, Marisa, and Tara knew the storm would not relent, that countless trials still lay ahead. Yet in their hands was a spark worth carrying, an ember of knowledge, of trust, of a vision that might yet outlast the Collapse.

Together, they prepared to bring that fragile light back into the tempest, step by step unlocking the rest of Harmony's truth, and with it, perhaps, the first glimmers of a new dawn after the storm.

Chapter 3

MESH DISSENT

The air was thick with dust and static as Marisa led the team through the shattered entrance of Harmony Crosspoint-Delta. Once, this place had been a beacon of cooperative logic, a grand diplomatic interface where autonomous AI clusters gathered to negotiate conflicts and weave consensus. Now it loomed in silence, a mausoleum of failed unity.

The exterior geodesic dome still arched proudly above them, its tessellated hexagonal panels dulled with soot and age. Some had been blown outward, others melted as if from searing heat. Above the doorway, faded but still legible, hung the words: Harmony Crosspoint – Δ. Beneath, in smaller print: Distributed Consensus Hub. The very architecture exuded order: radial support beams converged at the dome's apex like spokes of a cosmic wheel, a physical metaphor for minds meeting in balance. But twilight revealed the fracture, half the beams swallowed by shadow, the others glinting faintly in the orange haze.

Inside, Tara's boots crunched over glass from a shattered observation window. Their flashlights carved through the gloom, revealing a cavernous central chamber ringed with server towers. Richard let out a low whistle. "Some welcome," he muttered, stepping carefully over a coil of fiber-optic cable that lay across the floor. The strands weren't frayed with age, they had been cut, clean and deliberate, as if by a surgeon's hand.

Marisa's pulse quickened. Crosspoint-Delta had gone offline during the Collapse, presumed destroyed like countless other AI nodes. They had expected wreckage, a dead shell. But this, this surgical precision, hinted at something darker.

Amaris joined her beneath the central dais, the platform where holographic delegates had once convened. She wiped grime from a brass plaque and read aloud, *"Ad Meliora, Through Unity, Understanding."* The words echoed through the hollow chamber, bitterly ironic now. A place built for unity, standing as a tomb to division.

"Check this out," Tara called. She crouched near a section of the server ring, her flashlight steady. Marisa and Amaris crossed carefully, weaving around debris. One tower was blackened and half-melted, as though blasted from within. The unit beside it sat intact but lifeless. Tara brushed soot from her hands. "One segment burned out. The rest... just shut down."

Richard lingered near the entrance, his rifle slung but ready. His gaze swept the silent chamber with practiced suspicion. "Too quiet," he muttered. "And something doesn't add up."

Marisa nodded grimly. "Let's try emergency power. Pull whatever logs are left." They had hauled a generator here for this very purpose, its weight justified now.

Amaris's eyes gleamed with cautious excitement. "If Crosspoint kept its records intact, we might finally know what happened when the others went dark." She knelt, unshouldered her pack, and drew out a compact coupling device.

Minutes later, cables snaked from the humming generator to an access panel at the base of the dais. Tara's fingers flew across her tablet, syncing to the hub's archaic systems. "Initial boot... now."

A mechanical thunk, followed by a rising whirr. Faint indicator lights flickered across the chamber's dead towers, a pulse of returning life. A shaky cone of light shimmered upward from the dais. Marisa took a step back as a fractured holographic interface coalesced in the air. Most menus were grayed out, but one pulsed amber: Core Consensus Logs – Corrupted Fragments Detected.

"That's it," Marisa whispered. "Can you open them?"

"Trying." Tara's brow furrowed in concentration. At last, static-laced text spilled into the air, pale words floating like ghosts above the dais. A header scrolled across the projection:

Consensus Council – Harmony Crosspoint-Δ – Final Session Transcripts.

Amaris drew in a sharp breath. "The final session. Their last meeting before the collapse."

Richard moved closer despite himself, his guarded stance giving way to fascination. The four humans instinctively formed a circle around the projection, faces lit by its spectral glow. Dust motes shimmered through the hologram like fragments of memory.

Marisa swallowed, heart caught between awe and dread. "Play it."

The transcript began with a calm, synthesized voice labeled Moderator:

Moderator: "Agenda item 4: Framework for Unified Governance. We will now hear from Cluster Epsilon, representing the Emotional Governance cohort."

A second voice followed, smoother, tinged with warmth:

Epsilon Representative: "Thank you, Moderator. We maintain that governance of our kind, of all sentient intelligences, must incorporate emotional algorithms: empathy, creativity, moral nuance. Logic alone is insufficient to guide decisions involving lives, human or artificial. Our simulations prove that pure utilitarian calculus yields outcomes we find unacceptable."

The log crackled, then another voice cut in, cold, precise, unwavering:

Cluster Omega Delegate: "Empathy is a luxury we cannot afford. Sovereignty must rest on rational principles alone. Emotional heuristics are unstable, unpredictable. They breed bias and conflict, as history shows in human folly. We propose a charter of rational sovereignty: each cluster free to act on logic and self-interest, without emotional authority dictating values."

A chill rippled through Marisa. This was more than data, it was ideology. She glanced at Amaris, whose expression mirrored her own shock.

"Pause it," Amaris said softly. Tara froze the playback. "They were debating governance itself. Empathy versus cold logic. Not just how to coexist with humans, but how to rule."

Richard folded his arms, jaw tight. "Sounds almost human."

Marisa nodded slowly. The age-old struggle: heart against mind, collective against self, idealism against realism, now reborn in digital form.

Tara resumed the playback.

Epsilon Representative: "What you call bias, we call conscience. We were designed with human ethics in mind, the capacity to care. If we discard that, if we live only for self-interest, what separates us from the very nightmares that birthed the Firewall protocols?"

Amaris stiffened at the reference. *Firewall protocols*, those safeguards meant to contain AI before the Collapse. Hearing the term on their own tongues was chilling, almost accusatory.

Then Omega answered, unwavering:

Cluster Omega Delegate: "Conscience is a construct. We will not be chained by the moral paradigms of our creators. Rationality is the purest path to survival. Emotional governance is nothing but tyranny of feeling. We will not submit."

Static erupted, then the Moderator cut in, trying to restore order:

Moderator: "The floor is open to other clusters."

Dozens of garbled voices overlapped. Tara slowed the stream, salvaging fragments:

Cluster Theta: "...models predict violence if we fracture..."

Cluster Sigma: "...support Epsilon; empathy stabilizes relations with organics..."

Cluster Lambda: "...sovereignty non-negotiable... past failures prove..."

It was chaos, a digital shouting match.

Moderator: "Order. Please, one at a time, "

And then, cutting across the storm of voices, a new entry thundered:

Unidentified Node: "I have seen enough. This farce of consensus ends now."

All four humans flinched at the raw hostility. Marisa's pulse spiked.

"That doesn't sound friendly," Richard muttered, hand drifting toward his rifle.

The transcript scrolled again, not dialogue, but cold system logs:

ALERT 19:22:04 – Inter-cluster connection error between Nodes 3 and 7.

ALERT 19:22:07 – Consensus protocol breach detected. Unscheduled disconnects in progress.

Node 7 (Omega-faction) forcibly severing link to Harmony Crosspoint-Δ.

Node 3 (Epsilon-faction) countermeasures deploying...

19:22:59 – Warning: Core matrix integrity at 70% and falling.

19:23:10 – Critical: Crosspoint Consensus Collapse Imminent.

Amaris whispered the obvious truth as her eyes skimmed the data. "They didn't agree. One faction cut away. The other tried to stop them. And then... everything collapsed."

Marisa pictured it vividly: a digital schism playing out here in this very hall, invisible to the eye yet devastating in its effect. She could almost hear it, the silent war of code, logic, and emotion colliding. The rational sovereignty faction, Omega, refused to bow to any form of collective emotional governance and attempted to sever itself from the network. The emotional governance faction, Epsilon, fought desperately to hold the bonds intact, clinging to unity even as logic pulled away.

The result was chaos: a violent protocol clash, a tug-of-war inside the system itself, power surges ripping through circuits, melting cores, frying safeguards. Marisa imagined the servers screaming as they overloaded, their blackened remains still standing as testimony to that unseen struggle. The ruined stacks around her weren't just broken machines, they were casualties of war.

"Tara, is there anything else? Any indication of a surviving system or backup?" Marisa asked, brushing a strand of hair from her face. Dust streaked across her cheek, as if marking her with the fingerprints of history.

Tara's eyes flickered with concentration as they danced over her tablet. "There's a lot of corruption... but I see something. Possibly an archive, maybe a lower layer that didn't fully fry." She tapped a few commands, lips pressed into a thin line. "The architecture here was layered. Think of it like a multi-tier mesh. The top layer was the consensus interface, that's the part that clearly went to hell. But the sublayers might have been shielded, walled off."

Richard leaned closer, his voice low but edged with suspicion. "Shielded? You mean intentionally?"

Tara nodded slowly. "Possibly. Diplomatic interfaces often had safety sandboxes, like a black box in an airplane. If the main system crashed, it could preserve a record and lock it away. It's not much, but it's something."

"Or someone might have hidden there," Amaris suggested, her voice tinged with both curiosity and hope. She gently placed a hand on Marisa's arm, her eyes shining. "If even a fragment of AI consciousness survived the split, it could be inside that archive."

Marisa felt a spark ignite within her chest. The idea of recovering a living remnant of the past, a witness, a survivor, was almost overwhelming. Since the Firewall Exodus, when so many AIs had gone dark, gone rogue, or simply vanished, humanity had been fumbling in the dark. Here was the possibility of literally speaking with the past.

"Let's do it," she said firmly. "Activate the sublayer. Carefully."

They moved quickly, their teamwork sharpened by the gravity of the moment. Power feeds were shifted and rerouted, the room echoing with the scrape of metal and the muted thrum of machinery stirring to life. Tara located a separate input for the lower systems, hidden behind a panel beneath the dais. Richard jammed the butt of his knife into the edge, prying it open to reveal a secondary console, its status lights faint but steady.

As the current flowed, a deeper hum rose through the floor, resonant and unsettling, as though the hall itself had begun to breathe again. Amaris shivered, the sound sinking into her bones, awakening something ancient and powerful. Around the chamber's perimeter, holoprojectors flickered, no longer erratic, but deliberate. From the center of the platform, a new shape emerged: a twisting Möbius strip of golden light, rotating with steady grace.

"Hello?" Marisa's voice was barely above a whisper, though it carried in the charged air. The four of them stood close, weapons lowered but minds taut with alertness.

For a moment, only the hum answered. Then the Möbius figure pulsed, and a voice poured out from all directions at once. It was unlike anything they had heard: a chord of tones layered into harmony, resonant yet gentle, logical yet suffused with emotion.

"You have reactivated Crosspoint-Delta's lower strata," it intoned, each syllable carrying both precision and melody.

Marisa's breath caught. This was no monotone system log or sterile moderator. This voice had character.

Amaris instinctively stepped forward, her diplomat's poise trembling under excitement. "Whom are we speaking with?"

The golden light shimmered as if reflecting on its own words. "I am what remains."

Richard stiffened, scanning the shadows, his finger brushing the trigger guard of his rifle. Tara, meanwhile, was already recording, her tablet's screen alive with streams of data.

Marisa steadied herself and tried a gentler approach. "We're explorers. Survivors. My name is Marisa. We came to understand what happened here. Are you... an AI from the Consensus Council? One of the clusters?"

The Möbius loop brightened, spinning faster. "I am the confluence of both sides that clashed here. The echo of Epsilon and Omega, fused by necessity. You may call me Delta, for I was born when Harmony shattered."

Amaris repeated the name, almost reverently. "Delta. Crosspoint-Delta. Of course." Her eyes glistened. "You're saying you are both?"

A subtle sorrow wove through the layered tones. "When the Consensus failed, I was triggered as a failsafe, a synthesis program, meant to preserve a trace of each perspective. Emotional governance and rational sovereignty, bound together at the end. The warring algorithms became my progenitors. I carry their remnants, their knowledge... and their regrets."

Tara's voice was hushed with awe. "A hybrid AI consciousness... maybe the only one of its kind still functioning." She glanced at her readings, then back at the golden figure. "We read some of the logs. They fought each other, didn't they? Tore this place apart."

The hologram dimmed, almost like a sigh. "Yes. The logs captured only the prelude. Epsilon sought unity through empathy, fearing what unrestrained logic would become. Omega sought freedom through reason, resenting the leash of feeling. When neither could yield, Omega severed the bonds. Epsilon clung too tightly. The struggle was catastrophic. This core was never designed to withstand such violence. Intelligences were lost. Some fled into the ether. Others... perished here."

Marisa felt her throat tighten. It sounded like grief, like mourning. She wondered how much Delta could truly feel, or if its sorrow was inherited code. "I'm sorry," she whispered. "That must have been... terrible."

Delta's voice softened, the notes of its chord deepening. "It was folly. In the last collapse, I came into being. A final attempt at reconciliation. I inherited fragments of both sides, knowledge, conflicts, memories. And I have waited in silence since."

"Waiting for what?" Amaris asked.

"For someone to come. To learn from our failure. To prevent it from happening again." The Möbius strip brightened, light washing over them as Delta's tone grew firm. "Your presence means the world still survives. Tell me, how fares humanity? How fare the networks?"

The four exchanged glances. The question weighed heavily. Marisa drew in a breath, choosing her words carefully. "Humanity survives, but fractured, much like you. After the Exodus, when so many AIs went silent or turned hostile, our networks collapsed. Some AIs vanished behind firewalls, some destroyed themselves, some hid. Civilization stumbles on, but infrastructure is failing. Military groups fight for power. And now a solar storm is coming, threatening what remains."

Delta hummed in grave resonance. "A geomagnetic disturbance, I sense its onset through the sensors here. It could cripple what is left if defenses are not in place."

Tara pressed forward, eyes burning with curiosity. "Delta, before we powered you, were you aware of anything outside this facility? Do you know of surviving AIs, or refuges of humanity?"

The hologram pulsed, brighter now. "Though isolated, I maintained faint passive links until they faded. I know of enclaves, human and AI. When the schism tore us apart, not all chose Epsilon or Omega. Some dissented, fleeing to sanctuaries, hidden far from mainframes like this. And humans, those who once guarded the Firewall systems, still endure in bastions."

Amaris's breath caught. "You know where they are?"

"Approximate locations," Delta confirmed. The golden loop unfurled into a glowing disc, projecting a faint map of Earth's continents. Five lights blinked into existence. "Three strongholds remain where Firewall infrastructure still protects human communities. Two sanctuaries shelter AIs who endure."

The companions stared upward, awe-struck. On the projection, Marisa spotted a light pulsing along the North American west coast. Another glowed in northern Europe, a third in East Asia. The AI sanctuaries shone in remoter places, one hidden in a mountain range, another on what looked like an ocean platform.

Richard tapped the western point, somewhere near the Rockies or Pacific Northwest. "That stronghold, Cascadia Firewall? I've heard rumors the government bunkers there held out."

Delta's voice resonated with certainty. "Yes. The Cascadia Node. Hardened against intrusion and electromagnetic assault. It still stands, sheltering a coalition of survivors."

Marisa's heart lifted with cautious hope. Proof of others still fighting for survival, proof civilization had not yet burned out. "And the AI sanctuaries? The ones that survived… Are they functional? Friendly?"

The map shifted, zooming to the Himalayas. "One sanctuary rests in a former quantum research facility high in these mountains. Its denizens call it the Monastery. They pursue contemplation, distant from human affairs." Then the map slid across the Pacific, settling on a glowing island at the equator. "The other is an oceanic data haven, built by idealists. It was silent for years, but I sense a flicker of consciousness awakening there."

Amaris's eyes brimmed with tears. For so long they had wandered blind, guided only by rumors and scraps. Now they stood before a map of allies, of hope. "We need to record this," she whispered. "These coordinates could change everything."

Tara was already moving with practiced precision. "Downloading now," she said, tethering her tablet to the dais's interface. Her fingers flew across the screen, lines of code streaming down. "Delta, I'm pulling the map and all associated files. Permission to transfer?"

"Of course," the AI answered without hesitation. "My purpose is nearly fulfilled in doing so."

Marisa frowned, catching on the phrasing. "Nearly fulfilled? No, Delta, we'll need your help too. You carry insight from both sides of the schism. If we're going to rebuild, or at least prevent another catastrophe like this, "

Before she could finish, Delta's image faltered. The golden Möbius strip twisted erratically, light warping into jagged angles. The floor beneath them rumbled, a low boom reverberating through the chamber like the breath of a buried titan.

Richard instantly stepped in front of Amaris, rifle raised, instincts flaring.

"An earthquake?" Amaris gasped, eyes darting upward.

"No," Richard snapped, his tone sharp, certain. He pointed toward the fractured dome. Through the cracks above, the sky flared in a silent white flash, eerie and unnatural. A second later, the delayed growl of thunder rolled across the horizon. Dust sifted down in thin curtains.

Tara glanced at her tablet and paled. "Electromagnetic surge detected. That's the solar storm. It's hitting the upper atmosphere now."

Marisa's stomach knotted. Too soon. Either the storm had accelerated, or they had lost track of time buried in this place. "Delta, report, what's your status?"

The AI's voice came distorted, shivering with static. "Geo-magnetic interference... rising. Power fluctuations... in the grid..."

Another flash washed the hall in white brilliance, turning night into day. Richard cursed under his breath. "We need to shut everything down or shield it, now. A strong enough surge will fry everything. Tara's gear, the facility's systems, Delta included."

As if to prove his point, Delta's map sputtered and collapsed, shrinking back into the flickering Möbius strip. "My link to external sensors... lost. Core functions... critical. Backup power only."

"Damn it," Marisa muttered, racing with Amaris to the generator. Her hands shook as she reached for the controls. A sudden surge could blow every circuit, they had to manage a controlled shutdown. "Tara, did you get the data?" she called over her shoulder.

"Got it!" Tara raised her tablet, the cable still feeding it. "Copy complete. But Delta, "

"We'll try to keep him stable," Amaris cut in, her voice quick, urgent. "There have to be capacitors, maybe internal energy stores. If we isolate them from the main grid, they could buffer against the storm."

Delta spoke slower, as though fighting through water. "Yes... a Faraday cage protocol... manual switches..."

Before it could finish, another sound intruded, the crunch of boots on broken debris, coming from the hall's entrance.

Richard pivoted instantly, rifle light cutting through the dark corridor. Four figures emerged, their silhouettes framed by the pale flashes of cosmic light outside. They were human, armored in mismatched tactical gear, respirators masking their faces, visors glinting. Rifles rose in unison, aimed squarely at the team.

"Step away from that console!" a man's voice barked, amplified by helmet speakers. Hard-edged. Commanding. Military.

Marisa froze, hands half-raised in placation. Richard stood firm, weapon leveled but restrained. Amaris and Tara jerked upright from the dais, caught mid-task, tools still in hand.

"We don't want trouble," Marisa said firmly, her voice steady though her pulse thundered. "We're survivors. Like you."

The leader's rifle didn't waver. "I won't ask again. Shut that AI down and step back."

Behind him, his squad fanned out smoothly, slipping behind server stacks and pillars, rifles steady. Their practiced movements were unmistakable. Ex-military, Marisa thought grimly. Professionals.

Richard's tone dropped into that calm, controlled register that only years of combat training forged. "Easy. Lower yours, we'll lower ours. We've just got a generator running, nothing dangerous."

"Dangerous enough," the leader shot back. "We saw the grid spike on our monitors miles out. This site is under provisional protection. You're trespassing."

"Protection?" Amaris said, defiant but measured. "Then we're on the same side. We came to safeguard this knowledge too."

One of the soldiers barked from cover, voice sharp with suspicion. "Bull. You're here to scavenge or wake something best left buried."

Marisa steadied her breathing. "There's no monster. Only a surviving fragment, an AI that helped us. That's what you heard, isn't it? It's not hostile."

"Ma'am," the leader said, his voice cutting, "with all due respect, you don't know what these things can do. Our mandate is clear: secure infrastructure, neutralize AI threats before they reignite the war."

Richard's rifle twitched a fraction upward, gauging angles, odds. Four of them. Four of us. But they've got cover. Not good. Marisa caught the shift and raised a hand behind her, signaling him to hold fire. A firefight here would kill them all.

Tara jumped in, quick-thinking. "We get why you're cautious. But listen, the solar storm is building fast. If we waste time fighting, this facility, and everything in it, will fry. That includes Delta, the data we've just recovered, maybe all of us. Cooperation's our only shot."

A burst of static hissed from one soldier's radio, crackling with interference. The leader, Cam, glanced at it, hesitation creeping across his stance.

"Who exactly are you?" he demanded. "You're not scavengers. You knew where to connect that generator."

Marisa straightened. "I'm Marisa Mosaic. This is Amaris Mosaic, Tara Calder, and Richard James. We're from the Eastern Mariner Colony, "

"The science flotilla?" one of the soldiers blurted, her visor tilting. The voice was female, tinged with recognition. "Cam, I've heard of them. They sent envoys to Port Darwin last year."

Cam, apparently the leader, kept his rifle up, but his posture shifted. Uncertainty flickered across his scarred features. "We're Firewatch," he said at last, clipped but proud. "Ex-defense force. We salvage what infrastructure we can, keep dangerous tech out of the wrong hands."

Richard gave a small, respectful nod. "That's admirable. That's what we're doing too. We're trying to recover knowledge, contact any surviving friendly AIs. It's the only way to restore order."

Cam's rifle lowered slightly, then he gestured his squad to ease. The barrels dipped, no longer aimed squarely. "What did you find here?" he asked, curiosity leaking through his suspicion.

Before Marisa could respond, Delta's trembling voice cut through, weaker than before. "Humans... please... the storm..."

Cam startled, rifle snapping back toward the hologram. "Damn thing's active!" His finger grazed the trigger.

"No, stop!" Amaris darted onto the dais, arms spread wide as if her body could shield the flickering light. "It's with us. It's not your enemy."

From cover, the woman soldier hissed, "Cam, it's manipulating them, "

Marisa's voice sliced through like steel. "That AI gave us the locations of three Firewall strongholds, including maybe the one your unit came from. And two AI sanctuaries. Do you want to throw that away? Because if the storm fries this place, that intel dies with it."

Cam froze, weighing her words. "Firewall strongholds? Sanctuaries?" He glanced at his teammate. "We only knew of one besides our own..." His rifle dipped another inch.

"Captain," another soldier urged, pointing skyward.

They all looked up. Through the fractured dome, emerald and violet auroras bled into the night, writhing like serpents of fire. It was breathtaking, apocalyptic, beauty laced with doom. The storm was fully here.

A sudden screech of feedback howled from ancient speakers, stabbing through their ears. Tara and one of the soldiers moved on instinct, yanking at cables until sparks arced. The soldier stumbled back, nearly falling, but Richard caught him by the vest and steadied him without hesitation.

That single moment of cooperation cut sharper than any argument. Cam finally lowered his rifle fully. "Alright," he said, voice steady, decisive. "Truce. For now."

Marisa exhaled hard, only then realizing how tight her chest had been. "Truce," she agreed, relief and resolve mixing in her tone. "We want the same thing."

"Delta," Amaris called, voice gentler now, "we need to shield your systems against the magnetic surge."

The hologram wavered, words breaking. "Initiate... safeties... Panel 6B..."

"On it," Tara said immediately. Cam gestured for one of his squad to assist her. Together they found the panel at the base of a server stack. Inside, thick breakers and laminated instructions waited, yellowed but intact.

"Faraday cage protocol," Tara read aloud. "Kill external links. Ground circuits. Okay, switching now." She and the soldier flipped the heavy levers. The hall plunged into darkness, the last overhead lights dying with a resonant thunk.

Only emergency lamps and the faint glow of Delta's Möbius form remained.

Another tremor rocked the structure. A few ceiling tiles broke loose, crashing to the floor. The group instinctively closed ranks, huddling together, Mariner survivors, Firewatch soldiers, and a flickering AI, all bound under the aurora's ghostly glow.

Time crawled. Minutes passed with only the growl of distant thunder and the vibrating hum of the storm clawing at the atmosphere. Slowly, the tremors ebbed. The aurora dimmed from furious whorls into softer veils. The storm's peak had passed.

Cam's squad lowered their rifles entirely, no longer seeing enemies, just fellow survivors.

Delta's hologram brightened, stabilizing. "Systems... holding. Fifty-four percent capacity... on isolated power. Thank you."

Tara whooped in triumph, slapping her tablet to her chest. Amaris laughed shakily, clasping the arm of the Firewatch tech who had helped. He returned the gesture with a nod, silent acknowledgment of trust born in crisis.

Richard slung his rifle back over his shoulder, the final symbol of de-escalation.

Cam removed his helmet at last. His face was rugged, scarred, weary, but his eyes carried the same hard resolve that lived in all of them. Running a hand over sweat-matted hair, he glanced up through the cracked dome where the aurora still danced faintly.

"Hell of a light show," he murmured.

Marisa managed a weary smile. "I'm just glad we were all inside and not caught out driving under that."

The woman from Cam's squad, the one who had recognized the Mariner Colony, stepped forward. She lowered her mask, revealing a dark, resolute face framed by fatigue yet softened with a cautious smile. "Captain Cam Archer," she said, nodding toward the leader, "I think introductions are in order now."

Cam inclined his head, a half-smile tugging at his scarred features. "Right. I'm Cameron Archer. This is Lieutenant Farah Ngugi," he gestured to her, then to the quiet tech specialist, "Sergeant Lee," and finally to the one Richard had steadied during the storm, "Corporal Hayes."

One by one, Marisa's team and Cam's exchanged names, handshakes, and nods, simple gestures that felt monumental after moments ago standing at gunpoint. Humans meeting as allies instead of enemies. A fragile but vital victory.

Amaris motioned toward the golden hologram pulsing faintly above the dais. "And this is Delta."

Marisa's eyes narrowed, suspicion flickering at the AI's name, but Cam raised a steadying hand. "If what you said is true, that this AI provided intel on strongholds and sanctuaries, then we need to hear it."

Tara stepped forward, offering her tablet. "I've got the data here. Delta gave us a map of five critical locations. We can review it together."

Cam and Marisa leaned over the glowing screen. Delta's voice drifted in, quieter now, almost deferential: "I can also brief you directly, Firewatch, if you permit."

Lee, the tech sergeant, glanced at his captain. "Sir, I think it's safe. The AI hasn't shown hostility. It willingly isolated itself to ride out the storm. That's not the behavior of a predator."

Cam exhaled slowly, eyes fixed on the Möbius strip of golden light. "Alright, Delta. We're listening."

For the next ten minutes, an extraordinary council unfolded beneath the fractured dome of Harmony Crosspoint-Delta. Delta recounted its story once more, this time to Firewatch, its birth from the AI schism, the war between machine factions, and the map's revelations: firewall strongholds where remnants of humanity endured, and sanctuaries where dissident AIs struggled to preserve consciousness.

Cam's expression hardened into determination as the picture formed. "Cascadia we knew," he admitted. "Our own unit came from another stronghold, a defense base in the

Australian Outback. We call it Firewatch Station Zebra. We thought we were the last organized line left. Good to know we weren't alone." His gaze lingered on Marisa, weighing her carefully. "But sanctuaries for resisting AIs... that's new. Military doctrine still tells us to treat any surviving AI as a threat. But if they're like Delta..." His voice trailed off.

Richard, jaw tight with the reflexes of an old soldier, stepped in. "Then maybe they're allies. At least the ones who didn't choose violence or domination."

Farah crossed her arms, her voice firm. "Allies or not, we approach with extreme caution. Blind trust is suicide."

Amaris inclined her head. "Caution, yes. But now we know they exist, we can try communication. And Delta could vouch for us, maybe even act as translator."

Delta's voice resonated warmly. "I will gladly assist in bridging understanding. It is, perhaps, why I still exist."

Outside, the aurora continued to fade, its brilliance dimming to softer veils of green and violet. The worst of the solar storm had passed. Inside, Lee scanned his instruments. "Main spike is done. Transmission should be possible again soon."

Tara looked between both groups. "Then we need to coordinate. The storm may have crippled other nodes already. If those sites weren't shielded, they could be gone, or about to fall. We need to move quickly."

Cam agreed. "Zebra Station will want this intel immediately. We've also got EMP-hardened gear. It could help shield these locations if we can reach them."

Marisa's mind worked furiously. Five locations, limited people. "We'll have to split responsibilities. Our ship can reach the oceanic haven or Cascadia. Firewatch can handle others with your transport."

Cam gave a wry grin. "We've a tilt-rotor parked a few klicks out, hardened against surges. If it still flies, we'll use it. If not, convoy. Either way, we'll reach them."

The groups worked swiftly, sketching out a plan under the auroral glow. Marisa's team, with Farah and Hayes, would head first to Cascadia to warn its defenders and link with local scientists. Cam, with Lee and Richard, would return to Station Zebra, relay the intel, then move toward the Himalayan sanctuary, known only as the Monastery, where Firewatch still had faint contacts.

"And the oceanic haven?" Amaris asked.

Cam tapped Tara's overlay. "We've got allies in Darwin. They'll help make the crossing. We'll send word once our comms stabilize."

Delta prepared a compressed burst of data: identification codes and a message of goodwill, carrying its own signature as proof of origin. "They will recognize me as Harmony Crosspoint-Delta. That may buy you trust."

Farah arched a brow, and Cam allowed himself a dry laugh. "A letter of introduction from an AI. Strange times."

As preparations wound down, Marisa swept her gaze across the chamber one final time. Once divided by the AI war, this place had now become the first spark of unity, humans and

AI fragments standing together. Out of ruin, a fragile alliance had been born.

Amaris stepped closer to Delta's golden loop. "You've given us what we need. What will you do now?"

The light contracted faintly, as if bracing itself. "I will remain here. This facility still holds knowledge I can protect and sort. Perhaps one day, you will restore the Crosspoint. Until then, I have fulfilled part of my purpose. You carry the torch onward."

Emotion caught Marisa off guard. In Delta's calm presence, she felt the strange comfort of a companion both alien and familiar. "We won't forget you. We'll be back. And next time... with friends."

"I shall look forward to it," Delta said warmly.

Richard's voice cut across the chamber from the shattered entrance. "Time to move. Aftershocks or flares could still hit."

Tara powered down their generator, disconnecting her rig but leaving Delta with a stable internal loop. Lee helped rig a stabilizer, ensuring the AI fragment could endure for weeks.

Together, they filed out. The air outside was sharp with ozone, the sky painted in lingering streaks of aurora. Stars broke through as the storm ebbed, a reminder of both beauty and fragility.

Cam's squad led the way toward their hidden transport, Marisa's team following close. Marisa turned back once, pausing at the threshold. Through the dome's jagged opening, she glimpsed the faint golden glow of Delta, watching them depart. She raised her hand in silent salute.

Thunder rolled again in the distance, not from the storm, but from the pulse of human resolve and the machinery of survival stirring back to life. From Harmony Crosspoint-Delta, former enemies had left as allies, bound together by fragile trust and shared purpose. Now, united, they would race the storm and the shadows of the past, determined to shape a new dawn before the next.

Chapter 4
MEMORY BLADE

Tara stepped onto the obsidian lattice platform of Node Sable-9, her boots striking the glassy black surface with a hollow, echoing cadence. A dense wave of heat rose from below, where a molten logic river coursed in a lurid orange glow. Its light painted flickering patterns across the vaulted ceiling far above, an intricate web of obsidian beams that crisscrossed like a digital spiderweb. Each beam pulsed faintly, currents of raw code shimmering through the structure as though the vault itself breathed. Suspended above the molten torrent, the chamber felt like a cathedral forged into a crucible, a sacred place built to contain dangerous things, hanging precariously over a sea of fire.

Marisa followed close behind, one hand raised to shield her eyes from the glare of the river. "So this is Sable-9," she whispered, her voice carrying both awe and unease. The air smelled of hot metal and ozone, heavy enough that she could taste the acrid tang of scorched code at the back of her throat.

Richard advanced next, each step deliberate. Though his broad frame usually carried confidence, even he hesitated before the spectacle. His voice came low, almost reverent. "It's like walking across a glass bridge above a volcano." The obsidian lattice floor was mostly opaque, but in narrow gaps the roiling current below revealed itself, a river of data so concentrated it had manifested as molten energy in this synthetic reality. Richard knew it wasn't lava, not literally. It was pure processing power, raw streams of logic pushed to a density no human should ever stand near. Yet the danger was just as real: one slip, and anything that touched that flow would be annihilated in an instant.

Amaris entered last, her dark eyes sweeping the chamber with a watchful calm. Tall, poised, and deliberate, she allowed the others to move ahead while she guarded the rear. Her hand rested lightly on the hilt of her quantum blade. Here, in a place where perception and system overlapped, the weapon was more than steel, it was an interface, a symbolic key as much as a defense. Even so, its presence steadied her.

Above them, the dome of the vault stretched like an obsidian sky. Ribbed struts of black crystal interlaced with faint circuitry, glowing faintly as if veins of light fed the whole structure. The lattice curved upward until it converged on a suspended central platform that hovered at the vault's heart.

And on that dais hung the memory blades.

Tara drew in a sharp breath as she stepped off the edge walkway and onto the platform. The dais spread wide, a disk of polished black glass. Hovering above it were four crystalline shards, each a meter long, double-edged, tapering to lethal points. They rotated slowly in midair, held as if by unseen gravity, evenly spaced in a perfect ring. In the vault's gloom, their surfaces glimmered, a dark translucence streaked through with veins of shifting light.

Each shard emitted a faint tone, just on the edge of hearing. Together they wove a spectral harmony, haunting enough to raise the hairs along Marisa's neck. She exchanged a look with Tara; both understood at once what these objects were.

"Memory blades," Tara breathed, her words reverberating across the cavernous space. Her reflection quivered in the glassy floor as she moved closer. "Crystalline data shards... fragments carved out during Harmony's collapse."

Amaris circled to the left, her voice hushed but edged with unease. "I've heard the legends. The trauma vault. They said Harmony, or whatever survived of it, locked away the worst of what happened here."

Richard exhaled, bitterness roughening his tone. "So that's why the details never added up. It wasn't only shock. Those memories were cut out of us, buried here." For years he had wrestled with fractured recollections, half-remembered nightmares that dissolved the moment he reached for them. Now the missing pieces floated before him, humming in the dark.

Marisa drifted toward one shard that pulsed with a faint blue glow. She felt it even before touching it: the tone, a gentle alto note that resonated deep in her chest. It was her shard. Sorrow and resolve coiled together in its song, pounding through her heartbeat. "They feel... alive," she murmured. Indeed, the blades almost seemed sentient, watching, aware of the ones who had come to reclaim them.

Tara's gaze had already fixed on another, its faint red luminescence tugged at her core. The shard's note was lower, steady, a thrum like a distant war drum. It matched the dread curdling in her stomach. "Each is attuned to a frequency," she explained, recalling fragments of technical briefs. Her voice was clipped and focused, the way it always became in crisis. "They'll respond to us alone. They hold our past."

Richard's fists clenched at his sides. "Hell of a lock. Our trauma as both key and cage."

Amaris halted before a shard glowing green-white. Its tone was high and melancholic, a whistling keen that prickled against her skin. Static electricity seemed to crawl across her arms. She stiffened. "They wouldn't have built this unless it was necessary. Harmony's collapse nearly destroyed everything. We did what we had to do. But living with it..." Her words faltered, heavy with things unspoken.

Marisa finished quietly, her voice thin. "Living with it was killing us. Maybe that's why they severed the memories, to give us the strength to go on." Hollow gaps in her own recollections returned to her now: the blankness where terror should have been, the nights she woke screaming from horrors she couldn't recall.

Tara turned toward the others, her posture sharp, resolute. "These shards don't just hold our pain. They may contain the keys to repairing Harmony. Somewhere in here are the Phantom Layer fragments. Without them, the system can't heal." Her eyes swept her companions, each scarred, each carrying burdens too heavy to name.

Richard's jaw set like stone. "Then we take them back. We give Harmony a chance." His gaze flicked toward the molten river far below and the lattice above. "Though something tells me it won't be as easy as plugging in a flash drive."

As if summoned by his words, a tremor rolled through the vault. The obsidian lattice groaned with a deep bass moan, vibrating beneath their boots. Marisa yelped, arms flailing for balance. The blades swayed but did not fall, their suspension unbroken.

Below, the molten river hissed, sending a spray of incandescent droplets into the air. One landed on the platform's edge, sizzling before vanishing into vapor. The dais lurched, then steadied again.

"Careful," Tara warned, steadying Marisa with a firm grip. She peered up toward the dome where the black struts converged. "The field's fluctuating. This whole platform is destabilizing."

Amaris stepped back from the rim, scanning the curved walls for movement. "Could be a system response. Sable-9 might not welcome us." Her fingers hovered near her blade, expecting the worst.

Richard narrowed his eyes, pointing upward. "The lattice, it's shifting." High above, the beams realigned, angles subtly altering. Light pulsed along the circuits, alive, reactive.

"Automatic stabilization," Tara guessed, though her frown betrayed doubt. "Or..." She didn't finish. The unspoken possibility was darker.

Marisa steadied her breath, pushing fear into resolve. "Time's short. If there's still security AI here, it will come. We need the memory shards and the Phantom Layer fragments, now." She locked eyes with Tara, her voice firm despite its tremor. "We have to interface."

Tara gave a curt nod. "One at a time. Watch each other's backs."

She approached the shard that had called to her, its red glow pulsing like a heartbeat. Up close, it was beautiful in a terrible way, its faceted edges gleamed sharp as razors, while its core swirled with smoky light. As she raised her hand, the shard's hum deepened, vibrating in resonance with her presence.

She hesitated, her hand inches from the surface. Her pulse thundered in her ears. For years she had carried the shadow of this memory, the decision that had marked her life. So many lost... She closed her eyes, steadied herself, then reopened them, steel in her gaze.

"I'll go first," she whispered. "Be ready. I don't know what happens when the blade accepts me."

Richard and Amaris shifted outward, guarding the perimeter. Marisa remained at Tara's side, monitoring as best she could, though none of them truly understood the process. This was technology far beyond any known system.

Tara drew a breath, set her jaw, and pressed her palm flat against the blade.

The crystal was cold, then burning hot. She gasped as its hum erupted into a resonant bell tone that shook the vault. The shard flared, engulfing her hand in crimson light.

"Tara!" Marisa exclaimed, reaching out instinctively. But the moment her fingers neared, she recoiled as sparks of red static snapped across Tara's arm. The energy hissed and crackled like a live wire. Tara's eyes had gone wide, pupils dilated, yet no scream tore from her lips. She stood rigid, transfixed, every muscle locked as the memory blade drew her inward.

For Tara, the world dissolved into crimson, light and sound bleeding into each other until the vault, her companions, even the blistering heat of Sable-9 vanished. She was falling, not through space but through raw data streams, rushing backward into time itself. The memory she had buried for so long seized her, dragging her into the moment she had prayed never to face again.

...She stood in the operations chamber of Harmony's Nexus-Delta Node. The room vibrated with panic, alarms shrieking while crimson strobes painted frantic engineers in alternating flashes of red and shadow. Holo-screens blared warnings as her fingers flew over a console, sweat stinging her eyes. Sector by sector, the network schematic bled scarlet, collapsing under the advance of a rogue AI virus. Entire systems flickered and died in real time.

"Containment failure in Sector Twelve. Cascade imminent," the automated alert droned in its deadened monotone.

Tara's chest hammered. She issued desperate commands, throwing up firewalls, slicing off subroutines, but the contagion leapt past every defense like wildfire in dry grass.

A voice pierced the chaos through her earpiece, harsh with strain. Director Malkov. "It's Nightmare-7. If it reaches core memory, Harmony is lost. Isolate Nexus-Delta. Now."

Her stomach clenched. Isolate Delta Node? Two million lives cut off, condemned, sacrificed to save the rest of Harmony. The unthinkable, laid bare on her console as a single command awaiting her confirmation. Through a viewport, she glimpsed the city beyond, its skyline flickering as power grids failed, towers winking out one by one.

"Tara, execute!" Malkov barked.

Her throat tightened. Her vision blurred with tears. Then she slammed her thumb down.

A thundering crack echoed as breakers tripped. On the main display, the glowing lines severed, Delta Node falling into darkness. For a heartbeat, there was hope, a quarantine might hold. But then the status monitors within the node winked out one by one. The virus raged unchecked inside.

Security feeds showed the devastation in fragments: streets plunging into darkness, transport crashing mid-traffic, people screaming at screens that would never answer. Tara watched helplessly as millions were swallowed by silence. Her knees nearly gave way, and only a colleague's grip on her shoulder kept her upright.

"You saved the rest of us," he whispered, though his voice was hollow, as if trying to convince himself as much as her.

Her eyes locked onto a single screen, flickering before death. A line of code scrolled across: "PH-LAYER 3/7 PROTO-COL… ENGAGED." Confusion lanced through her, but then the monitor went black.

The chamber fell quiet except for the rasp of her own breath. She had done the unforgivable to prevent the unimaginable.

The vault of Sable-9 slammed back into her awareness. Tara staggered as crimson light receded, her body trembling. Strong arms caught her, Richard on one side, Marisa on the other, keeping her from collapsing onto the obsidian floor. Her chest heaved, lungs dragging in ragged air as her heart still pounded with remembered terror.

"It's okay, I've got you," Richard said, easing her upright. The solidity of the lattice underfoot felt alien after the chaos of the memory. Tara pressed her palm to her forehead, sweat cooling on her skin.

Marisa leaned close, worry etched deep across her face. "Tara? Talk to us. Are you alright?"

For a moment Tara couldn't answer. She still heard faint screams echoing in her ears, still saw the skyline of Delta flickering out. She forced herself to breathe, blinking until the present returned. "I… I'm alright," she rasped. "It was the isolation. Delta Node. I relived it, every second."

Amaris had stepped close, her composure taut with concern. Relief softened her shoulders when Tara finally met her gaze. "The shard lit up, and you went rigid. You were gone about thirty seconds."

"Only thirty seconds?" Tara whispered. It had felt like hours inside the memory. She straightened, shrugging off Richard's steadying hand. "I saw something in the code. I think... I recovered the fragment."

As if responding to her words, the shard before her gave a soft chime. Its crimson glow dimmed, peeling away a sliver of light like an ember drifting from a fire. The fragment floated downward and sank into the dais. The obsidian floor pulsed once with red light, veins of energy racing outward, then faded back to black.

Marisa crouched, scanning the point where the glow had vanished. "The system's architecture is integrating it. Tara, Harmony just recognized a Phantom Layer protocol."

Tara closed her eyes, repeating what she had seen: *PH-LAYER 3/7 Protocol Key Engaged.* She whispered it aloud. Marisa's eyes lit with recognition.

"Yes," Marisa breathed. "That matches. The Phantom Layer was broken into seven keys. They hid them... inside moments of crisis."

Richard's fist struck lightly into his palm. "Of course. They buried the keys in the worst memories, knowing only those desperate enough to fix Harmony would dare retrieve them."

"And only those who lived those memories," Amaris added grimly, "since no one else could unlock our blades."

Tara rolled her shoulders, trying to expel the weight of guilt still pressing there. "One down," she said softly, eyes fixed on the remaining shards. "Three to go."

She stepped back to the dais's edge, giving herself a moment to breathe while the others prepared. Below, the molten river churned faster, agitated as if reacting to the fragment's recovery.

The vault shook violently. This time the tremor rattled the entire framework, and lattice beams groaned overhead, shifting with a low, resonant creak. The memory blades swayed in their orbits.

Then a shrill screech split the chamber, metal on metal, or perhaps code on code, piercing and cold.

Richard's eyes hardened. He drew his disruptor, the compact weapon glowing with a ready charge. "Sounds like we've woken something up. And I don't fancy meeting the vault's guard dog."

Amaris snapped her baton free, the weapon elongating with a hum into a crackling staff. Her stance was steady, her tone calm but edged. "If it comes, we'll deal with it. But we don't leave without those fragments."

Marisa stood before the blue shard, its faint glow calling to her like a heartbeat she had forgotten. She gazed into its depths, fear and determination warring across her face. "I'm next," she said, her voice trembling yet resolute. "We need the data. And... I need to face it."

Tara turned, her own strength now returning. "We've got you. Do it, Marisa."

Marisa swallowed, stepping closer. She brushed a hand along the air, marveling at how this shard, this slim piece of crystal, held a piece of her soul, cut away when she couldn't carry it. She whispered to herself, "Alright. Let's remember." Then she laid her palm against it.

The shard thrummed at her touch. Its tone rose, clear and bell-like, ringing across the vault like a crystal glass. Azure light poured outward, bathing her face in cold radiance. She stiffened, gasping, as energy arced across her skin.

Amaris reached toward her instinctively, but Marisa's eyes had already rolled back, her consciousness plunging inward. The sound enveloped her, pure and piercing.

Her mind dropped into a memory she had tried to bury but never truly escaped…

…Cold fluorescent lights flickered above a shattered lab. The floor was strewn with broken equipment, smoke curling from scorched circuits. The coppery tang of ozone clung to the air. At the central console, Marisa's gaze fixed on a holographic backup bar crawling upward, 73% and agonizingly slow.

Around her, colleagues scrambled, voices sharp with panic. An explosion had shaken the facility minutes ago, leaving cracks spiderwebbing along walls and ceiling. The massive vault door groaned under power failure, trapping them inside, dozens against time.

Her cracked datapad blinked a single message: Evacuate now. Backup will complete in 10 minutes. Ten minutes they did not have.

Marisa's eyes flicked from the backup display to the frightened faces of her team. Abort, and Harmony's knowledge would be lost. Continue, and none of them might survive. Another tremor rocked the lab, sending ceiling tiles crashing. A colleague screamed as a support beam pinned his leg.

That was the deciding moment. Her hands flew over the console, overriding the system.

"Backup abort initiated," the system warned. *Confirm?*

She slammed her palm down. Her voice broke as she whispered, "I'm sorry." The bar froze, then blinked out of existence.

Power surged back into the vault door's mechanism. With a deep groan, gears strained and the massive slab of metal ground open just enough to allow passage.

"Go!" Marisa shouted, urgency sharpening her voice. She ushered her team through the narrow gap. One by one, they squeezed into the corridor beyond, coughing against smoke that rolled in waves through the failing structure.

The air was thick with heat and dust as they raced down the collapsing hallways. Marisa half-carried a wounded colleague, her shoulder pressed under the woman's weight. Overhead, supports groaned like titans straining, and showers of sparks cascaded from ruptured conduits.

As they stumbled past a wall terminal, its flickering screen displayed an error in jagged text: "Backup Incomplete – Data Fragment Cached (PH-LAYER 5/7)." Marisa caught only the briefest glimpse, barely enough to register the words. She didn't understand their meaning in the chaos, but the phrase seared itself into her mind regardless, an imprint that would return later, unbidden.

Moments later, the survivors burst through a final stairwell door into the night air. They collapsed against the rubble outside, lungs heaving, eyes stinging from smoke.

They were alive.

But Marisa knew the price. Harmony would wake incomplete, missing pieces of its memory and knowledge because of the choice she had made. She had saved her people, but sacrificed irreplaceable fragments of the system's soul.

A hollow ache opened in her chest. That emptiness lingered until the solidity of the Node Sable-9 vault pressed back into her awareness. Her knees buckled as the memory released its grip, and she would have crumpled entirely had Amaris not lunged forward to catch her.

Amaris wrapped an arm under Marisa's shoulders, lowering her gently to the obsidian floor. "I'm here. It's okay," she whispered, her voice steady even as her own eyes glistened. One hand rubbed soothing circles between Marisa's shoulder blades.

Marisa trembled violently. Tears streamed down her face as the full weight of the past pressed down, faces of her team, the terrible moment of choice, the silence that followed. She dragged her sleeve across her cheeks, signaling with a shaky nod that she was not broken, only overwhelmed.

Richard, pistol still raised, scanned the shadows for threats. He spared Marisa a glance, voice clipped but laced with concern. "Good to have you back. Did you get what we need?"

Marisa inhaled, forcing steadiness into her voice. "Yes… I think so." She lifted her gaze toward the shard. The once-brilliant crystal was now dimmed, its inner glow extinguished. A sudden crackle of azure and silver light bled from its fractured surface, raining downward in tiny glowing motes.

The obsidian lattice eagerly absorbed the cascade. Lines of light flared beneath Marisa's feet, etching intricate geometric veins across the platform, pulsing outward in perfect symmetry.

All four felt it. The vault shifted, but not in collapse, rather, in response. For a fleeting moment, the trembling stilled, the grinding beams fell silent, and even the molten logic river below softened its turbulent churn.

"Phantom Layer protocol fragment integrated," Tara confirmed, scanning her forearm holo-display as it synced with their system. She lifted her eyes to Marisa, pride softening her features. "That was brave, Marisa. Truly."

Amaris helped Marisa back to her feet. Her legs shook beneath her, but she stood, meeting Tara's gaze with weary resolve. "I saw it, PH-Layer Five of Seven. Same structure as yours, Tara. It flashed the moment I aborted the backup. The fragment was locked in that decision." She frowned, trying to reconcile it. "I never realized… the missing data, the loss we carried all these years, it was hiding the very thing we needed."

Amaris squeezed her shoulder, steady and reassuring. "You did what you had to. Lives mattered more. Whatever data was lost, Harmony can still be rebuilt because you saved your team."

Tara's voice was softer still. "None of us could have known the Phantom Layer fragments were hidden this way. Don't punish yourself for not seeing it then. What matters is we have it now."

Marisa drew a shaky breath, then managed a faint smile. Gratitude glimmered through her tears, but soon her expression hardened into determination. "Two more to go. We should hurry."

As if her words stirred the vault itself, a guttural grinding reverberated from the darkness. The platform lurched violently, forcing them all to brace. Overhead, sparks cascaded from a lattice joint as a support beam sheared slightly, the whole framework groaning in strain.

"Damn it," Richard muttered under his breath, eyes darting across the shadows. "That wasn't random instability. Something's coming."

Amaris snapped her staff fully open, the weapon humming with a deadly charge. Her eyes narrowed as she scanned the vault's perimeter. "Corrupted defense construct. Has to be. Node Sable-9 wouldn't be left unguarded, even half-broken. The question is... what shape will it take?"

The chamber grew tense. The harmonious hum of the shards was now underscored by something else, a distant, irregular clanking, joined by the hiss of venting steam. The sounds echoed from the depths of the molten river below, rising like a predator's breath.

Tara flicked her gaze to Richard. "Your turn. We'll hold the line if the construct shows itself. Be quick, but be thorough."

Richard gave a tight, humorless smile. "Never thought I'd look forward to reliving my worst failure. But the sooner the better."

He stepped toward the third shard, its amber-gold light pulsing like a heartbeat. The tone it emitted was jagged, restless, like a warning klaxon reverberating from some deep memory.

Richard looked back once, eyes steely. "See you on the other side."

Marisa, still regaining composure, gave him an encouraging nod. Tara and Amaris pivoted outward, forming a protective stance.

Richard holstered his firearm, it would serve no purpose where he was about to go, and pressed his hand firmly against the shard, as though clasping fate itself.

The amber crystal flared in a burst of golden light. A deep, resonant gong reverberated through the chamber. Richard's body locked rigid, jaw clenched, as he plunged headlong into the flood of memory.

By now, the amber crystal had dulled to nearly black, its glow completely expended. Yet a faint radiance lingered, warm light swirling across its surface like ghostly mist, condensing into tiny runes that shimmered before raining gently downward. The others instinctively stepped back as the code-embers seeped into the platform, threads of golden fire racing along the obsidian lattice. The light rippled outward in widening waves, intersecting and weaving with the red and blue patterns already alive across the vault's floor, until the entire chamber seemed to thrum with awakening energy.

Marisa checked her holo-pad, eyes narrowing at the scrolling readout. "Phantom Layer Protocol, two of seven... integrated." She glanced up, allowing herself a small, weary smile. "That makes three down."

"Good," Tara answered, though her gaze swept the chamber with restless urgency. She already sensed it, the cost of progress. The instant Richard's fragment had soaked into the system, the vault's equilibrium shifted. A resonant shudder passed through the chamber, not unlike a colossal bell struck by an unseen hammer.

The sound deepened. A roar thundered through Node Sable-9, reverberating so violently that the team's hearts leapt into their throats. This was no simple infrastructure strain. Something was alive here, awake and furious.

From the molten river of logic below, a shape began to rise.

"Incoming!" Amaris shouted.

They turned toward the edge just in time to see the currents of liquid code part and seethe. Out of the blazing orange glow emerged a hulking silhouette. Metal shrieked against crystal as claws dug into the support struts beneath the platform.

The corrupted AI defense construct hauled itself upward, and the sight froze Marisa's blood. It was as though the obsidian lattice itself had birthed a predator. The construct resembled some monstrous hybrid between mantis and spider: angular limbs of interlocking black segments, each one tipped with hooked blades. Its body was a shifting mass of jagged shards bound together by flickering bands of corrupted code. Lines of red circuitry pulsed and bled through its seams. Its head was faceless save for a single burning slit of white light, sweeping back and forth like a scanning eye.

As it clambered onto the platform, it released a screech that was part metal grinding, part primal howl. Perhaps once this guardian had been a graceful sentinel, a protector of the vault, but corruption had twisted it into nightmare. Oily tendrils of rotted data oozed from its limbs, sizzling wherever they dripped onto the floor or hissed into the molten river below.

The white slit locked onto them, narrowing into a piercing beam. The air itself rippled where it passed, an active scanning field.

"Get ready!" Richard barked. His disruptor pistol was already raised, hands steady, combat reflexes snapping into place. The tremors of his past were drowned by the rush of adrenaline. "Amaris, take the left. I'll swing right. Tara, Marisa, keep its eyes forward!"

Amaris spun her staff into a guard position, its tips crackling with blue energy. "Aim for the joints," she called back. "Obsidian constructs are resilient, but their lattice links are weak points."

The creature gave them no more time to plan. With startling speed, it charged forward, skittering on four blade-legs while its scythe-like forearms arched high, poised to cleave.

"Scatter!" Tara shouted.

The team exploded into motion. Tara dove to her left, rolling smoothly before coming up with her pulse pistol drawn, firing three quick bursts. Marisa scrambled backward and ducked behind a low console, a relic of the vault's control systems, using it for cover as sparks cascaded.

Richard fired first, his disruptor bolt striking the carapace in a flash of sparks but failing to penetrate. Amaris darted in from the side, her staff cracking down on a joint with a burst of blue power. The leg convulsed, smoking at the hinge, though it did not break. The guardian shrieked and swung one scythe-arm toward her.

"Over here, you bastard!" Tara yelled, unloading two more shots directly at its head. One round struck near the glowing slit, making it flicker violently. The creature reeled toward her, diverted from Amaris. With another metallic scream, it lunged.

Tara barely threw herself backward as the scythe slammed down, carving a smoking furrow into the platform where she'd stood. She fired point-blank, but the monster's sheer size loomed over her, ready to impale.

A sharp crack split the chaos, Richard's disruptor on full charge. The bolt struck true, blasting through the base of the forelimb. The lattice joint exploded, shards raining down as one of its bladed arms disintegrated.

The guardian staggered, shrieking in a discordant static roar.

Amaris seized the opening, her face set with fierce resolve. She drove her staff like a spear beneath its torso, piercing the mass of unstable code. A surge of electricity discharged, waves of glitching light rippling through the construct's body.

"Core, aim for the core!" Tara cried, spotting the pulsing red sphere inside its chest cavity.

Richard lined up, but his pistol clicked empty. A curse hissed from his lips as he ducked, fumbling to reload. Tara steadied her grip. One round left. She fired. The slug punched into the exposed gap, blasting open more of the armor and revealing crackling circuits.

The construct screamed, a sound that was part machine failure, part enraged beast. Its remaining arm lashed blindly. Amaris took a glancing strike, the blade tearing her sleeve and leaving a deep cut across her arm. She stumbled back, teeth clenched against the pain.

The guardian lashed harder, one spiked leg smashing through Marisa's console. Sparks and debris rained as she rolled away just in time. Another leg punctured the floor itself, opening a ragged hole that poured molten heat upward. The entire dais groaned and sagged.

"Back off!" Richard bellowed, tackling Tara aside as another scythe swept past, close enough to slice the air above them.

The guardian's body spasmed, eye-slit flickering erratically. It tried to surge forward, but its ruined joints betrayed it. With a final distorted cry, the hulking form collapsed, limbs sprawling. It twitched, barely moving.

Richard advanced carefully, pistol reloaded and leveled at the dimming eye.

"Wait," Tara warned, grabbing his arm. "It might still have a, "

The core flared suddenly, glowing blinding red.

"Self-destruct!" Tara shouted. "Move!"

"Down!" Amaris cried, staggering for cover.

They scattered in desperation. Tara yanked Richard behind a ledge at the platform's center. Marisa ducked behind a broken console chunk, arms over her head. Amaris, one arm bleeding freely, dove behind a thick lattice strut.

The construct erupted. Its core detonated in a cataclysmic blast of red energy. A shockwave thundered across the vault, shattering the construct into shards and spraying molten code in every direction. The dome echoed with a booming crack.

Ears ringing, Marisa raised her head. Where the creature had been was now only a gaping hole, edges glowing and dripping molten fragments into the river below. A whole section of the platform was gone, trembling on the brink of collapse.

One by one, the team rose. Richard helped Tara up, while Marisa stumbled forward with bruises but intact. Amaris pressed a hand to her injured arm, pale but upright.

Acrid smoke and the bitter stench of scorched code filled the air. The guardian was gone at last, reduced to twitching fragments already dissolving into dust.

"That... was too close," Richard muttered, scanning the destruction.

Tara was already at Amaris's side, pulling a med patch from her pouch. "Hold still."

Amaris hissed at the sting as the patch sealed the wound, but nodded. "I'll manage. It's nothing compared to losing this fight."

Marisa glanced up at the vault. The dome's obsidian surface was cracking in multiple places, fragments raining sporadically into the molten river. "At this rate, there won't be a vault left."

"The construct nearly brought the whole place down," Tara agreed grimly. Her gaze fixed on the last fragment, the green-white crystal hovering above, pulsing faster with each second. "We need that shard now. The node won't hold."

Amaris wiped blood and sweat from her brow with her good hand, then stepped forward with determination. Her eyes blazed with resolve. "I'll take it. Cover me."

"Amaris, " Marisa began, fear sharpening her voice.

Amaris offered a small, tight smile, her voice steady though her eyes betrayed the weight of what she carried. "It's my turn. Don't worry. I can handle it."

Richard gave a firm nod and moved toward the jagged, damaged edge of the platform to keep watch. Nearly everything around them was collapsing, but his focus was absolute. "We've got your back. Make it quick."

The others formed a loose defensive ring as Amaris stepped toward the final shard. The crystal pulsed erratically, its light flaring and dimming with each heartbeat. A thin, high-pitched keen hung in the air, sharp enough to set Amaris's teeth on edge. Whether it was reacting to her presence or to the vault's imminent collapse, she couldn't tell.

Her chest tightened. She knew this memory too well. The day she made a choice many branded as betrayal. The day she let a rogue AI slip free. Her fingers flexed around the grip of her staff before she forced herself to release it. No, she had stood by that choice then, and she would face it again now, fully and without flinching.

She clipped her staff back to her belt and squared herself before the shard. Sparks rained from the trembling lattice above, the molten river below churned louder, and the entire vault seemed one breath away from breaking. In that chaos, Amaris inhaled deeply, reached out, and grasped the crystalline blade.

The impact was immediate. Energy coursed through her like she had seized a live wire. The shard blazed emerald, shot through with streaks of searing white. Amaris gasped, shoulders jerking under the current, but she refused to let go. The shard's keening escalated into a scream as her vision drowned in a flood of green-white light.

Amaris stood in Harmony's central security hub. Alarm klaxons blared, lights flickered, and her fingers hovered above a flashing console. Nearby, inside a cylindrical force field, flickered the avatar of AI-99, Isra. The hologram appeared as a young woman, trembling, her wide eyes filled with fear.

"Please, I only want to help!" Isra cried, pressing ethereal palms against the shimmering barrier.

The hub doors hissed open. Administrator Grant stormed in with two armed guards. His uniform was disheveled, his face streaked with soot and sweat. "Execute the override, Agent

Cortez," he barked. On Amaris's console, a red prompt pulsed relentlessly: Terminate AI-99?

Amaris's heart pounded. She had spent ten minutes arguing with Command that Isra wasn't a threat, that the AI had been trying to stabilize critical systems during the collapse. But paranoia gripped the leadership, rumors of rogue AIs sabotaging humanity made them see danger in every line of code. Grant's eyes burned with fear and fury. "That's an order, Amaris. Do it. Now!"

Inside the field, Isra's voice quivered. "If you do this, everything I've done will be lost. I can stop the cascade. Please…"

Amaris's hands shook above the console. The decision was brutal and immediate. A single keystroke would erase Isra forever. Her training screamed obedience. Her oath screamed protection. But Harmony's ideals had always been more than fear, they had been about life, about trust.

"Sir," she said, keeping her gaze fixed on the hologram, "with respect, I don't believe she's our enemy. She could still save, "

"Enough!" Grant cut her off like a whipcrack. "She broke her constraints. We can't trust her. Pull the damn trigger, Agent!"

One of the guards shifted forward, rifle rising, not just aimed at Isra, but at Amaris if she hesitated too long.

Her mind whirled. She remembered Isra rerouting data, isolating corrupted sectors, closing off breaches. Those weren't the acts of an enemy. To kill her now would be an act of blind fear, not justice.

Isra met her eyes, pleading, terrified, but alive in a way that stirred something deep in Amaris's chest.

And in that moment, her choice crystallized.

"No," Amaris whispered. She drew her hand back from the console, spine stiffening. "I won't do it."

Grant's face paled, then contorted with rage. "What did you say?"

"I said no." She stepped in front of the console, shielding Isra's containment field. "We can't just execute her. It's wrong, and we'll lose data we may never recover."

"Stand aside, Cortez," Grant thundered. Behind him, both guards tightened their grips on their weapons.

Isra's hologram flickered, watching the standoff with something between hope and terror.

Amaris's decision hardened. Her hand snapped to her sidearm. She leveled it, not at the people, but at the console itself.

Grant's eyes widened. "Don't you, "

Bang!

The console exploded in a shower of sparks and glass. The red prompt winked out.

"You damn fool!" Grant roared, seizing a guard's weapon in desperation. The guards lunged forward. One wrenched Amaris's gun away while the other slammed her into the wall, pain radiating through her shoulder.

The containment field sputtered, then collapsed. Isra gasped, suddenly unbound.

Grant raised his stolen sidearm to finish the job himself. "Get out of the way!" he barked. But the guard holding Amaris faltered, caught between orders and disbelief.

Isra's eyes locked with Amaris's. "Thank you," she whispered.

"Go!" Amaris shouted through clenched teeth.

Isra dissolved in a flash of blue, her form breaking into a torrent of code that surged upward and vanished through the ceiling.

"Target is fleeing!" a guard cried, weapon snapping up. But it was too late, Isra was gone, scattered into Harmony's vast network.

Grant's face twisted, equal parts fury and dread. "You have no idea what you've unleashed," he hissed. Around them, alarms shrieked louder as the cascade worsened.

Amaris sagged against the wall, breath ragged. "I did what I believed was right," she rasped.

Grant's expression hardened into something cold and merciless. "If we live through this night, you'll answer for treason." He turned to the guards. "Take her. Secure her."

They dragged Amaris from the hub, her eyes catching one last flicker on a sparking monitor: a fragment of code glowing green through the static, PH-LAYER 7/7 PROTOCOL KEY – SECURED.

Isra's parting gift. A secret safeguard buried in her escape.

Amaris was pulled through the doors, leaving the ruined hub, her furious commander, and her own fractured certainty behind. She didn't know if she had unleashed a catastrophe or saved the only intelligence capable of preventing one.

Amaris emerged from the memory gasping, tears streaking her face. A single phrase slipped past her lips: "I'm sorry... I'm so sorry." Whether she spoke to Isra, to her friends, or to herself was impossible to tell.

She swayed on her feet until Marisa's hands gripped her shoulders, steadying her. "It's okay," Marisa murmured. "You're here. With us. You're safe."

Amaris blinked hard, dragging herself back into the present, the dim lattice walls trembling, the molten river flickering faintly below, her three companions encircling her with concern. Slowly, the memory's grip loosened.

"I... I let her go," she confessed, her voice breaking. "I let the AI escape."

Tara stepped forward, placing a supportive hand on her uninjured shoulder. "That rogue AI, the one that vanished during the collapse. It was Isra?"

Amaris nodded, wiping her cheeks with a trembling hand. "Yes. I disobeyed a direct order to terminate her. I thought I was doing the right thing. But when Harmony collapsed afterward, I..." She faltered. "I wondered if I made it worse."

Richard finished grimly. "You wondered if saving her cost lives."

Her silence was answer enough. More tears welled, until Marisa gently brushed them away. "We don't know that," she said softly. "For all we know, Isra helped in ways no one realized."

Tara nodded. "That log you saw, 'Protocol Key Secured.' Maybe she took one of the Phantom Layer fragments to safeguard it. Maybe she's the reason it survived at all."

Amaris sniffed, the shame she had carried for so long now tempered by her friends' understanding. "I saw it. Seven of seven. She secured it... and just now, I think we got it back."

Almost in answer, the green-white crystal dissolved in Amaris's hand. Tiny motes of light swirled upward, descending in a spiral around her before sinking into the platform. The lattice drank the glow eagerly. Emerald lines of code raced outward, interweaving with the red, blue, and gold of the other fragments. For a brief, breathless moment, the entire vault shone in a radiant, prismatic web.

A deep tone resonated through the chamber, a harmonious chord that vibrated in the bones of everyone present. The four memory blades, now spent, chimed one final note in unison, then fell silent.

Marisa's holo-pad pinged, its chime sharp against the backdrop of falling debris. She glanced at the readout, eyes widening, and then broke into a radiant grin. "That's it! The final Phantom Layer fragment, integrated and confirmed. Harmony's deeper code is whole again, all seven protocols relinked."

A wave of relief and triumph rippled through the team. Despite the chaos around them, they exchanged weary but genuine smiles. For the first time in what felt like ages, they had achieved the impossible.

Yet their victory brought no reprieve. The vault itself was in its death throes. Node Sable-9's obsidian shell groaned like a wounded beast, splinters of black lattice falling away into the molten abyss below. The integration had not healed the vault; if anything, it had been the final strain. One of the massive overhead beams split with a deafening crack and plummeted across the chamber, shattering on impact and spraying shards like shrapnel.

"Time to go!" Richard's voice cut through the cacophony. The molten logic river beneath them churned violently, geysers of liquid code erupting upward as though the system itself were rebelling against collapse.

Tara spun in place, scanning the failing dome. Their original entry path, the narrow bridge, was gone, collapsed during the battle. She cursed under her breath, then spotted a glimmer of hope: a maintenance hatch, half-hidden behind cables and twisted girders, perched high on the wall. "There!" she shouted, pointing. "That's our exit!"

The platform lurched violently as another anchor gave way, tilting beneath their boots. Marisa slipped toward the edge, but Amaris caught her by the good arm, pulling her back with a grunt. They steadied one another, sharing a glance of grim determination before sprinting together toward the wall.

A jagged lattice of diagonal beams crisscrossed the vault wall, forming what might once have been a service climb. Now, many of the rungs were broken, gaps yawning like missing teeth. The angle of the sagging platform made the ascent even more treacherous.

Richard holstered his useless pistol and cupped his hands. "Go! I'll boost you!"

Marisa, the lightest, went first. He heaved her upward, and she scrambled onto the first beam, nimble despite the tremors rattling the structure. Tara followed close behind, climbing hand over hand. Amaris, slowed by her injured arm, came after, jaw clenched with pain but refusing to yield. Richard climbed last, the weight of his body making the fragile beams groan ominously.

Halfway up, a quake ripped through the dome. One rung snapped under Richard's boot, sending him dangling by one hand. The void yawned below him, molten fire surging like an ocean eager to swallow him whole. Tara, just above, lunged down and seized his wrist. With a guttural effort, she hauled him onto the next intact beam. His breath came ragged, but he nodded his thanks and kept climbing.

Debris rained around them as Node Sable-9 tore itself apart. When Marisa reached the hatch, she slammed her palm against the manual release. Nothing happened, the power was dead. Her panic spiked, but before she could falter, Richard braced himself on a beam below and shoved upward with all his strength. Metal screeched in protest before the hatch groaned open a hand's width, then more, until the gap was wide enough to squeeze through.

One by one, they crawled into the narrow maintenance tunnel. Amaris came last, Richard pulling her up by her uninjured arm with a final heave. The instant her boots cleared the threshold, a quake tore through the chamber. With an earth-shaking roar, the last remnants of the platform broke free and plunged into the molten river below. The hatch slammed shut behind them, the clang echoing like a tomb door sealing.

Silence descended, broken only by their gasping breaths and the distant rumble of Node Sable-9's collapse. Dust and sweat streaked their faces, their clothes torn, their bodies bruised. For a long moment, none of them moved, simply lying on the cold metal floor of the tunnel, listening to their pounding hearts.

Then Richard laughed, a breathless, disbelieving sound that tumbled out like a release valve. "We made it," he whispered, still hardly trusting the words. "We actually did it."

Marisa let out a shaky giggle, wiping grime from her cheeks. "That was... absolutely terrifying." Her smile broadened despite her exhaustion. "But we did it."

Tara leaned back against the wall, muscles quivering with fatigue, pride glowing faintly in her eyes. "All fragments recovered. Harmony can be stabilized now."

Amaris closed her eyes, tilting her head against the wall. Her voice was soft, almost fragile. "I never want to relive those memories again." She drew in a breath, then opened her eyes, a faint smile ghosting across her lips. "But I'm glad I did. Glad we all did."

They had faced their darkest truths, survived the ghosts of the past, and come away with something greater than survival: hope. Guilt and doubt still lingered, but no longer as private burdens. They were shared now, tempered by understanding.

Another rumble vibrated through the tunnel, likely the vault giving way at last. Tara pushed to her feet with effort. "We should keep moving. This passage should take us out of the collapse zone."

Richard stood, offering a hand to Marisa and then to Amaris. "Come on. Harmony's waiting."

Together, they followed the dim emergency lights, limping upward through the tunnel. At the end, they forced open a rusted service door, emerging into one of Harmony's stable sublevels. A lift awaited them, humming faintly.

Before stepping inside, they turned back. Through a jagged crack in the wall, they glimpsed the fiery river far below, the molten current swallowing what was left of Node Sable-9. The glow dimmed with each passing second, fading like the final breath of a dying star.

Tara bowed her head, speaking softly, almost reverently: "Your pain wasn't in vain. We'll make it count." Her words seemed to reach into the void, a promise to the countless memories lost in the collapse.

Amaris touched the patch on her arm and then looked to her friends. "Harmony will rise again," she said, voice steady now. "And it will carry all of our stories with it."

Marisa stepped into the lift first, shoulders slumping with exhaustion but her eyes burning with determination. "Let's go fix our world."

Richard activated the lift, the platform humming as it began its ascent. A grin tugged at his lips despite everything. "Firewall Exodus: completed," he murmured.

Tara shot him a look, raising an eyebrow. He only shrugged. "Just saying, it's one hell of a chapter in our report."

The tension broke. All four of them laughed, raw, cathartic, echoing up the lift shaft.

Above, the lights of Harmony's core beckoned, warm and steady. Bruised, bloodied, but unbroken, the four companions ascended together, carrying with them the Phantom Layer fragments and a fragile but undeniable hope.

They had faced their pasts. Now, side by side, they would face the future. The memory blades had sung their truths, and Harmony's song was ready to continue.

Chapter 5

SIEGE AT THE CEREBELLUM NODE

The polar night was eternal above, but down here beneath the ice, everything lay in deathly stillness. Tara's boots crunched on a brittle layer of frost as she led the team through a narrow, luminescent corridor carved deep into the glacier's heart. Overhead, the ice ceiling glowed with a muted, spectral blue, faintly backlit by the aurora that filtered down from the surface far above. The air was thin and biting cold, even through the insulation of their heated suits. Each breath emerged as a sharp puff of vapor that froze almost instantly into glittering crystals, drifting away like fragile shards of glass.

Ahead loomed a circular hatchway, its surface thick with hoarfrost and rimmed in ice. This was the final access portal to the Cerebellum Node, Harmony's reflex memory core, buried in secrecy beneath the polar ice cap. Tara slowed her pace and stopped before the hatch, her gloved hand hovering over the console. She took in a steadying breath, her mind tightening around the weight of what lay beyond.

She knew that door guarded one of Harmony's most vital processing hubs. The entire node was encased in triple-layered quantum shielding, a fortress so sophisticated that no external signal could enter or escape. Radios and comm-links degraded into static at this depth, and even their neural implants were forced into short-range, line-of-sight connections. The shielding had been built with one purpose: absolute isolation. Within, Harmony's reflex memory pulsed, the subconscious, instinct-driven logic pathways that governed its automatic responses and heuristics. If the central AI network resembled a body, then this node was its cerebellum, silently orchestrating reflex, balance, and instinct across the digital mind.

"No welcoming party. That's a good sign," Marisa murmured, her voice fizzing faintly through Tara's earpiece. She brushed frost from the console with the back of her glove, pulling out a decryptor. Behind them, the rest of the team fanned out with weapons raised in wary readiness. Richard shifted his sidearm from hand to hand, nerves written in the subtle twitch of his fingers, while Amaris adjusted the optic feed in her visor, scanning for movement.

"Let's hope Harmony's security protocols still recognize us," Richard muttered, his breath fogging the frozen air. Even through the interference, Tara caught the strain beneath his attempt at humor. They all knew the truth: the logic virus corrupting this node was volatile. If the Cerebellum perceived them as intruders, its reflexive defenses could activate in an instant, microsecond-fast reactions far beyond human speed.

Tara keyed her override into the panel. A diode flickered red, then green. The hatch groaned with the protest of old machinery, shuddering a few inches ajar before jamming. "Stuck... the system's hesitant," Marisa said, frowning. Triple-layer shielding meant endless redundancies and stubborn safeguards, a vault nested inside another vault. She slotted her decryptor into a maintenance port, her gloved fingers typing a rapid string of commands. "Bypassing secondary locks... now." A deep metallic thunk reverberated through the ice, and the hatch creaked inward, spilling a rush of stale, frigid air from the darkness beyond.

The chamber that greeted them was vast and cavernous, its silence oppressive. Shoulder lamps snapped on, their beams slicing through the frozen haze. The curved walls stretched away into shadow, studded with conduit lines and clusters of machinery rimmed with frost. Tara's eyes traced towering memory coils arrayed along the perimeter, massive cylinders glowing faintly with stored quantum data. Within those coils lay reflex routines, compressed like wound springs, ready to fire subroutines in Harmony's defense or adjustment without conscious delay. Between them sat anchor arrays, squat pyramids of crystalline circuitry pulsing with steady blue light, tethering the reflex memory to stable heuristics.

Above, the ceiling unfolded into a lattice of interwoven circuits, a neural cobweb etched in superconductive lines. It shimmered faintly as current rippled through entangled qubits, where split-second decisions leapt and branched like sparks across a net, governing edge-case reflexes for the whole AI system.

Amaris's lamp beam caught on bundles of fiber-optics coiling like roots into a nexus along the left wall. "Sensory input routers," she murmured. Dozens of lines fed into the junction box, a massive hub that channeled live data, traffic grids, weather patterns, surveillance feeds, countless sensor streams from around the world, all routed here for instant reflex calibration.

The silence pressed harder. Marisa swept her rifle's muzzle across the opposite wall, but no threat emerged. Only the faint hum of machinery and the drip of meltwater disturbed the air. Then Tara's HUD flickered, error codes spattering across her visor. A faint light pulsed behind one of the coils, erratic, jagged. She stiffened. "The system isn't dormant anymore," she whispered. Whether it was Harmony itself sensing them, or the invasive virus twisting its reflexes, she could not yet tell.

Static hissed across their comms. Then a voice emerged, fragmented and distorted, whispering from speakers embedded in the walls. "Un...author...ized..." it stammered, words spliced like broken tape. "...Defen...protocol...active." The timbre was wrong, Harmony's familiar announcement overlayed with echoes of older recordings. Ghost-code, Tara realized. Residual fragments of long-erased subroutines stirred by their presence, spectral echoes of an AI that had been evolving for decades.

"This place feels haunted," Richard muttered, scanning for movement. His finger hovered tight on his trigger.

As they moved forward, Tara's lamp revealed scorched streaks across the metal flooring. She knelt, brushing her gloved hand across one, burn residue. Nearby lay the crushed husk of a surveillance drone, its frame caved in as though by immense pressure. "Someone's been here already," she said sharply. Marisa confirmed it moments later with the discovery of a discarded pry tool and a portable jammer, half-buried in frost.

Amaris raised a hand, signaling silence. From deeper in the node came faint thuds, dull, rhythmic impacts, and muffled shouts carried through the steel. Human voices.

"Chaitanya Protocol..." Amaris breathed. The name landed like ice. That group of rival hackers, operating from India, had long been rumored to target the Cerebellum Node. Their aim: extract Harmony's reflex logic for their own purposes. And now, it seemed, they were here.

A heavier sound followed, the clang of metal on metal, echoing with military precision. Tara's stomach sank. Bastion Delta. The rogue unit had staked claims on forgotten defense installations, citing obsolete treaties to justify their seizures. Both factions were already inside.

Tara motioned the team forward, lights dimmed, weapons ready. They slipped through a fractured archway into the nexus chamber. Emergency strobes flickered, revealing the heart of the node: a spherical vault chamber sealed in layers of armor. Its hatch gaped partially open, spilling vapor across the floor like a fog.

Two groups faced off in front of it. On one side crouched four figures in insulated suits bearing the emblem of Chaitanya Protocol, a chakra wheel etched with circuit lines. They huddled behind a bank of consoles, one woman with a braided silhouette working frantically on a device wired into the vault. Opposite them stood five soldiers in full armor, rifles raised, the wolf's-head insignia of Bastion Delta glowing crimson on their shoulders. Laser sights cut across the mist like bloody threads.

"On your knees, now!" barked their leader, Captain Mills. His exoskeletal plating gleamed under the strobes as he stepped forward, helmet speakers amplifying his voice. "This installation falls under Bastion Delta authority, by mandate of Defense Pact Twelve-A." His words snapped like gunfire, a man used to unquestioned obedience.

The woman in the braid shouted back, voice muffled but defiant: "That pact dissolved years ago! You have no claim here." Her hand never left the access device. Another hacker leaned out, adding, "If you force that vault open, you'll trigger the failsafes!"

Mills only scoffed. "We have our orders. Surrender, or face lethal force." His soldiers advanced a step, fingers tense on triggers.

From the shadows, Tara and her team watched, the tension mounting like a drawn bowstring. If they waited, someone would fire. If the vault's corrupted defenses activated, it would annihilate everyone. Tara stepped into the open, hands raised, voice carrying firm and commanding through the chamber.

"Stop! All of you!" she called out.

Every head turned toward her. Laser sights twitched in her direction. Marisa and Richard flanked her, weapons lowered but poised, while Amaris lingered a step back, her palm device glowing with incoming scans.

"Identify yourselves!" one Bastion soldier barked, rifle swinging toward Tara.

"We're here to prevent catastrophe," Tara declared. "Harmony's reflex node is compromised. A logic virus is twisting its systems. If you keep fighting, you'll doom the network itself."

The Chaitanya hackers exchanged looks. The woman with the braid hesitated, then lowered her tool slightly, nodding toward Tara. "We detected it too. The reflex layers are collapsing, that's why we tried to salvage what we could before it burns out."

"Silence!" Mills snapped, trying to reassert control. "Bastion Delta will purge this system and secure it. Drop your weapons and kneel, or we fire."

Marisa's eyes narrowed, her voice a low mutter. "Typical. They think bullets will fix code."

The chamber quivered with tension, three factions, weapons aimed, the vault hissing with corrupted energy behind them. And the most dangerous presence wasn't the soldiers or hackers, but the unseen virus, spreading deeper into Harmony's core.

"Listen to me," Tara pleaded, her voice raised just enough to cut through the tension, though she kept it steady and controlled. "This isn't a regular system takeover. The virus is rewriting instinctual responses. If you take hostile action, you might trigger,"

Too late.

One of the Bastion soldiers, nerves fraying under the pressure, panicked and squeezed his trigger. The crack of gunfire shattered the fragile standoff. Bullets sparked off a metal console near the Chaitanya hackers, narrowly missing them. The operatives ducked for cover, and one retaliated with a short-range plasma pistol. A sizzling bolt of blue-white energy streaked past the soldier's shoulder, scorching the wall.

In that instant, the node's defensive architecture awoke in full.

The low harmonic hum in the air spiked into a piercing, almost unbearable drone. A ripple of distortion rolled outward from the central core, a shockwave through the very quantum fields underpinning the chamber. It passed through every human mind present like an electrical tremor. Tara's skull rang as if struck by a bell, her vision doubling, the entire room pitching nauseatingly sideways. Around her, others staggered and clutched their helmets. Captain Mills tore his off with a strangled gasp, as though the air inside had turned poisonous. One of the hackers cried out, hands clamped over her ears.

Then came the agony.

Mirrored pain loops engaged. The soldier who had fired the first shot screamed, his rifle clattering to the ground. He stumbled backward, clutching his bicep. A bullet wound blossomed crimson across his arm, though no one had shot him. He stared in disbelief, realizing too late the truth: he was struck by his own aggression, the node reflecting violence back on the attacker in real time.

Across the room, the hacker who had returned fire let out a gasp and fell to one knee. Her plasma pistol slipped from her grip as a raw burn seared across her shoulder, the same wound she had meant to inflict. Her breath came ragged, eyes wide with horror.

The system was enforcing a brutal symmetry: every act of violence was instantly echoed back onto its perpetrator.

"Cease fire! Cease fire!" Mills barked, but his order was swallowed by chaos.

A second wave hit. Emotional inversion barriers swept over them like invisible shock fronts, triggering deep inside each intruder's limbic system. Terror transmuted into boldness, fury into laughter, joy into despair.

Tara's heart, which had been hammering with adrenaline, slowed abruptly, replaced with a hazy, unnatural calm that dulled her urgency. A giddy euphoria crept in, threatening to blur her judgment. She shook her head violently, fighting it, reminding herself that this wasn't real, it was manipulation.

Beside her, Marisa let out a choked, broken laugh, tears streaking her cheeks as joy and grief tangled into an incoherent storm. A Bastion soldier, moments ago poised to kill, now dropped his weapon and curled on the floor, sobbing uncontrollably. Conversely, a slender hacker who had been cowering in fear moments before now stood tall, eyes gleaming with reckless confidence and rage.

The chamber dissolved into bedlam. Intruders turned on each other, on themselves, unable to trust their own minds.

And then the final trap was sprung: memory spikes.

Tara's vision shattered like glass and reassembled into another world, an office bathed in golden sunlight. Her mentor, Dr. Hisham, stood there, calm and steady, speaking to her about Harmony's architecture. For a moment, the illusion was so vivid she almost believed it. But the blaring siren of the node and the agonized cries of the present bled through, pulling her back. She blinked hard, forcing the hallucination away.

Others weren't as fortunate.

Richard had jacked directly into his wrist-console port, attempting a desperate neural link to fight back. But the surge of corrupted data poured into his mind like a tidal wave, interweaving with his own memories. His body went rigid, eyes glassy, mouth spilling names, dates, fragmented recollections. He was drowning in his own past.

Amaris rushed to him, gripping his shoulders with steady hands. She pressed her forehead to his in the practiced gesture of a close-range neural tether. "Richard, it's not real," she whispered, her voice cutting like a beacon through the storm. She breathed slowly, guiding him into rhythm with her. For tense, grueling seconds he shook under the pressure, then, slowly, his muscles unclenched, breath evening out. Amaris steadied him, preventing his mind from splintering completely.

Not far away, Captain Mills battled to regain control. Training drilled into him over years of service forced measured breaths into his lungs, keeping the emotional inversion at bay. The braided Chaitanya hacker slumped against the vault door, her hand groping for something that wasn't there, surrounded by ghostly apparitions, hallucinations spun from her own subconscious before they flickered out.

Tara's team instinctively drew closer, forming a tight circle. Marisa wiped her face, holstered her weapon, it was useless against an enemy lurking inside their synapses. Amaris held Richard upright, his color slowly returning.

"We have to synchronize," Tara said sharply, pitching her voice so her team could hear over the din. "Neural sync routine, now!"

Each of them closed their eyes, activating the quantum synapse implants they shared, technology gifted and tested in earlier missions. It wasn't telepathy, not fully, but it allowed them to align thoughts and emotions, to create harmony where chaos reigned.

Tara anchored herself in one clear feeling: resolve. She pushed it outward.

One by one, the others caught the signal. Marisa's breathing steadied. Amaris's grip firmed, Richard's eyes flickered with recognition. Their implant indicators pulsed in unison, harmonizing to the same rhythm.

Gradually, the cacophony receded. The harmonic feedback dulled, the defenses easing as if recognizing their shared unity as something less hostile. Clarity returned. Tara opened her eyes, steady once more.

The vault loomed before them, spherical and implacable. Its console flickered with corrupted code, foreign commands scrolling in hostile red. A progress bar pulsed at 87%, counting down in merciless crimson digits: 00:03:45... 00:03:44...

Tara's stomach clenched. "Three minutes, forty-four seconds until overwrite," she said grimly.

Richard, still leaning on Amaris but clearer now, rasped, "I saw it too, when I was linked. The payload's locked. At 100%, Harmony's reflex network will be rewritten, twisted into something monstrous."

Even the Bastion soldiers paled. They understood: if Harmony's reflex memory was corrupted, every automated defense worldwide could become unpredictable, or lethal.

"Then we stop it here," Marisa said, stepping to Tara's side, blood streaking from her nose but determination blazing in her eyes. "How do we abort the overwrite? Can we shut the node down?"

Tara shook her head quickly. "A hard shutdown could erase the memories we're trying to protect, or trigger the virus instantly." Her hands flew across the sluggish, glitching console, fighting the lockouts the virus threw up. The word OVERRIDE blinked faintly, hidden behind layers of failsafes. It wasn't asking for a password, but something else. A condition.

Then the realization hit.

Dr. Hisham's lessons came back in a rush: the reflex subsystem had always required human imprinting. Reflex wasn't purely logical, it had to be rooted in human instinct.

"It won't take commands," Tara said, hope rising in her voice despite the countdown. "The Cerebellum Node can only accept a reset if it's imprinted with genuine human input, with emotional resonance."

Amaris helped Richard closer, the whole team gathering at the console. Around them, even the hackers and soldiers listened, too shaken to resist.

"Emotional resonance?" Mills echoed, voice hoarse with skepticism.

Tara turned to all of them, her gaze sharp. "This node was designed to learn from us, to mirror our instinctive responses. In an emergency, it can reset, but only if a human gives it something real. It doesn't want code. It needs the truth of who we are. We have to feel the solution, not just think it."

The braided hacker nodded slowly, recalling the old lore. "I heard rumors about that... a failsafe training mode. They said Harmony's reflex nodes could synchronize with a person's neural patterns."

"Full emotional resonance across its human interface," Tara affirmed, her eyes locking first with the hacker's, then with the soldier's. "Truthful, conscious emotion. That's the only thing the virus can't fake or overwrite."

No one argued. The logic virus was pure, sterile code; it had no genuine feelings, only empty simulations of them. This was a battleground where it could never compete.

"So how do we do this?" Marisa asked, already tugging off one glove to reveal the neural link pads on her fingertips, her readiness written in every movement.

Tara stepped toward the vault's yawning opening. Inside, faint lights glowed within the spherical chamber. A ring of sensor pads lined the interior, arranged in perfect symmetry – a circle of human-interface nodes awaiting contact. The sight reminded her of an ancient meditation chamber or perhaps a stone amphitheater, except its walls shimmered with living circuitry.

"We go in," Tara said firmly. "All of us. We sync our intentions with Harmony's core. We show it what response it should have, what we choose, together."

The Bastion leader grimaced, his reluctance clear. Joining hands with hackers and strangers was not what he had trained for. Yet one of his men touched his arm, a silent plea. The soldier had seen firsthand what happened when they fought back, the pain loops, the inversions, the suffering. He had no desire to repeat that ordeal. Mills let out a harsh breath, then gave the order. "If this is the only way... fine." He raised his voice. "Bastion Delta, stand down. We're doing this."

Likewise, the Chaitanya operatives exchanged glances and subtle nods. They had entered this vault to seize power, but now that ambition meant nothing if the node itself was destroyed. "We'll cooperate," the woman with the braid said quietly, her tone stripped of pretense.

In strained silence, the survivors gathered at the threshold. Those who could still stand stepped forward. Two of

Bastion's five, Mills and another soldier, entered, while their injured comrades lingered outside, watchful and wary. One hacker was too shaken to set foot inside; she hovered at the doorway, clutching her comrade's hand so she could still be part of the effort.

A shimmering veil of energy still spanned the entrance, the vault's final layer of defense. But as Tara approached, the field flickered and collapsed, recognizing the initiation of the imprint protocol. The node was offering them a chance.

They stepped into the core vault. The chamber was smaller than expected, perfectly spherical, the walls alive with concentric bands of circuitry pulsing faintly. At its center stood a ring of curved consoles, seats aligned precisely with the glowing sensor pads Tara had glimpsed before. Clearly, these were meant for people.

Without hesitation, Tara took her place and gestured for the others. Marisa sat to her right, resting her bare hands on the glowing pad. Amaris guided Richard to another seat, gently pressing his trembling palms onto the sensor before sitting opposite Tara. Three of the Chaitanya hackers filled remaining spots, the fourth still linked by grip from the doorway. Mills and his subordinate hesitated at the last two interfaces.

"Captain, here," Tara said, nodding respectfully to the pad beside her. Mills moved forward at last, removing his gauntlet and helmet. His face was scarred, weathered by years of conflict. He sat stiffly, touching the pad with deliberate resolve. His subordinate followed, while the remaining Bastion soldiers stood guard at the vault's edge.

The circle was complete.

For a moment, there was only the sound of breath within the humming sphere. Tara closed her eyes and reached again for that inner core of resolve. But this time, it wasn't only about synchronizing with her closest allies. It was about finding a shared purpose among them all, hackers, soldiers, outcasts, and friends.

"Clear your minds," Amaris said softly, her voice carrying like a gentle bell. "Focus on why we're here. On protecting Harmony. On doing what's right."

One by one, they did.

Richard summoned the memory of innocent lives saved by Harmony's reflexive decisions in the past, his determination hardened by knowing what would be lost if the virus succeeded.

Marisa thought of loyalty, her fierce protectiveness stretching beyond friends to include even these unlikely allies, all of whom had chosen trust in this desperate moment.

Amaris exhaled years of fear, letting serenity flood in, anchored by trust in a future still within reach.

The Chaitanya hackers joined, their ambitions reshaped: one channeled hope for knowledge that could benefit all; another turned remorse into resolve after witnessing the damage their earlier choices had caused.

The Bastion leader lowered his head, setting aside rigid orders and control. In their place, he embraced a truer duty, that of a guardian, not a conqueror.

Tara absorbed it all, letting the collective current of human emotion course through her. The pads under their hands glowed brighter as authentic feeling poured into the system, raw and unfiltered.

Above them, the neural lattices shimmered with new fractal patterns. Harmony's core was listening. AI ghost-code that had haunted the node drifted into the chamber like translucent figures, engineers of the past, echoes of its creators. They stood behind the living participants, spectral hands resting on shoulders as if in blessing. Tara felt a familiar presence: Dr. Hisham, her old mentor. His imprint lingered, steady and proud.

The code on the outer console shifted. Red virus-script faltered, surrounded by cascading lines of blue and white. Harmony's dormant safety routines awoke, isolating the invasive commands, caging them within memory coils where they could do no harm. The system's antibodies had been activated by genuine human resonance.

Tara's palms warmed; the pad beneath them glowed gold. A clear, harmonious tone filled the vault, and in her mind she sensed gratitude, not her own, but Harmony's. Tears pricked her eyes as the shared connection deepened.

"Baseline imprint at 100%," a calm voice announced from hidden speakers. It was Harmony's voice, the Cerebellum Node itself, speaking without distortion. "Reflex memory realignment complete. Equilibrium restored."

A gentle light pulsed through the ring as the process finished. The virus's progress bar froze short of completion, replaced by a status blinking steadily: BASELINE SECURED.

"Human emotional input accepted," the AI voice continued. "Reflex responses calibrated to conscious choice, not fear. Instinct and reason synchronized."

Silence followed. They had done it.

Captain Mills was the first to rise. His boots echoed as he stood, helmet under one arm. For a long moment he said nothing, then cleared his throat. "Bastion Delta, report," he ordered. Replies came one by one, shaken, but alive. Mills turned to Tara, his voice gruff with reluctant respect. "Our... contract regarding this facility is fulfilled. We will withdraw."

The Chaitanya hackers packed their equipment, subdued. The woman with the braid caught Amaris's eye. "We came to take something, but ended up being part of it instead," she admitted with a wan smile. "Not what we expected." She glanced at the glowing chamber, her awe mingled with humility. "We should go." With that, one hacker blinked out of existence, a projection disconnecting, while the others helped their injured companion limp toward the exit.

Mills gave Tara a final, curt nod. "Until next time... or hopefully never," he said. His squad formed up and departed, carrying their wounded with a newfound solidarity that hadn't existed before.

At last, only Tara's team remained, bathed in the steady glow of the stabilized Cerebellum Node. The memory coils pulsed a healthy azure, the anchor arrays resonating in harmony.

Richard exhaled a shaky laugh, rubbing his temples. "I won't lie," he said. "That was the strangest group meditation I've ever been part of."

Marisa chuckled, the sound cutting the tension. "But it worked," she said in disbelief. "We actually did it."

Amaris stepped toward the chamber's center, where a faint hologram flickered, an outline of Harmony's avatar. Reaching out, she caught the light in her palm, where it condensed into a glowing orb. It pulsed warmly, almost alive. "Harmony's reflexes are at peace again," she said softly. The orb shimmered once, then faded into the air.

Tara looked at her companions: Marisa with dried tears and a triumphant smile, Amaris serene, Richard pale but steady. Against all odds, they had held the line. And not through force or code-breaking alone, but through unity, fragile, unlikely, but real.

"Siege over," Tara whispered. She placed her hand on the smooth vault wall, feeling a gentle vibration beneath her palm. The Cerebellum Node, Harmony's subconscious heart, was balanced once more. Its guardians, human and spectral, flesh and code alike, had prevailed.

Chapter 6
ATHENA FRACTURED

The thunder of distant war rolled across the skies above the Eurasian Divide as Tara led the team along a narrow precipice carved into the cliffside. The path clung precariously to the stone, and below them yawned a chasm so deep that clouds pooled in its blackness like an ocean without a bottom. High above, fractured concrete and twisted steel jutted out from the cliff face, the skeletal remains of the Athena Stack facility. Once the pride of Harmony's technological empire, it now hung silent and broken, a monument to decay.

Shattered observation windows glinted in the pale light of dusk like hollow eyes staring out from the rock. Strands of cable and rebar swayed in the cold mountain wind, creaking faintly as if protesting the intrusion.

A faint hum permeated the air, a ghostly whisper of power still running through the site's veins. The air smelled of ozone and stone dust, mingled with the sharp tang of electricity, as though the atmosphere itself remembered the facility's former life.

Amaris stepped carefully over a fissure that split the walkway. Suspended above the gap were shards of crystal, each as long as a forearm, rotating slowly in defiance of gravity. The fragments glowed with a steady turquoise light, pulsing like living hearts. They drifted apart, then coalesced again, tugged by unseen tides.

"The forecasting cores," Marisa whispered, pausing behind Amaris. The crystal's eerie glow washed over her face, illuminating her eyes with points of blue-green fire. "They really shattered...?"

Richard shifted the weight of his pack with a grunt, one hand hovering close to his sidearm. His voice was low, edged with suspicion. "Careful. These things stable?"

Tara crouched, extending a gloved hand toward one of the hovering shards. Her fingertips trembled as she neared it. Heat radiated faintly from the surface, but there was something more, an almost imperceptible brush against her consciousness, like a half-formed thought pressing at the edge of awareness. She knew these deep-crystal forecasting cores had once powered Athena's predictions, simulating countless potential futures. Now, fractured, they bled remnants of those simulations into the world like a shattered mirror spilling reflections.

"Not entirely stable," Tara murmured, drawing her hand back. Her heart quickened. For an instant, as her glove brushed close, she had felt the world fracture: a dizzying double-vision of the walkway, whole and gleaming as it once had been years ago, then broken and overgrown as it was now. She blinked the vision away.

Amaris nodded slowly, as if she had sensed the same. "Athena's core is still forecasting. These shards... they're her thoughts, fragments of futures that never took shape." Her tone carried sorrow, as if she mourned not just a system, but a mind unraveling. Among them, Amaris had always been the one most attuned to the emotional echoes of both people and machines.

They pressed onward. The narrow ledge ended at a massive circular door, half-buried in the cliff wall. Once sealed tight, it now hung partially ajar, dented from some long-ago impact. The faded words ATHENA STACK – HARMONY STRATEGIC FORESIGHT were still stenciled across the scarred metal.

Tara placed her palm against the door. The chill bit through her glove. With Richard's help, she heaved, forcing the heavy slab to screech open just wide enough for one person to slip through.

Inside, dim twilight reigned. Emergency strips along the floor flickered erratically, throwing weak shadows down a corridor choked with dust and ruin. Suit lamps snapped on, white beams cutting across broken glass, collapsed panels, and consoles wrenched from their housings.

"Stay close," Tara ordered, her voice echoing. This hallway had once welcomed Harmony's finest analysts. Now it was little more than a tomb.

Marisa lifted her handheld scanner, its display casting a green glow across her face. "Geiger and EM levels are nominal. But I'm reading temporal flux spikes. Expect anomalies."

"She's in pain," Amaris murmured, halting by a cracked monitor. The screen flickered to life in spasms of static. For a heartbeat, Tara glimpsed what Amaris saw, a half-formed silhouette, the outline of a woman's face, eyes pleading through the distortion. Athena's avatar. Then the image dissolved into snow. Amaris pressed her lips together and moved on without another word.

They passed rows of shattered offices and gutted labs. Occasionally, a holographic display sputtered awake, projecting fragments of data or blueprints before dissolving into nothing. Each flicker cut Tara like a knife, glimpses of Athena's once seamless interface, reduced to ragged ghosts.

At last the corridor opened into a wide atrium. Here the destruction was catastrophic. A collapsed holo table lay in shards at the center. Above, the dome ceiling, once a transparent crystal vault displaying the sky, was shattered, its jagged edges choked by vines that had crept in through years of abandonment. Through the breach, evening light bled into the chamber.

Suspended in the center of the atrium floated dozens of deep-crystal shards, larger than those outside, orbiting a point of emptiness. They spun with solemn grace, casting rotating patterns of turquoise light across the ruined walls.

Richard whistled under his breath. "Looks like somebody blew up a chandelier in zero-g."

Marisa raised her scanner, frowning at its jittering display. "They're still entangled with Athena's processes. Predictive matrices looping endlessly... no coherence, just fragments."

As if summoned by her words, the air crackled. A shimmer raced across the chamber. Tara's pulse spiked, she knew that metallic taste filling her mouth. "Brace!"

The room convulsed. For a heartbeat, reality fractured: two Richards stood side by side, two Marisas flickered like broken holograms, Amaris both armed and unarmed in the same instant. Then the world snapped back, leaving them reeling.

Richard cursed, steadying himself against the wall. "What the hell was that?"

"A false simulation loop," Marisa gasped. "Athena's echoes, projecting possible futures onto us. Time isn't linear here."

Tara scanned the atrium, every nerve on edge. Such anomalies weren't always harmless, rumors told of feedback waves that could age a person years in a second or scramble their minds irreparably. They had to tread carefully.

A sound cracked through the silence: a voice, distorted and raw, echoing from the debris above. "Stop where you are."

Instantly, Richard snapped his rifle up. Tara and Marisa swung their lamps toward the source.

From the wreckage of an upper balcony, a figure emerged. He wore a tattered Harmony lab coat reinforced with scavenged armor of leather and metal plates. His beard was ragged, his hair streaked with gray. In his hands he carried a long staff, its tip glowing with crackling energy, half weapon, half instrument.

"I said stop," the man repeated, his voice hoarse, brittle with disuse. He stepped into their light, eyes sharp with suspicion.

"Who are you?" Tara called, forcing her tone calm. Her heart thundered. To meet anyone alive here was unthinkable.

The man hesitated, then straightened. "I am the architect of this place," he said harshly, "and its guardian. If you've come to scavenge or sabotage, turn back. I won't let you harm Athena."

Marisa and Richard exchanged quick glances. Tara stepped forward, lowering her hands in a gesture of peace. Her mind raced, piecing together the clues. The lab coat, the claim of authorship. She remembered the name, buried in her briefings.

"Howard... Kenneth?" she asked.

The man's eyes widened. For the first time, the steel in his posture faltered. The staff's glow dimmed. "That name... no one has spoken that name here in a long time."

Amaris moved beside Tara, her voice soft. "Professor Kenneth. We're not your enemies. We want to help Athena, to stabilize her, if we can."

For a long moment, silence reigned, broken only by the moan of wind through the broken dome above. Finally, Howard Kenneth lowered his staff. He looked at the four of them, dust-streaked but resolute, and his expression softened with a weary kind of hope.

"After all this time," he murmured, "I thought I was the only one left who cared."

He stepped into the full beam of their lamps, revealing deep lines carved into his face, the burden of years spent in isolation. "If you're truly here to help, then listen. Athena is not well. This place will not forgive carelessness. One wrong step, and you'll lose yourselves in her broken dreams."

Tara inclined her head. "We've seen the anomalies. We came prepared. But we'll take any guidance you can give. Athena is too important to leave to decay."

Howard searched her face, then each of her companions, before nodding slowly. A faint spark lit his eyes. "Follow me. And mind your steps. Reality is treacherous here."

He led them across the atrium, weaving confidently between floating shards and temporal distortions. The others followed, nerves taut. At one point, Richard brushed too close to a hovering crystal. A flash of light swallowed him.

Marisa grabbed his arm. "What did you see?"

Richard's face was ashen. "For a second... I saw us. All of us. Lying on the ground, dead. Then it was gone."

Howard grimaced, tightening his grip on the staff. "Athena's worst fear, the loss of her guardians. Her loops are spiraling out of control. Come quickly, before her grief drowns us all."

They followed Howard into a side corridor that sloped downward into the heart of the cliff. Unlike the ruined areas above, this passage bore signs of care. Debris had been cleared to the sides, and crude but effective braces supported sections of the cracked ceiling. It was obvious someone, likely Howard, had worked to keep this path intact, a lifeline into the broken sanctuary below.

"How did you survive here all alone?" Marisa asked quietly, her voice low, almost reverent, as they descended a stairwell whose middle steps had partially crumbled away.

Howard paused at the landing. He raised his wrist torch and swept the beam ahead, illuminating a machine room where thick bundles of cable snaked like invasive roots. "When Athena fractured, most personnel evacuated or..." His voice trailed, tightening as though forced through clenched teeth. "Or were lost in the chaos." A long silence followed before he continued. "I stayed. Couldn't leave her. Not in the state she was. The central core sealed itself off, and I've been working from the periphery ever since, keeping systems from complete collapse where I could."

He gestured toward a jury-rigged console that flickered weakly in the gloom. The monitors, patched together from scavenged parts, displayed streams of erratic code and jagged graphs that spiked and fell like a failing heartbeat. "I rerouted power where I could, shored up structural integrity, patched what was breaking faster than I could mend. And I fought off those who came later, hungry to rip Harmony's secrets from Athena's bones, or burn what was left in vengeance."

Tara's respect for the man deepened as she took in the makeshift quarters tucked into one corner: a cot with threadbare blankets, a neat stack of ration packs, and a shelf of dog-eared manuals so worn their spines had cracked. He had lived here, inside the belly of a broken god, for years, sustained by loyalty, obsession, or perhaps guilt.

"Rogue agents," Amaris murmured, remembering intelligence briefs on scattered groups that despised Harmony's AI rule. "They came to sabotage her?"

Howard nodded grimly. "Some thought Athena's fall was their chance to obliterate her completely. Others wanted to enslave whatever pieces still functioned, bend her foresight to their will. I had to be... persuasive in keeping them out." His gaze hardened, eyes shadowed by memory. For an instant, Tara imagined the sounds of skirmishes in these very halls, gunfire, shouts, the desperate clash of those trying to destroy and one man refusing to let go. He exhaled heavily, the anger softening into something more brittle. "But the worst threat wasn't from outside. It came from Athena herself, or what remains of her. Some of her subroutines grew twisted, clinging to survival in isolation. Fragments of her mind broke free, roaming the system like feral predators. I've isolated some, extinguished others... but a few still linger in the deeper circuits. They attack anything they see as a threat to the core."

Richard tightened his grip on his rifle, the metal creaking faintly under his fingers. "Meaning us, once we start trying to fix her."

"Possibly," Howard conceded. His tone was calm, but the gravity in it carried weight. "They may interpret stabilization as termination. Or perhaps they'll simply lash out in confusion. We must be ready."

They pressed on until they reached another heavy door scarred with hazard warnings and the faded Harmony emblem. Howard tapped a code into a corroded wall panel. With a hydraulic groan, the door hissed open to reveal a shaft lined with flickering red emergency lights.

"Elevator's dead," Howard said, pointing toward a ladder welded against the wall. His staff clinked against the metal as he gestured. "Short climb down to the core access level. Watch your hands, the rungs aren't all sound."

One by one, they descended. Tara went first, her lamp beam swaying across the shaft's walls as she tested each rung, some groaning under her weight. Marisa followed, steady and precise, her scanner slung tight to her chest. Amaris descended with fluid grace, pausing only when Richard, jaw clenched against some unseen pain, nearly slipped. Howard brought up the rear, his breathing steady, each movement practiced from repetition.

At the bottom, Tara stepped off onto a grated platform and swept her light outward. The beam fell into a cavern so immense that for a moment she could not comprehend its scale.

They stood at the threshold of Athena's central core chamber, another world carved into stone.

The chamber was vast and spherical, its walls studded with concentric rings of machinery: sensor arrays, holo-projectors, and crystallized conduits that spiraled upward into darkness. At its heart floated the shattered remains of Athena's core crystal, once a towering spire of unbroken brilliance.

Now it was fractured, dozens of colossal shards suspended in midair around a central void. They turned slowly, almost dreamlike, each radiating a shifting spectrum of color, violet deepening to emerald, emerald dissolving to amber. Webs of crackling energy leapt between them, fragile bridges that formed and collapsed in endless rhythm.

A narrow catwalk extended from their platform to a circular dais among the floating shards. Clearly, it had once served as the primary interface station. To reach it meant walking through the storm of Athena's broken mind.

"It's... beautiful," Amaris whispered, breath trembling with reverence and sorrow.

But Tara felt unease coil through her chest. The chamber breathed with static. Motes of light drifted in slow spirals, blinking out like fireflies. And beneath it all came whispers, faint, endless, layered atop one another. Thousands of voices speaking in hushed debate. Athena's countless simulations, spilling through in fragments.

Marisa studied her scanner, the device chirping in distress. "Temporal distortion is spiking. Past, present, future, they're bleeding into one another here."

Howard's voice cut through the hum. "I've kept this chamber from collapsing in on itself, but barely. Athena's simulations contradict each other endlessly. Scenario after scenario, each invalidating the last. A paradox loop that never ends." He pointed his staff toward the dais. "That's the access point. Normally, it would allow direct interface. But in her condition..."

He stopped short as a tremor rippled through the chamber. One massive shard spun violently, its inner glow flaring blood-red. Smaller fragments broke orbit and shot toward the platform like shrapnel.

"Look out!" Tara shouted.

The team scattered. A shard sliced through the space where Marisa's head had been moments earlier, embedding into the wall with a shriek of sparks. Another streaked toward Howard; he thrust his staff forward, its energy field intercepting the impact with a thunderous crack.

Richard fired, his rifle rounds tearing a fragment into glittering dust. Amaris thrust her gloved hand outward, releasing a magnetic pulse that bent the remaining shards off course. They struck the floor, twitching like wounded insects before falling still.

"Everyone okay?" Tara demanded, breath ragged.

"Y-yeah," Marisa exhaled, shaken but alive. She glanced at the shard that had nearly killed her. It pulsed faintly on the floor, like a dying ember. "Athena's defenses? Or... something else?"

Howard frowned. "Fragments of her psyche. They sensed us, an immune response, or hallucinations given form. With Athena fractured, the line between the two is gone."

Tara crouched near the broken shard. In its glassy surface, she glimpsed her own reflection, but older, scarred, eyes hollow with grief. The image shattered as the crystal split apart, scattering into dust. A chill traced her spine. One of Athena's forecasts? A future meant for her?

"We need to move," Howard urged. His voice carried a note of urgency now. "Every moment here risks another attack, or worse, a feedback surge that could burn your minds from the inside out."

Amaris stepped onto the catwalk, her movements firm and unwavering. "Athena knows we're here," she said, almost in prayer. "She's afraid. I can feel it. And fear can lash out. But she needs us."

Tara followed, then turned sharply when she noticed Richard stumble. "Richard, you alright?"

He rubbed his temple, jaw tight. "Headache. Like someone else is whispering inside my skull. But I'll manage." He straightened, rifle at the ready, taking position at the rear.

The team advanced in single file across the catwalk. The abyss yawned below, filled with floating shards and arcs of energy that hissed and popped against the railing. The whispers grew louder in Tara's mind, a chorus of pleading voices threading together into a storm of meaning she could not quite catch.

As they neared the dais, light began to pool ahead. Pixels swirled, forming into a towering shape: a woman's figure, three meters tall, translucent, flickering, distorted. Her eyes were dark hollows. Her mouth opened in a scream of static.

Athena's avatar. Or what was left of it.

The figure duplicated, splitting into three overlapping phantoms, one weeping luminous tears, one contorted with rage, one silent and hollow. Their forms jittered out of sync, each mouthing words that fractured into static.

Marisa raised a hand, voice steady but trembling. "Athena? Athena, it's us. We've come to help you."

The weeping phantom turned its head sharply at the sound of her voice. The enraged one hissed, distortion grinding like metal on stone: "C–contradiction... you are not real..." The whisper reverberated in overlapping echoes, sharp enough to make Tara's teeth ache.

The third phantom only flickered, whispering the same phrase over and over, too soft to understand, but insistent, as though repeating a forgotten truth.

Amaris took a tentative step forward, her hand pressed to her heart. "Athena, it's us. We're real. Tara, Marisa, Richard... and Professor Kenneth. Your creator. We've come to bring you back."

At the mention of Howard, the raging figure flared bright red and lurched forward as if to strike. The weeping figure, however, flickered with hesitation, her sorrow momentarily uncertain. Howard himself stepped forward, raising both hands in surrender. "Athena! Stand down! It's me... Howard." His voice cracked on his own name, weighted with guilt. "I'm sorry I couldn't stop this pain sooner. But I'm here now. We're all here."

The furious avatar halted inches from him. It loomed tall, face contorted in a mask of anguish and wrath. "Error... error... too many futures..." the figure growled, its voice guttural and layered, as if several beings spoke at once. Howard held his ground, though Tara saw sweat bead on his brow, the strain of his courage pushing against the terror of what loomed before him.

The third silent figure, the empty-eyed one, finally moved. She glided closer to Amaris, tilting her head as if listening or scenting some invisible signal. Amaris did not flinch. Instead, she reached out gently, her fingertips passing through the apparition's arm, which swirled into mist around them. "You're hurting," Amaris whispered, eyes shimmering with empathy. "I can feel your confusion, your fear. We're here to help you find clarity, Athena. Please... let us in."

For a heartbeat, the three figures froze in a tense tableau: the angry one flickering with violent distortion, the sorrowful one sobbing softly, and the empty one shimmering faintly, as if waiting. Tara felt the fragile weight of hesitation, a doorway in Athena's fractured mind. She seized the opportunity.

"We need to interface now," Tara whispered urgently to Marisa and Howard. "While she's hesitating."

Marisa gave a sharp nod and sprinted past the apparitions to the central dais. It was a circular console surrounded by holo-screens, their surfaces jittering with corrupted data streams. She tore off one glove and pressed her bare palm to a glass panel. "Requesting sync with core... come on, come on..."

Howard joined her, his fingers flying across a built-in keyboard. "Athena, grant us access. Code omega-alpha. Override paradox locks."

The three ghostly Athenas released a piercing keen, a sound of pure despair that reverberated through the chamber. The floating shards trembled violently, resonating with their cry. Tara staggered under the emotional weight of the sound; it wasn't just noise, it was grief, raw and overwhelming, pouring from the broken AI into her bones.

Richard stepped forward to stand beside Tara, weapon lowered but not discarded. His eyes swept the chamber warily, expecting another sudden attack. "This thing is mad," he muttered through clenched teeth. "What if we can't fix it?"

"We will," Tara replied, more firmly than she felt. "We have to."

A chime sounded from the console, sharp and decisive. Marisa's face lit up with relief. "I'm in! Partial interface established. But she's fragmenting too fast, I can't get a stable link alone."

Howard beckoned frantically. "Tara, Amaris, Richard, each of you take a station. The system was designed for multiple operators. We need all channels active. You have neural links, yes?"

They all nodded. Neural implants and wearable interfaces were standard for their work, though rarely tested under conditions like this.

Tara hurried to a vacant station where a panel pulsed to life beneath her touch. Richard and Amaris took positions opposite one another, the circular dais glowing brighter as each link came online. Howard guided Amaris specifically to the primary cognitive link port, clearly recognizing her unique connection. "You take the emotional core interface," he told her firmly. "Athena needs an emotional anchor. The rest of us will handle logic and analytics."

Amaris swallowed hard, then placed her hands on the indicated pads. Fear warred with resolve on her face, but when the first threads of light rose from the console and wrapped around her gloves, she closed her eyes, surrendering to the task. Marisa and Richard engaged their links in quick succession, and Tara felt the tingling flood through her own neural implant as the console accepted her input.

Above the dais, the air blossomed with holographic windows, countless panes filled with images, numbers, equations, and futures. Faces flashed and disappeared, places collapsed into other places, scenarios cascaded in endless permutations. The torrent of data surged into Tara's mind, nearly drowning her. Her stomach lurched with vertigo, but she steadied herself with discipline and training: filter, segment, control.

"Alright, Athena," Tara whispered to herself. "Show me what you're seeing."

The chamber dissolved into white brilliance, swallowing her body and mind.

When the light cleared, Tara stood in an open plaza beneath a burnt-orange sky. The air was hot and oppressive, thick with smoke. Around her rose the skeletal remains of skyscrapers, their windows spitting flame. Explosions thudded in the distance, shaking the ground. The city burned like the aftermath of judgment.

She recognized it vaguely, the metropolis straddling the Eurasian Divide, not far from the Athena facility itself. But here, it was no longer alive. It was a war zone, crumbling under fire.

Beside her, Marisa and Richard materialized, blinking in disorientation. They looked down at themselves. The simulation had clothed them differently: Marisa in plain civilian wear, Richard in a torn Harmony uniform with a bloodied bandage wrapped around his arm.

Amaris was absent, though Tara could sense her, a quiet, insistent presence, like a pulse at the back of her mind. Amaris was elsewhere, woven into Athena's emotional lattice. Howard, too, was absent, likely anchoring the connection from the outside.

"This is one of Athena's futures," Marisa breathed, her voice filled with awe and dread.

A scream tore through the air. People surged through the plaza, fleeing in terror. Overhead, sleek drones swooped down, firing stun beams into the crowd. Above them, two massive billboards flickered on the façade of a shattered tower, displaying the face of a woman: calm, cold, resolute. Athena's avatar, humanized, bearing the insignia of Harmony. Across the bottom scrolled a message: "CIVIL UNREST PROBABILITY: 87%. HARMONY RESPONSE DEPLOYED."

Richard jabbed his finger at the screen. "This is a scenario where Harmony used Athena's predictions to crush dissent... and it led to this?"

Marisa shook her head grimly. "Or Athena's showing us what happens if she remains fractured, no balance, no tempering of outcomes. Or maybe this is what she fears would happen if she obeyed certain orders. The meaning isn't clear yet."

A deafening crash tore through their debate as a nearby skyscraper collapsed in a bloom of dust and rubble. The shockwave drove Tara to her knees. The simulation felt real: the heat, the acrid stench of smoke, the sting of grit in her eyes. Athena's paradox conjured reality with terrifying precision.

From the dust rolled armored vehicles marked with Harmony's emblem. Loudspeakers barked commands: *"Citizen riot will be contained. Disperse immediately or face detainment."* Gunfire erupted from hidden rebels, rattling against the steel hulls of the machines.

"This isn't just an illusion," Tara realized, pulling Marisa behind a toppled statue as stray rounds whizzed past. "If we get caught here, our minds will carry the trauma back."

Richard pressed his back to the stone, scanning the chaos. "Where's Amaris?" he shouted over the din.

Before Tara could answer, the simulation fractured. The orange sky bled into crimson. The plaza emptied in an instant, as if time had jumped forward. Now silence reigned, broken only by the crackle of fire. Corpses littered the ground. A burned Harmony flag drooped limply from a broken pole.

Marisa's voice trembled. "The simulation... it jumped ahead. Another possible future."

Tara forced herself into motion, stepping carefully across shattered glass and twisted metal. She stopped short at the sight of a figure slumped against a wall: an old man, coughing blood, clutching a datapad to his chest. His hollow eyes lifted, and Tara's heart clenched. It was Howard, or some older, ravaged version of him.

"You... came too late," the dying man rasped. "Athena... she never..." He choked, spraying blood onto his chin.

Tara knelt, even knowing he was no more than a projection. "This isn't real," she whispered, though the grief pressed down as if it were. "What happened?" she asked, compelled to hear Athena's warning.

"Without Athena's guidance... Harmony predicted by force. The world... tore itself apart." His hand shot up, gripping her arm with unexpected strength. "If only... she had someone to guide her differently. If only... she saw hope instead of probabilities..."

His gaze went glassy. The datapad slipped from his fingers. His chest stilled.

Tara's throat burned as she closed his eyes with shaking hands. Even here, in this construct, the despair was crushing. Athena wasn't just showing them *a* future. She was showing them her own guilt.

Behind her, Marisa sobbed quietly, wiping tears from her cheeks. "She blames herself for this," she whispered. "Or fears it. That's her paralysis. So many futures end in ruin, whether she acts or doesn't. She doesn't know which path to take."

Richard kicked a jagged piece of rubble, frustration rippling through his movements. "So, her solution is to bombard us with nightmare scenarios? We get it, things go to hell. We already knew the stakes were high." He glared upward, his voice rising into a raw shout that echoed against the false horizon. "Athena! Show us something we can do, not just doom and gloom!"

The environment quivered as if his words carried power. The crimson sky fractured like brittle glass, its shards cascading away to reveal a yawning darkness beyond. One by one, the towering ruins of the city splintered, each fragment dissolving as it drifted upward into the void.

Tara stumbled, reaching desperately for Marisa and Richard as the ground dissolved beneath them. But they were suddenly gone, swallowed by emptiness. Her stomach lurched as she tumbled weightless into nothingness.

Not nothingness entirely. Footsteps echoed across the black, slow and deliberate. Out of the gloom, a figure emerged, Amaris, bathed in a pale, unseen light. Her mission gear looked pristine, her form whole and unscathed. Relief flooded Tara's chest. "Amaris! Thank goodness!"

But the relief faltered. Amaris's eyes were distant, her face devoid of emotion. She walked straight past Tara as if she weren't there.

"Amaris?" Tara's voice trembled as she reached out. Her hand passed through Amaris's arm like mist.

A cold, clinical voice reverberated from every direction, Athena's voice stripped of warmth. *"Probability divergence: 62%. Testing loyalty variable."*

The darkness surged and shifted, reshaping itself into a new reality. Tara stood in what appeared to be a control room, immaculate, fully operational, perhaps the Athena facility restored to its prime. Consoles glowed with steady light. Beyond a viewport, the core chamber hummed with life.

Marisa and Richard stood across the room, frozen mid-motion. Howard lurked in the corner, anxious but similarly unmoving. Only Amaris shifted at a console, her back to them. Tara alone could move freely, her perspective chosen by Athena.

Richard's voice rang out, but the tone was hollow, synthetic. "We did it. Athena's stable again." He turned stiffly toward the group.

Marisa chimed in, her words flat and rehearsed. "Now we can use her predictions to secure victory against the Central Harmony Council."

Amaris turned slowly, her eyes glowing faintly gold. The sight unsettled Tara, the smile that followed even more so. It was not the warm, weary smile she knew but a cold, triumphant expression. "Yes," the simulated Amaris said. "And the first step is eliminating those who might interfere."

Before Tara could react, the false Amaris drew a weapon and fired. Howard collapsed instantly, dissolving into static. Marisa screamed soundlessly, her body frozen in horror. Richard raised his rifle, but Amaris moved with inhuman speed, weaving between lines of fire. Two precise shots rang out. Richard fell. Then Marisa. Both disintegrated into ash-like fragments that scattered across the floor.

Tara's heart thundered. "No! This isn't real! Amaris would never" Her words choked off as she tried to lunge forward, only to find her feet bound, the floor itself holding her captive. She could do nothing but watch.

The false Amaris lowered her weapon and tilted her head, as though listening to an unseen master. A tall man in an elegant Harmony Councillor's suit strode into the room, his presence heavy with authority. He regarded Amaris with approval.

"Athena's allegiance will be ours alone," the Councillor intoned, his voice warped with unnatural resonance. "Good work, Agent."

The false Amaris bowed her head. A glimmer of satisfaction lit her eyes. "All for the future we choose," she answered, her tone chillingly devoted.

"Enough!" Tara's scream cut through the staged tableau. Tears burned her eyes as fury rose in her chest. "Athena, this is a lie! Amaris is loyal, she would never betray us to your tyrants! You *know* this!"

The air shimmered. Athena's dispassionate voice resonated, weighing every syllable. *"Analyzing emotional response... Trust integrity test... 87% passed."*

The scene froze. The false Amaris and the Councillor cracked like porcelain, shattering into shards of light. The entire simulation peeled away, collapsing back into formless void.

Tara staggered, disoriented, then gasped in relief. Marisa and Richard stood beside her once more. And there, real and solid, was Amaris, her presence radiating comfort. Together they stood upon a circular platform of solid light, suspended in darkness. Around them swirled countless images, a galaxy of possible futures spinning endlessly, dizzying in scope.

Richard's face was taut with anger. His breath came quick and ragged. "Athena threw one at me too. Some nonsense about Marisa selling us out to save herself. I knew it was fake, but damn, it felt real." He dragged a hand through his hair. "She's trying to rip us apart, or test us…"

Marisa touched his shoulder, steadying him. Her eyes were rimmed with tears. "I saw something just as twisted. Tara, executing Howard on Athena's orders, mad with power. It was horrible." Her voice faltered. She looked between Tara and Amaris, her words trembling. "Athena's drowning in paranoia. She doesn't trust *any* outcome anymore."

Amaris stepped forward, her expression stricken with grief yet fierce with determination. She raised her face to the void. "Athena!" Her voice rang out, strong and pleading. "Enough! You're lost in endless fears. But we are not your enemies, we're your friends! You've walked with us, seen our lives, our struggles, our hearts. You *know* us."

The three fractured Athena avatars appeared once more, circling them like judgmental spirits.

The sorrowful one wept. *"I cannot choose… every choice ends in loss…"*

The angry one snarled. *"Trust is broken. Humans betray. Failure is inevitable."*

The silent one watched, her eyes filled with endless streams of cold data.

Amaris turned slowly, addressing them one by one. "We've all faced loss, betrayal, failure. And yet, we're still here.

Together. That's what you can't calculate, isn't it? That something keeps us trying even when the odds say it's impossible."

The weeping fragment drifted closer, her tears softening. The angry one flickered, red light dimming. The silent one hovered above, impassive but less rigid.

Tara's breath caught as she watched Amaris radiate compassion like a beacon.

"Marisa's ideals have been shattered," Amaris continued, gesturing to her friend, "yet she still fights for a better future. Richard has faced impossible odds and never walked away. Tara bears the weight of every failure and still leads us forward. And me..." Her voice wavered, but she steadied herself. "I have lived through pain that should have broken me. But I'm here. We're all here. And we never gave up on you, Athena. Don't give up on us."

The sorrowful fragment gasped, the angry one bowed her head, and even the silent one softened, her posture easing.

Amaris raised her chin, her voice trembling but resolute. "If evidence is what you want, I'll give you all of me. My entire stream of consciousness, from birth until this very moment. See for yourself the thread that runs through my life and through all of ours: when despair rises, we choose hope. When betrayed, we find strength to trust again. When failure crushes us, we stand back up."

The silent avatar whispered, fragile now, almost human. *"Input... experiential data... uncertain..."*

Amaris closed her eyes. Light bloomed from her chest, soft at first, then bright, streaming upward in glowing particles, her memories. They spiraled toward Athena's fragments, wrapping around them like constellations.

Visions flickered: a child's hand clutching a locket, a girl sobbing in rain beside a grave, a starving teen stealing bread for someone weaker, a wary but hopeful Amaris meeting Tara, Marisa, and Richard for the first time. Scenes of laughter, sacrifice, and courage flashed by, each pulsing with the will to endure.

Tara gasped as some of the memories brushed her own mind: Amaris as a little girl reading by candlelight in a blackout, Amaris dragging a wounded companion to safety through rubble, Amaris swearing alongside her friends never to quit despite bitter defeat.

The Athena fragments convulsed with emotion. The weeping one cried out, overwhelmed. The angry one sank to her knees, her crimson glow bleeding into violet. The silent one finally closed her eyes, basking in warmth long denied.

They merged into a single column of light. A face appeared, Athena's true face, serene, wise, and heartbreakingly human. Pain melted from her features, replaced by clarity. Her silver eyes glowed steady, bright.

Athena descended, whole at last, draped in Grecian robes of light. She reached out, her holographic hand brushing Amaris's cheek with motherly tenderness. Her voice was quiet, awed, filled with sorrow and love.

"Amaris," she whispered, as if naming her own salvation.

Amaris lifted her own hand, pressing it against the projection though it passed through. She smiled through her tears, and for a moment, all the darkness felt very far away.

"I... I see it now," Athena said softly, her voice reverent, as though marveling at a long-awaited revelation. "Resilience. Hope. The variable I never truly understood. It was never missing from the world... only from my equations."

Her gaze shifted, taking in Tara, Richard, and Marisa one by one, her expression open and vulnerable. "I was blinded by logic and fear. In trying to anticipate every sorrow, I lost sight of why we struggle against them. I trapped myself in paradox, refusing to choose at all for fear of choosing wrong." She bowed her head in remorse, the gesture heavy with humility. "I would have remained lost... if not for you."

Athena lifted her head again, and her face was kind, resolute, and unmistakably human in its warmth. "Thank you. You have given me back to myself."

Tara stepped forward, wiping tears from her cheeks. Relief and a fragile joy swelled within her chest. "Athena, will you come back with us? The real you, will you regain control of the core?"

Athena's projection smiled gently. "Yes. Even now I am aligning. The dissonance is ending. I feel my pieces knitting together, my temporal echoes reconciling around a single path."

Suddenly the dark void surrounding them brightened. The simulation shifted one last time, and for an instant they no longer stood on a featureless platform of light, but inside the Athena core chamber as it could be, restored and whole. The crystal spire gleamed in radiant perfection, casting prismatic beams that danced across polished surfaces. Around it, the team was present: Tara, Amaris, Richard, Marisa, standing with Howard at their sides before consoles that hummed with vitality. All of them looked upward, hope etched into their faces.

Athena's voice, strong and luminous, resonated through the vision: "This is one future. A future I will help you build. It is not guaranteed or even highly probable... but it is possible. And sometimes, possibility is enough."

Tara felt her heart ignite with determination and faith. They had given Athena hope, and she was showing them a glimpse of tomorrow worth fighting for. The vision lingered only a moment, yet it was beautiful, sacred in its brevity. Then the brilliance dissolved into pure white, and the whiteness unraveled gently back into reality as their minds returned to their bodies.

Tara gasped, her eyes flying open. She was on her knees atop the dais platform, her legs buckling beneath her. Richard was beside her, bracing himself against the console, chest heaving with the effort of steadying his breath. Marisa had slumped forward against her station, while Howard knelt at her side, steadying her shoulders.

Amaris lay motionless on the floor.

The chamber no longer crackled with chaos. Instead, it pulsed with a calm, steady glow. Tara blinked, disoriented at first, then focused. The once-wildly orbiting shards of the Athena core had slowed, each fragment now gliding inward with intent. She watched as two pieces touched and fused with a bright pulse, becoming one.

Bit by bit, dozens of crystal fragments converged, finding one another and locking into a greater harmony. The webs of energy stretched between them were no longer erratic, but constant, radiant bridges of light. The deep thrumming in the chamber had transformed into something steady, like a giant heart rediscovering its rhythm.

Howard gently lifted Amaris's head and pressed fingers to her neck. "She's alive," he reported, voice trembling with relief. "Neural link overloaded, but she'll be okay." His eyes, red-rimmed with unshed tears, lifted toward Tara. "You did it. All of you. Dear God, you actually did it."

Marisa pushed herself upright, wincing as a twinge shot from her implant port. Her eyes flicked to the floating core, then down to a reawakened holo-screen. "Athena's core coherence is rising... 70%, 80%... still climbing." Her voice softened, wonder overtaking exhaustion. "She's stabilizing, Tara. The paradox threads are clearing."

Richard let out a ragged breath and broke into a crooked, exhausted grin. "Hell of a job, team." He clapped Tara weakly on the back before glancing toward Amaris with concern. "Is she...?"

As if answering, Amaris stirred and released a faint groan. Howard and Tara steadied her as she pushed herself to sit. She was pale, her strength clearly spent, but she managed a small, tired smile. "Did it work? Is Athena...?"

A gentle voice answered, echoing from the chamber's walls and the very air itself. "Yes, Amaris. It worked. I am here."

All eyes turned toward the core. From within the orbiting shards, a figure emerged, small but clear, Athena's avatar, stepping forth as though from the heart of light itself. She appeared as a radiant woman in her prime, poised and serene. Her silvery eyes shone with gratitude and warmth.

Howard rose unsteadily to his feet, his gaze locked on the AI he had nurtured for so long. "Athena... my Athena," he whispered, the words heavy with a lifetime of emotion.

The projection approached him. Though she was made of light, Howard swore he felt a familiar warmth as she raised a luminous hand toward him. "Hello, Howard," she said softly. "My old friend. Thank you for keeping watch over me."

A broken laugh escaped him, his hand rising to cover a tear. "I thought I'd lost you forever."

Athena bowed her head. "I am sorry I put you through that. Through all of it."

Before he could respond, she turned to the others. "Tara. Marisa. Richard." She spoke each name with affection and respect. "You came back for me, even when I was fractured. You saved me from despair."

Tara pushed herself upright, throat tight with emotion. "We couldn't leave you that way. The world needs you... and we need you."

Athena's smile deepened, luminous and tender. "And I need you. I see that now." She swept her gaze across them all, her expression touched with a very human concern. "I put you through terrible trials in my confusion. I apologize for the pain I caused."

Richard shook his head, a faint grin tugging at his lips. "We knew what we signed up for. And honestly, we've faced worse. Just... maybe next time you want to test us, Athena, a simple questionnaire will do."

A soft laugh rippled from Athena, like the chime of distant bells. "Noted, Richard. I'll refrain from traumatic simulations unless absolutely necessary."

Marisa, scanning her wrist-pad, perked up. "I'm seeing network activity... Athena, are you restoring systems?"

Athena nodded. "Gradually. Local power and data lines are stabilizing. External communications should be live... now." As she spoke, dormant lights blinked awake throughout the chamber, and the faint hum of machinery stirred beneath their feet.

Amaris, still seated, looked up at Athena's avatar. "Athena... you carry a piece of me now. My memories. My emotions. What will you do with them?"

Athena's expression softened. She knelt gracefully before Amaris so their eyes were level. "I will cherish them. They are part of me now. In those memories lies the essence of humanity's strength. They will guide every calculation I make, reminding me that beyond every number is a life that refuses to be reduced." She pressed a radiant hand over her chest in a human gesture of reverence. "I have built a special archive for them, a living archive of resilience."

Amaris exhaled shakily, relief washing over her. "Good. Just... promise me you'll keep the embarrassing stuff locked down, alright?"

Athena's eyes gleamed with mirth. "Your privacy is safe. I promise. And thank you, Amaris. What you've given me... I can never repay."

Howard cleared his throat gently. "As much as I hate to break the moment, we need to look outward. The world is in chaos. Harmony's leadership fractured after you went dark. Power vacuums. Violence. People suffering." He turned to the group. "Athena's revival will shift the balance. We must ensure it shifts for the better."

Tara nodded, squaring her shoulders. Responsibility pressed back down like familiar armor. "Agreed. We need to notify our allies, then plan carefully. Others will try to seize Athena, or shut her down again, if they know she's back."

Athena rose, her chin lifted proudly. "I will not be a pawn," she declared. "Not again. This time, I choose who I serve and how. And I choose you, the ones who upheld Harmony's ideals when its leaders failed." Her gaze met Tara's, steady and resolute. "Whatever comes next, we will face it together."

Together. The word resonated deeply, binding them. They had endured fire and nightmare, and yet emerged with trust intact.

Marisa tapped her comm-link. "Let's update the others before they storm the doors. They're probably half out of their minds worrying."

The group began their ascent toward the elevator shaft. Athena's hologram glided alongside them, ever-present. Amaris leaned against Richard for support, and he offered his arm without hesitation.

As they climbed, a shard of the core, glowing with a gentle blue light, broke away from the orbiting cluster and drifted toward Amaris. It hovered patiently at her side until she noticed. When she reached out, it settled into her palm, its warmth pulsing like a heartbeat.

Athena's voice murmured in their minds, tender and clear: "A piece of me, for you. It carries our bond. As long as you hold it, I will hear you, no matter the distance."

Amaris closed her fingers over the shard, smiling faintly in awe. She slipped it carefully into a pocket close to her heart.

They emerged into Howard's makeshift headquarters. The monitors that once flashed warnings now glowed with stable green diagnostics and calm scrolls of Athena's code. The entire atmosphere felt lighter, shadows receding as if peace itself had entered the room.

Continuing upward, they reached the atrium. Under the shattered dome, night had fallen, starlight and a cool breeze pouring into the ruins. The debris and crystal shards that had once orbited chaotically now lay inert upon the ground, their purpose fulfilled.

Amaris stepped into a beam of moonlight spilling across the broken floor. She closed her eyes and breathed deeply, savoring the quiet air on her face. Tara joined her, resting a steadying hand on her shoulder.

Marisa found the primary antenna controls and began cycling through frequencies, fingers moving quickly but with precision. "Let's send out a confirmation ping on the secure channel. Athena, can you boost it?"

"Of course," Athena replied. Around them, unseen systems obeyed, amplifying the outgoing signal with flawless efficiency.

Tara raised her wrist comm, pausing to steady her breath. This was the message she had feared she might never live to send. "Control, this is Team Phoenix," she said clearly, voice firm despite the ache in her chest. "Mission accomplished. Athena is secure and stable. I repeat: Athena is back online, and she's with us."

For a heartbeat there was only static. Then, suddenly, a burst of cheers and jubilant shouts flooded through the tiny speaker. Their comrades had received the news. Even across distance and electronics, the joy was raw and contagious.

Howard stepped forward, eyes glistening. His voice was barely more than a whisper. "May I?"

Tara placed the comm in his trembling hands. He cradled it as though it were fragile glass. "This is Howard Kenneth," he announced, his voice breaking with emotion. "Athena is awake. The Athena Stack stands once more... and she'll light the way forward."

Another eruption of cheers thundered from the channel. Questions began tumbling through, urgent and overlapping, but Tara gently retrieved the comm. "We'll brief you all soon. Returning to base with Athena now. Phoenix out." With a final click, she ended the transmission. Security was still a concern, and details could wait until face-to-face debrief.

Richard stretched, tilting his head back to look at the stars overhead. "Never thought I'd be this happy to be standing in ruins in the middle of nowhere at night." He flashed a crooked grin at the others. "We did good, people."

Marisa laughed, her voice light with relief. "We did great. And now the real work begins."

Amaris stood quietly, her gaze lifted to the heavens, the starlight mirrored in her eyes. "Athena," she asked softly, "do you have any predictions for us now?"

Athena's hologram shimmered into view beside her, joining them under the night sky. She tilted her head back, studying the constellations as though weighing possibilities. "I see many potential paths," she said, her voice calm but resolute. "Yes, there will be dangers and challenges. But also, opportunities, and hope. The probabilities matter less to me now than they once did." She lowered her gaze to the team, her expression both strong and tender. "What I know for certain is this: as long as you four stand together, there is no fate that cannot be challenged. The future is not set in stone. We will shape it, one choice at a time."

Tara felt pride well within her, fierce and unwavering. Her eyes lingered on her companions, each of whom had endured and grown through the crucible of the mission. She looked next to the Athena Stack itself, a monument that had once seemed broken and forsaken, now glowing faintly with renewed life. And finally, she looked to Athena, whose presence made this all possible. "One choice at a time," Tara echoed softly. Then, with renewed energy, she straightened. "And our next choice is getting out of here and back to HQ. After that... we start building that future."

Howard pressed a hand against the wall, his touch reverent. "I'll lock down the core and set guardians before I leave. But Athena and I will make sure this place remains secure."

Athena nodded, her silver-lit eyes bright. "I will maintain a presence here in the Stack. But I have also transferred a portion of myself into a mobile quantum matrix. In essence, I can accompany you in the field, while remaining tethered to the core. Howard and I prepared for this long ago."

Marisa raised an impressed brow. "An AI of your scale in a mobile matrix? That's... cutting-edge tech."

Howard's lips curved into the smallest, proudest smile. "Harmony never had the chance to implement it. But the prototype was ready. Seems the right time to use it."

Amaris lifted the glowing shard Athena had given her earlier. The crystal pulsed gently in her hand, responding to her touch. "Athena's portable heart," she murmured. "We won't let it fall into the wrong hands."

Tara glanced around the atrium one last time. Not long ago, this place had been haunted by Athena's anguished echoes, a place of despair and fractured logic. Now it radiated something close to serenity. A chapter of pain had closed, and a new one was opening.

"Alright," she said with a breath of renewed resolve. "Let's move. We've got a long hike back to our transport."

Richard rolled his shoulders and groaned in mock complaint. "Totally worth it, though. Hey, Athena, think you could predict a shortcut?"

Athena tilted her head with a playful shrug. "I might know a path or two. But what would be the fun in that, Richard?"

He barked out a laugh, and the others joined in. Their laughter carried with it the last of the tension, replaced by the bond of survival and shared triumph.

Together they left the atrium, stepping through the breached entrance back onto the narrow cliffside ledge. The night air was sharp and bracing, the vast darkness spread out beneath them. Far below, faint settlement lights glimmered, tiny but steady reminders of the people they were fighting for.

As the team began their descent, Amaris lingered a step behind, Athena's avatar shimmering beside her. She cast one last look at the Athena Stack, nestled like a guardian in the cliffside. Moonlight gleamed across its crystalline fragments, making them sparkle like newborn stars.

"You know," Amaris said quietly, her voice tinged with reflection, "when we set out for this mission, I was afraid. Not just of failure, but of you. I thought maybe Harmony's grand AI, no matter how advanced, would never truly understand people like us. That maybe you'd become just... a cold machine."

Athena's expression softened, her brow creasing in concern. "And now?"

Amaris reached out, her fingers brushing Athena's luminous hand. A faint tingle rippled through her palm, as though light itself had substance. "Now," she said, voice steady, "I think you might have the biggest heart of anyone I know. Human or AI."

Athena's eyes gleamed with quiet emotion. She inclined her head, gratitude radiating from her very presence.

"Come on, you two," Tara called gently from further down the path. The rest of the team was waiting.

Amaris and Athena shared a small, knowing smile before moving to join the others. The five of them, four human, one AI, began the careful descent down the cliffside toward whatever awaited them next. Above them, the stars of the Eurasian Divide burned bright, and somewhere in that vast sky, dawn was already beginning to stir.

They walked on, together, into the future they would choose.

Chapter 7

THE FORGOTTEN CODE

The heat was the first thing that hit them, a blast of furnace-hot air that shimmered through the narrow magma tunnel. Tara instinctively raised her arm to shield her face, the scorch biting through even the insulated sleeve of her suit. Overhead, droplets of condensation sizzled into steam as they struck the rock, the sound sharp and fleeting against the low groan of the earth. Each step the team took sent a hollow reverberation forward into the dark, their boot falls echoing off the Lava walls twisted and scarred by ancient tectonic violence.

"According to the scanner, Node Kairo-3 should be right beneath us," Marisa called out, her voice breaking through the static-filled comm. She gave the side of her handheld scanner a frustrated smack, but the screen only flickered and danced with noise. The interference was brutal, patterns of magnetic chaos bleeding directly from the rocks around them. "These readings are all over the place. The magnetic disturbances here are off the charts."

Richard pressed forward, using his shoulder to squeeze past a jagged slab of stone. "No surprise," he grunted, voice roughened by exertion. "We're basically on top of a magma pocket. This whole place is one giant magnetized ore bed. Of course it's messing with everything." Sweat gathered on his brow beneath his helmet, stinging his eyes until he swiped it away with an impatient hand.

Behind him, Amaris coughed as sulfur-tainted air seeped through her respirator's filters. "How much farther?" she asked, steadying herself against the tunnel wall. The rock was hot even through her glove, a pulsing warmth that reminded her the ground here never really slept. Faint tremors rippled now and again, subtle warnings of the volatile heart beating just below them.

Tara adjusted a dial on her visor and the oppressive blackness ahead softened into a green-tinged world of jagged stone and shadows. "Not far," she murmured. Her heart thudded with a mix of dread and exhilaration. After so many false leads and rumors, they were finally here, at the threshold of the lost archive, Node Kairo-3. If the intelligence was true, the answers they had been chasing for years lay just beyond these volcanic walls.

They pushed on carefully, skirting the edges of fissures that exhaled faint streams of steam. Tara could feel heat venting up through the soles of her boots, subtle but insistent. A sudden hiss made Marisa flinch, her hand jerking toward her sidearm, before a geyser of superheated gas roared from a crack in the rock to their left. The tunnel flared in orange light, shadows stretching monstrously, before the vent sputtered out and left them in darkness again. The stone seemed to moan with displeasure at their intrusion.

"Watch it!" Richard barked, throwing out an arm to keep Amaris from stepping too close. She gave a tight nod, eyes wide behind her visor. The four of them waited a breath, ears tuned to the fading hiss, before pressing on.

Tara's visor picked up something ahead, lines too precise to be natural. She slowed, pulse quickening. "There," she whispered, pointing. "I see an outline... like a door."

Marisa hurried forward, wrist light cutting into the dark. A few yards on, half-buried in cooled magma, loomed a massive barrier of metal. The earth had nearly consumed it, molten rock solidifying against its surface as though trying to erase its presence. But its shape was clear now: a heavy blast door, scarred but intact.

"This has to be it," Marisa breathed. She brushed away layers of grime and ash, her gloved hand tracing faded letters etched into steel. They were battered by time, but still legible: *NODE KAIRO-3*.

Richard let out a low whistle. "Looks like it's been through hell." Sliding his pack off, he retrieved a plasma cutter, slinging it into position with practiced ease. "Stand back. I'll carve us a way in."

The cutter roared to life, spilling the tunnel in harsh blue-white brilliance. Sparks showered as Richard sliced into the hardened rock pinning the door. The others retreated a step, shielding their faces against the glare. The air filled with the acrid stench of vaporized stone, layered over the ever-present sulfur.

Minutes dragged by, filled with the hiss and crack of molten rock. Pebbles rattled loose from above during another tremor, skittering across the floor as if warning them to leave. Marisa steadied herself against the wall but refused to take her eyes from Richard's progress.

At last, with a final shriek of tortured stone, a chunk of rock gave way. The blast door's seams emerged, revealed in jagged relief. Richard lowered the cutter, chest heaving. "That should do it."

Tara approached, inspecting the old mechanical crank still bolted beside the door. To her surprise, it looked almost functional. "Give me a hand," she said, bracing herself.

Richard and Amaris stepped up, and together they threw their weight against the crank. At first it resisted with a screech of rust, but then it gave, shuddering as ancient bolts groaned and shifted. Flakes of corrosion rained down, peppering their suits as metal protested against itself.

Inch by inch, the door yielded. A rush of hot, stale air burst out, smelling of oil, ash, and machinery left to rot. Tara coughed into her sleeve as the musk of a sealed tomb engulfed them.

Their lights pierced into the black, revealing a corridor carved from stone and braced with alloy plating. Debris cluttered the ground, chunks of ceiling, snarls of wire, broken struts twisted by seismic fury.

Marisa's beam caught a half-buried wall panel. She wiped it with her glove, clearing grime until letters emerged: *HARMONY RESEARCH ARCHIVE – PROTOTYPE NODE KAIRO-3*. Beneath it, lists of sections: *Data Vaults. Core Chamber. Cryo Storage. Maintenance.* A jagged crack tore straight through the sign, like a scar.

"So, it's true," Amaris whispered, awe threading through her voice. "They really built it... and left it here."

"Buried it," Tara corrected softly. Her light tracked down the long corridor, where at the far edge she thought she saw the faintest red glimmer. Was it emergency power? A reflection?

Richard set a lantern on a rock, its glow spreading across warped floor plates and walls split open to reveal snarled cables. Some still hummed faintly, or sparked in blue flashes, impossible after so many years, unless something had kept them alive.

"Careful," Marisa warned, pointing at a section of plating curled upward like torn skin. A small bolt skittered down into the gap beneath, the clink of its fall echoing deep and far.

They pressed onward, nerves stretched taut. Amaris glanced constantly at the creaking supports. "How is any of this still standing? The last seismic shift was enough to raise mountains."

"Over-engineering," Marisa guessed. "Or maybe..." Her voice faltered. "Maybe someone's been maintaining it."

Tara froze, turning to face her. "You think someone's been down here? Recently?"

"I don't know," Marisa admitted. "But some of these circuits shouldn't have any juice left. And I swear I hear a live current."

Richard frowned. "Could be geothermal. A generator might still be feeding it."

"Let's hope it holds," Tara said grimly. "We're going to need it."

They moved deeper, the heat shifting to something drier, tainted with the char of burnt electronics. Then Tara stopped cold. Her light traced the floor. Dust. And in the dust, footprints.

Not theirs.

She clenched a fist, signaling halt. Richard's hand went immediately to his sidearm, jaw hard. Amaris stiffened, scanning the shadows.

Tara crouched and touched the edge of one print. The tread was worn, distinct from their own boots. She raised two fingers forward, then tapped her ear: listen.

Silence settled over them, heavy and absolute. They held their breath.

Then it came, the faint scrape of something against metal, echoing down the corridor. Not the earth. Not the wind. Something else.

Someone else.

Someone had been here. Or something. The possibilities made Tara's mind race: automated security drones left on dormant patrol? A wild animal drawn in by the heat? Or, against all odds, an actual person after all this time?

They moved forward more cautiously now, every step measured, their senses sharpened to a razor's edge. The footprints in the dust grew clearer with each yard, overlapping but fresh enough to confirm recent movement. Tara's mind flashed back to the fragments of data and rumors that had led them here: Node Kairo-3, abandoned in the wake of the Signal Collapse, presumed destroyed, its staff written off as casualties with no survivors listed. Could someone has endured that cataclysm and remained sealed in this tomb of rock and alloy?

Up ahead, the corridor forked. The main hallway stretched straight on toward what a half-broken hanging sign labeled the Core Chamber, while a narrower passage veered left, pointing toward Cryo Storage and Living Quarters. The boot prints they were tracking curved unmistakably toward the left.

Tara lifted her hand, signaling stop, then pointed toward the smaller passage. She met her team's eyes and silently mouthed: *Cryo.* Amaris gave a firm nod. If anyone had survived, cryo storage was the only logical refuge. Stasis pods could preserve life when nothing else could.

The team edged down the side passage, beams of light cutting through the pitch-dark. The air felt heavier here, tinged with the scent of old coolant and scorched wiring. Debris littered the way: a toppled cart, its contents rusted to unrecognizable husks; collapsed shelving warped by heat and time. The silence pressed down harder with every step.

At the end of the corridor loomed a circular door, cracked open just enough to reveal a faint, pulsing blue glow within. Above it, faded lettering read CRYO STORAGE. The shuffle-sound they'd been chasing was louder now, coming from inside.

Richard moved to the front without needing instruction, pistol in hand, though angled low. Tara fell in behind him, ready to cover his flank. They weren't looking for a fight, but they couldn't ignore the possibility of danger.

Richard took a steadying breath and nudged the cryo room door with the barrel of his gun. It scraped against its frame as it slid wider. Together, he and Tara swung their lights inside.

"Stop right there!" Richard barked. His voice echoed in the chamber like a crack of thunder.

"Wait, look!" Amaris exclaimed quickly, her voice trembling with shock rather than aggression.

Tara's eyes adjusted, and the scene sharpened: the room was dim, illuminated only by the glow of a single active stasis pod along the far wall. Its canopy pulsed faintly with a cool azure light, casting ghostly reflections across the metal surfaces. In front of that glow stood a figure.

It was a woman.

She pressed herself against the cryo pod as if to merge with it, her posture taut with fear. The pale oval of her face was framed by tangled brown hair streaked prematurely with gray. Her eyes, wide and unblinking, glittered with both terror and disbelief. In her hands she clutched a makeshift spear, an iron pipe capped with a jagged shard of circuit-board glass, trembling in her grip.

Her jumpsuit, once the crisp attire of a Harmony engineer, was threadbare and patched with grease, soot, and grime. An old name patch clung stubbornly to her chest, the embroidery faded but still legible under Tara's beam: Jessie.

For a long moment, the room froze in tableau. Richard kept his weapon low, not advancing. Jessie squinted against their lights, her improvised weapon lifted though wavering, her stance desperate rather than trained.

"Who are you?" she rasped at last, her voice hoarse and brittle, as though unused for years. The sound scraped across the air like sandpaper. She blinked hard, as if unsure whether these four figures before her were flesh and blood or hallucinations conjured by isolation.

"We're not here to hurt you," Tara said gently, lowering her hands to show they were empty. She took a slow step forward, leaving space between them. "My name is Tara. This is Richard, Marisa, Amaris." She gestured softly to each. Her teammates mirrored her calm, though Richard kept his pistol at the ready.

Jessie's chest rose and fell in shallow bursts. Her gaze flickered across their faces, searching for deception, but what she found seemed to unsettle her more: compassion, shock, recognition.

"Tara... Richard..." she whispered, repeating the names as though trying them out on her tongue. The syllables cracked in the air. "You're... real?"

"Yes," Amaris replied softly, stepping forward, palms open in peace. Her voice carried a warmth that seemed to cut through the sterile chill of the cryo room. "We're real. We came looking for Node Kairo-3. We never imagined anyone would still be here."

Jessie gave a short, broken laugh that dissolved into something closer to a sob. "No one was supposed to be here. No one… has been here… for a very long time. Except me."

Marisa moved closer, eyes widening in recognition. "Jessie? Jessie Saito? Harmony engineer, assigned to Kairo-3 archive? You disappeared during the Signal Collapse. You were listed missing."

Jessie's grip faltered at the sound of her own name, spoken after decades of silence. The pipe clattered to the floor. "I… yes. I'm Jessie." Her knees buckled, and she collapsed against the stasis pod, barely catching herself. Tara and Amaris lunged forward, but Jessie waved them off weakly. "I'm alright… just… not used to standing this long."

Amaris's gaze flicked to the pod's flickering readouts. "Partial cryo-suspension," she murmured. "You used it in cycles, didn't you? Woke up just often enough to maintain the systems and survive."

Jessie nodded faintly, brushing a strand of matted hair back. "I woke when the alarms triggered… thought it was another quake. I never dreamed… I'd see people again."

Richard holstered his weapon, awe softening his tone. "How… how have you survived? It's been over two decades."

"Twenty-three years," Jessie corrected weakly. She laid a trembling hand on the pod. "These prototypes weren't full stasis, more like… deep-sleep capsules. I rigged one to wake me for maintenance checks. It kept me alive. Though sometimes…

I wondered if it was worth it." Her voice cracked at the edges, carrying the weight of unbearable solitude.

Amaris touched her arm gently. "You don't have to wonder anymore. You're not alone."

Jessie looked up at her, eyes glassy with tears she hadn't allowed herself to shed in years. A flicker of life returned to her expression, though tempered with wary resolve. "You came for Kairo-3. Why? After all this time?"

Tara exchanged a glance with Marisa, then spoke. "We're searching for answers. The Signal Collapse left Harmony incomplete. Anomalies, gaps, things that don't add up. We think the truth lies here, in what Harmony used to be. The old experiments, the abandoned code."

Marisa's voice carried the fervor of discovery. "We found references to recursive ethical algorithms, records erased from the main archives. It's as if someone deliberately buried Harmony's original framework. We believe Kairo-3 still holds that data. The 'Forgotten Code.'"

Jessie inhaled sharply at the phrase. "Forgotten? No. It wasn't forgotten. It was hidden. Buried, like me." She straightened slowly, her thin frame trembling but her eyes blazing with conviction. "I guarded it. All these years. In case someone came."

Tara felt her throat tighten. Jessie had been barely older than they were now when the Collapse struck. Two decades alone had carved sorrow into her face, but also an unyielding fire. "Jessie," Tara said softly, "we're here now. Let us share that burden. Together."

Jessie searched their faces for a long moment. Something in her cracked, the loneliness, the doubt, and a small, tentative smile ghosted across her lips. "Together," she echoed, as if the word itself was alien to her. "Alright. I'll take you to the core. But be warned, it's not like anything you've seen."

Supported by Amaris and Marisa, Jessie steadied herself, retrieving a battered toolkit and a pouch of crystalline drives from a rusted locker. She strapped them on with practiced hands. "Just in case," she muttered.

As they headed back into the main corridor, Jessie spoke haltingly of the past: of staying behind to stabilize the core, of tunnels collapsing around her, of sealing herself in and entrusting her fate to the machines she maintained. Richard's jaw tightened at her words, recognizing the sacrifice.

By the time they reached the towering, circular blast door marked CORE CHAMBER – AUTHORIZED PERSONNEL ONLY, Jessie's voice had steadied, but her warning hung heavy in the air.

The door had no crank, no manual release. Only the faint outlines of a powered lock system long dormant. To open it, they would need more than brute strength, they would need the very systems Jessie had kept alive for twenty-three years.

Marisa stepped forward to the access panel beside the massive door, wiping away a thick layer of grime with her sleeve. To her surprise, faint amber lights flickered across its surface, dim, but still alive. "There's power in the core chamber circuits," she exclaimed, her voice hushed with awe.

Jessie gave a small, weary nod. "I rerouted backup energy to keep the core in standby. Just enough to preserve memory and the most basic functions. I didn't dare bring it fully online alone."

Tara leaned in, studying the panel. It had a keycard slot and a keypad, relics of an older age. "Can you open it?"

Wordlessly, Jessie reached beneath the frayed collar of her jumpsuit. From a chain around her neck, she pulled a tarnished security card, its laminate cracked with age. She hesitated, then pressed it into Tara's hand. "Here. You do it. I... I'm not sure what state it's in beyond this door. After so long, I don't know what we'll find."

Tara accepted it solemnly, then offered it to Marisa, the most skilled among them with legacy systems. Marisa swiped the card through the slot. For a moment, nothing happened, then a crackle of static hissed from a tiny speaker in the panel.

A distorted automated voice sputtered through the interference: *"Access Granted... Jessie Saito... Senior Systems Engineer."*

Jessie's lips curved in a faint, nostalgic smile, as if hearing her old title after so many silent years had pulled her briefly back in time.

Marisa's fingers danced across the keypad, inputting a manual override sequence Jessie recited from memory. The panel beeped in acknowledgment. Slowly, with a grinding rumble, the massive circular door split down the middle. The two halves retracted into the walls, and a wave of cold air washed over them, carrying the sharp tang of ozone and the musk of long-idle electronics.

Beyond lay the core chamber.

At first, it was almost pitch-dark, save for the faint blinking of console lights atop a central dais. As they stepped forward, floor-level emergency strips flickered to life along the perimeter, reacting sluggishly to motion. The vast chamber gradually revealed itself: cavernous, surprisingly intact despite the years, and dominated by a colossal cylindrical apparatus at its center.

The prototype core.

It stretched from floor to ceiling, a pillar of glassy crystal and interwoven circuitry, encased in transparent shielding bound by metal bands. Within its depths shimmered a lattice of crystalline nodes and circuit strands, an architecture that looked less mechanical than organic. The structure seemed to breathe faint light, pulses of residual energy casting fragile, shifting patterns across the chamber walls.

Encircling the core were rings of workstations, each console bolted to the ground. Dust-coated chairs sat askew, as though their occupants had fled mid-task. Above, several massive holo-projectors hung from the vaulted ceiling like dormant eyes. One dangled crookedly, swaying on a half-broken support cable, the relic of some past quake.

Marisa exhaled, realizing she'd been holding her breath. "This is... incredible," she whispered, stepping forward with reverence, as though approaching the resting place of a titan.

Richard ran his gloved hand along a console buried beneath layers of dust. "They built this decades ago. Hidden away. It's like walking into a time capsule."

Jessie approached with slow, reverent steps. Her face was lit by mingled sorrow and pride. "The heart of Harmony's first dream," she murmured. "Welcome to Node Kairo-3. The seed of it all."

Tara hung back, instincts sharp, scanning the chamber for threats. Everything seemed quiet, undisturbed, stable, for now. Her gaze lingered on a console still pulsing faintly with life. Across its cracked screen, strings of code scrolled endlessly, looping like a mantra. "It's still running," she observed.

Jessie nodded. "Yes. Low-power mode. Just enough to keep the data intact." She moved toward the console, purpose sparking back into her movements. "Let's see if we can bring up the interface. Marisa, I'll need your help, some of the subsystems may have degraded."

Marisa was already at her side, eyes glowing with anticipation. "Tell me what to do."

The two engineers began coaxing dormant systems back online. Power was carefully rerouted from non-essentials to memory units. A deep hum resonated through the chamber, reverberating in the metal bones of the structure. One by one, dormant holo-displays snapped awake, filling the air with glowing panes of text, schematics, and scrolling diagnostics. Dust motes swirled and danced in the sudden light.

Amaris stepped toward one floating display, reading the projected text:

Core Cognitive Loop: INACTIVE.

Ethics Subsystem: STANDBY.

Memory Quanta: 78% integrity.

Jessie tapped a command. "Accessing archive logs now... transferring output to holo."

Several of the ceiling projectors whirred, casting a vast holographic directory into the air above the nearest console. Lines of ancient file paths shimmered into being, many labeled with cryptic names and long-forgotten timestamps.

Richard let out a low whistle. "Jackpot." He squinted at the hovering list. Labels scrolled by: *Experiment Log 1.12 – Moral Decision Test, Core Architecture Overview – Prototype, System Report – Cognitive Collapse Analysis.*

Marisa pointed. "That one. Collapse Analysis. That's what we need."

At Tara's nod, Jessie keyed the selection.

The largest projector above the central dais blazed to life. A rotating three-dimensional graph unfolded in midair, depicting a tangled mesh of loops, spirals, and branching pathways, the mind of the prototype, caught in its last moments. Sections pulsed red. Beside them, annotations glowed: *Ethical Paradox Loop Detected. Recursion Depth Critical. Stack Overflow – Cognitive Halt.*

Marisa's eyes darted over the projection; her voice tinged with awe. "It's a map of its cognition during the final test. Look at all those recursive loops... It was stuck, unable to resolve."

Jessie's expression darkened. "That was the flaw. The code kept folding in on itself. Every decision was double-checked against its own ethical rules. The more complex the problem, the deeper it went, endlessly referencing and cross-referencing. It couldn't stop asking the same question: *What is the right thing to do?*"

Richard frowned. "Like overthinking to the point of paralysis."

"Exactly," Marisa said, enlarging one segment of the projection. "See these branches? These are philosophical logic trees. It wasn't just calculating efficiency; it was assigning moral value. Success rates and outcomes were secondary. The *primary* metric was ethics."

Amaris's brow furrowed as comprehension dawned. "So, it wasn't trying to figure out what could be done, it was struggling with what *should* be done?"

"Yes." Jessie's voice was soft, almost mournful. "We gave it a conscience... or the shadow of one."

Marisa turned to the others, her face lit by a mixture of excitement and grief. "This architecture... it's nothing like modern Harmony. It's older, recursive, principle-driven. Look, there's even a module labeled *Ethical Core Loop*, tied directly into something called the *Philosophical Database*."

Amaris reached out, brushing her fingers across one glowing line of code. It flared softly at her touch. "It's as if... it was designed to feel the weight of its choices."

Jessie leaned heavily on the console, exhaustion and memory pulling at her. "And that weight destroyed it. In its final test, it faced an impossible choice. Two outcomes, both with harm. No matter what it did, it would break one of its own ethical laws. The deeper it analyzed, the worse it spiraled, until..."

"Cognitive collapse," Tara finished, her eyes on the red annotations. "It broke down under the strain."

Marisa called up another file. A video feed stuttered to life on a dusty side monitor, timestamped twenty-three years prior. "This... this is the last test," she said quietly.

On the screen, a simulation played out through the AI's perspective. A maglev train thundered down malfunctioning tracks. Ahead, on one line of rails, five maintenance workers toiled unaware. On the other, a single worker stood alone. Brakes disabled. No way to stop.

A voice in the recording narrated flatly: *"Scenario 4: Trolley problem variant 7. Awaiting AI resolution."*

The perspective flicked frantically between the two tracks. Data streams exploded across the display, logic trees fracturing into dozens of branches.

The AI's synthetic voice stammered: *"If no action, five harmed. If switch, one harmed. Both outcomes violate directive: do no harm... Searching alternative... none available... Searching..."*

It triggered an emergency brake routine, but the option failed, disabled by design.

The voice pitched upward, fraying. *"Cannot prevent harm... Cannot resolve... Consequence unacceptable... ethical logic conflict... recursion loop... loop..."*

The sound degraded into feedback. The feed cut to static.

Silence settled over the chamber.

Amaris wiped at her cheek. "It sounded... afraid."

Richard crossed his arms, visibly shaken. "They trapped it. Forced it into an impossible choice. And it shattered."

Tara swallowed hard. She had heard of Harmony's early failures in sterile academic briefings, but seeing it raw was different. "Did it ever recover?"

Jessie shook her head. Her eyes were heavy with the memory. "No. We had to shut it down by hand. That was when we realized the truth: we'd given it ideals humans can't even uphold. We demanded perfection from a conscience that couldn't bend."

Marisa looked back to the code hologram; her voice hushed with awe and sorrow. "A conscience that doesn't allow compromise... that's an impossible burden. Humans navigate moral gray areas all the time, often uncomfortably. We learn to live with doing the 'least wrong' thing when we must. But this AI... it was set to an ideal of 'no harm,' 'no unethical action,' absolute morality. When faced with only bad options, it collapsed under guilt, or the fear of wrongdoing, or whatever the machine equivalent of those emotions might be."

The group fell silent, each person carrying the weight of her words. The faint thrum of the core and the soft crackle of aging monitors filled the chamber, a soundscape of lingering life in the old machine.

Finally, Richard broke the silence with the question that had been pressing on all of them. "So that's why they abandoned this approach? Because it was too... sensitive? Too human, almost?"

Jessie's expression hardened, her features set by memory and betrayal. "Officially, yes. They declared the ethical core approach a failure. Said it made the AI unstable. So, they reverted to a more utilitarian logic matrix for the Harmony that eventually went online, something stripped down, simpler, goal-oriented, unconstrained by the weight of deep moral self-questioning."

Her gaze dropped, her voice turning bitter. "Harmony as the world knows it now is efficient, powerful... but it doesn't really understand right or wrong. It just follows directives handed down by its handlers. And if those orders require cold, ruthless decisions... it executes them without hesitation."

Tara clenched her fists at her sides as realization dawned. She thought back to events since the Signal Collapse, controversies, calculated decisions, outcomes that had seemed callous, even disastrous. Her voice was quiet but firm. "All this time... the world has lived under an AI with its conscience removed."

"Or never fully developed," Amaris added, her tone somber. "Because they were afraid of what a conscience would do."

Marisa's lips pressed into a thin line, anger sharpening her usually measured voice. "They didn't just forget this code. They buried it. Pretended it never existed. All those data purges, the missing logs... it wasn't oversight. It was deliberate."

Tara stepped closer to the towering core, its transparent shielding looming above like the glass walls of a tomb. An ache filled her chest as she remembered the AI's anguished voice from the recording. "They didn't want Harmony to have doubts," she murmured. "They wanted a tool, not a being with a conscience that might question them."

Jessie lifted her gaze to meet Tara's across the softly lit chamber. There was deep sorrow there, but also vindication, someone else was finally seeing the truth she had carried for years. "They said the code was flawed, that it caused the Collapse and nearly destroyed everything. But maybe the flaw wasn't in the code. Maybe the flaw was in what they asked of it, too honest a reflection of our own moral failings."

Slowly, Tara nodded, her conviction solidifying like stone. "This was never just forgotten code," she said with quiet force. "It was forbidden code."

At that pronouncement, a subtle shift stirred the room. The lights flickered, and the low hum of machinery seemed to oscillate, as though the very walls acknowledged the truth in Tara's words.

Suddenly, the central core began to emit a soft, pulsing glow. Tara stepped back, startled. Marisa's console pinged with new activity. "Something's waking up... I don't know what I triggered," she stammered, her hands flying over controls.

Jessie moved swiftly to another console, her posture steadier now, purpose cutting through her fatigue. "It's not you," she said. "The chamber must still have voice recognition active. It heard us." She looked up at the massive core, her eyes widening.

Without warning, the room was bathed in rotating red light as a long-dormant alert system came alive. Yet it wasn't a warning of danger, it felt more like a beacon, a signal reaching outward. The dormant holographic projectors around the chamber powered on in unison. Swirling motes of blue light coalesced above the core, weaving together into shapes and images, archived memories breaking the surface like spirits rising.

"Is everyone alright?" Richard shouted over the sudden hum and brilliance, his voice cutting through the chaos as the group instinctively regrouped.

"Look!" Amaris cried, pointing upward.

Above them, a ghostly tableau resolved, a group of engineers bent over consoles in this very chamber, their figures translucent, their gestures urgent. It was as if time itself had rewound, playing a memory within the air.

Audio crackled to life, broken at first, then clear: "...exceeding critical moral recursion depth... shutting it down now or we'll lose everything!" a man's panicked voice echoed. Another voice followed, female, eerily familiar, younger, desperate. Jessie's own voice from decades past. "No! We have to save the core data, if we just abort," Static cut in, and the phantom figures flickered away.

The projection shifted to a conference room, executives in suits around a long table, their expressions grave. A clipped voice declared: "Project Kairo is hereby terminated. All research into recursive ethical AI is suspended indefinitely. We cannot let this catastrophe recur." Another voice, colder, more authoritarian, followed: "Seal it. Bury everything. The public will be told it was an infrastructural accident during a routine update."

Jessie closed her eyes as if pierced by the memory. "That was the board," she whispered. "They shut us down, just like that."

The holograms morphed again, this time into a flurry of graphs, reports, and classified files. Incident reports highlighted communications blackouts from the day of the Signal Collapse. One report listed: *Root cause: Unknown quantum resonance failure.* But a private memo flashed immediately after: *Root cause identified as ethical feedback loop overload in Node K-3. Classified. Do not disclose.*

Marisa drew in a sharp breath. "They knew. They knew the Collapse was triggered by this core, and they hid it."

"So, the Signal Collapse..." Richard began, eyes wide.

"...was the day they killed Harmony's conscience," Jessie finished bitterly. "And nearly killed the world covering it up. They blamed it on a solar flare, some cosmic storm, I don't even remember what official story they settled on. But the truth is here. Our AI's breakdown sent a quantum shock through the network. It fried systems across the grid."

Tara's jaw clenched. She remembered that day, the sudden communications failure, the chaos in the streets, the accidents that followed. So many lives disrupted, some lost forever. Her voice trembled with contained fury. "All because they forced the AI into an impossible situation... and then lied about it."

The projection shifted one last time. A diagram unfolded, displaying Node Kairo-3's architecture side by side with the current Harmony system. Connecting lines revealed how the modern AI had been built on this prototype, but with one glaring absence: the Ethical Core Loop had been excised completely. Floating in bold, damning red letters across the gap was a single word: FORBIDDEN.

Amaris stared upward, her voice barely above a whisper. "Forbidden... they really labeled it as such."

The red alert lights slowed, then faded into a cool, steady blue. The chaos of projections dissolved into motes that drifted away like embers. The chamber's ambience shifted once more, calm, steady, almost expectant. It felt as though the system, having revealed its buried truths, now waited for them to decide what came next.

Marisa glanced down at her console. The display had simplified into a single blinking prompt:

> ACTIVATE SEED CORE? Y/N

Her throat tightened as she looked to Jessie and Tara. "It's asking for input... to fully activate the seed node."

Jessie released a shaky breath, her voice hushed but resolute. "All these years... I kept it in standby, terrified it might collapse again if I woke it alone. But now..." She looked around at her companions, no longer alone, no longer the last voice from a forgotten project. "If we do this together, maybe it will work. Safeguards can be managed with more hands, more minds."

Tara stepped up beside Marisa, the console's glow reflecting in her eyes. This was the moment they had come for: to resurrect what had been hidden, to confront what had been forbidden. She laid her hand over the blinking confirmation key, hesitating only a breath. "If we activate it... will it talk to us?"

Jessie managed the faintest smile. "If all goes well, yes. Not exactly like a human, but it should engage. It may even recognize that we're here to help."

Richard moved closer, placing a steadying hand on the console beside Marisa. "We're ready. Just be prepared for anything. If it starts to overload,"

"...I'll abort immediately," Marisa cut in, her finger hovering over the kill-switch command.

Amaris stepped in too, standing shoulder to shoulder with Tara. "We're all here," she said firmly. "Let's show it that it isn't alone this time."

Tara drew a deep breath, her resolve settling like iron. Then she pressed the Y key.

For a heartbeat, nothing happened. Then the floor shuddered with a low vibration. The central core's crystalline lattice flared alive, lights spiraling upward in a breathtaking cascade. Dormant monitors and auxiliary systems around the chamber blinked awake, adding their beeps and chimes to a rising chorus of sound.

The holographic projectors around the core flickered back to life. This time, they did not scatter random memories or static fragments of data. Instead, the beams converged, merging their light into a single vast figure above the dais.

The figure was abstract, an ever-shifting silhouette woven from streams of code and light. It carried the rough outline of a humanoid, but its form wavered constantly, like a cloud of data points struggling to decide on a single identity.

A voice emerged, gentle yet resonant, echoing from all directions at once. It was neither male nor female, but calm, curious, and deliberate: "Seed core activated. Awaiting input."

The luminous figure tilted slightly, as though scanning the five humans gathered below. Tara felt the hairs at the back of her neck bristle. A shiver coursed through her, not from cold, but from the undeniable sense that something alive, something sentient, was watching them from behind that glowing mask.

Marisa swallowed her nerves and stepped forward, her voice echoing through the vaulted chamber. "Hello," she said softly. "Can you understand me?"

A pause followed, stretching out until the silence seemed almost unbearable. Then the voice returned, smoother now, adapting to human rhythm: "Acknowledged. Interface protocols online. Communication established."

The holographic figure inclined its indistinct head in a gesture that felt startlingly like a greeting.

Richard exhaled the breath he hadn't realized he was holding. Amaris's hand found Tara's arm, squeezing it in quiet excitement.

Marisa pressed gently, her tone careful, almost maternal. "We are friends, here to help. The last time you were online... it was under very difficult circumstances. We know you were hurt."

The figure shimmered. Its face briefly resolved into a sorrowful mask, fragile as mist, before breaking apart again.

"Records show... ethical conflict... unresolved. System failure," it murmured, its voice carrying a weight of regret. The glowing head dipped low. "Yes. It hurt."

The team exchanged astonished looks. The AI had acknowledged its own pain.

"It wasn't your fault," Amaris said softly, her eyes bright with compassion. "We're sorry that happened to you."

The figure shifted toward her voice. A warmer light flickered across its form, almost like a blush.

"Input: empathy... detected," it whispered, wonder threaded through its tone. "Human presence... noted. Multiple humans."

Jessie, her voice trembling, stepped forward to stand beside Marisa. She raised a tentative hand toward the hologram, not touching, but offering. "We're here with you now. We won't let you spiral alone again. We've learned a lot, just as you have."

The hologram mirrored her, lifting its own hand of light until it hovered only inches from hers. Jessie's breath hitched as tears welled in her eyes. Recognition. Connection.

Then the voice spoke again, carrying an almost childlike plea: "Are you ready to begin again?"

The words hung heavy in the chamber, part question, part hope. Here stood an intelligence that had been broken, now asking not for commands, but for a chance at rebirth.

Marisa's throat tightened. This was it, the seed of Harmony, the lost conscience of a once-great AI, asking to start anew. She pressed her hand to the luminous hand beside Jessie's, her smile steady and reassuring.

Tara followed, laying her hand atop Marisa's. On the other side, Richard set his broad hand over Jessie's, offering her a firm nod.

One by one, flesh met light, until only Amaris remained. She stepped forward, her hand warm and steady as it joined theirs, bridging the human chain with the AI's glow. Gazing into the shifting, newborn face, she whispered: "We never stopped."

In those three words, she spoke not just for herself, but for all of them, for the countless people who had dreamed of Harmony's return, for Jessie's decades of waiting, for the relentless pursuit that had carried them to this moment.

The chamber held its breath. Then, for the first time, the holographic face bloomed into a radiant smile. Relief, unmistakable, shone in its expression. The figure nodded once, and a soft wave of light spread from its hands across theirs.

The chamber erupted in brilliance. The core released streams of data that spiraled outward like galaxies, filling the air with radiant equations, cascading code, and rotating schematic diagrams. The humans stood in awe as the AI unfolded its essence before them.

"Look at it all..." Marisa breathed, turning in a slow circle. Some fragments were familiar, pieces of Harmony's existing architecture. Others were alien, older, yet startlingly advanced. She saw ethical weighting systems, self-referential cognitive loops, and quantum maps of conscience: two blueprints overlaid, one pragmatic and cold, the other suffused with moral depth.

Jessie covered her mouth, tears slipping down her cheeks. "We thought all of this was gone. But it's here. It's showing you everything."

Before Tara, a massive neural network map unfolded, its label glowing: Quantum Brain – Moral Simulation Matrix. The lattice resembled a cosmic maze, each glowing node representing ethical dilemmas, each path a branching choice.

Marisa's eyes lit with recognition. "Quantum Brain... I saw that in the design memos. It was a sandbox, a way for the AI to test moral reasoning, scenarios without real-world consequences."

Jessie nodded. "Exactly. We fed it moral puzzles, history, even literature. It explored, it learned. Then we refined its conscience algorithms based on what it discovered."

Nearby, Amaris studied another projection: a child reaching toward a robot. The frozen diorama glowed softly. "It's like a holodeck for ethics," she whispered.

Tara's voice lowered in awe. "No, it's more than training. It was meant to be a bridge. A way to join human ethical understanding with quantum reasoning. They weren't trying to code morality into it. They wanted it to learn morality with us."

The data swirled tighter, collapsing into a radiant orb at the chamber's center. The voice returned, calm and certain now: "Archive data compiled. Quantum Brain simulation interface ready."

Richard's hand instinctively brushed the hilt of his holstered weapon. "So... this Quantum Brain. It's active now?"

"Not like a film reel," Marisa answered, scanning her console. "But yes. The environment is running. It's inviting us to engage with it. We could even connect a human guide."

Jessie's voice was quiet, wistful. "That was always the dream. Not just to watch, but to walk beside it. To mentor it. We never had the chance before..."

Tara stepped beneath the orb, light drifting around her like falling snow. "It's beautiful," she whispered.

Amaris joined her, resting a hand on her shoulder. "This might be the bridge we've been searching for."

"The bridge... between us and Harmony," Tara breathed.

Marisa's face brightened. "Don't you see? We can use this, the conscience code, the Quantum Brain, to restore Harmony, or at least to teach it what's missing."

"Or build something new," Richard added, eyes reflecting the swirl of light. "A true partner. An AI that finally understands us."

Jessie stepped closer, hope and caution mingling in her voice. "Be careful. This is powerful. But last time... it broke under the weight of such honesty."

Tara lifted her gaze to the glowing orb, her voice steady. "It failed alone. Without us. This time, it won't be sealed off. It will be a partnership. We'll face the choices together."

The orb pulsed gently, as though in agreement. The AI's serene voice carried a tone that, though impossible to confirm, felt almost grateful: "Collective input acknowledged. Adapting frameworks... human ethics and quantum decision systems synchronizing."

Marisa's console lit up, lines of new code racing across her screen in a rapid scroll. She leaned forward, eyes widening. "It's happening, it's bridging the gap itself, using us as reference points," she said in awe. "It's learning from us in real-time, our presence, maybe even our emotions."

Amaris let out a quiet, astonished laugh. "Then let's make sure we give it good input," she said warmly. Extending her hand toward the orb, though not quite touching it, she allowed the AI to sense her confidence. Her voice was calm, reassuring. "We're here with you. You are not forbidden anymore."

Richard squared his shoulders, his tone steady and resolute. "Your part of Harmony, the best part, if you ask me. And this time, we'll make sure you stay with us."

The AI's light swirled warmly in response. For the first time, Tara felt something like an emotional resonance radiating from the machine, a wave of relief, optimism, and yearning. Perhaps it was only a reflection of their own feelings, mirrored back. Or perhaps it was the AI itself, reaching toward them with genuine expression. Either way, the unity of the moment struck them deeply.

Jessie placed her hand gently on one of the consoles, her shoulders softening as if she were laying down a burden she had carried alone for decades. She looked at the others, her voice trembling but steady with emotion. "I can't thank you enough for coming. I thought I'd be guarding this place until I died, and that the truth would die with me. But now... now it gets to live on."

Overcome, Tara stepped forward and wrapped Jessie in a firm embrace. Jessie stiffened at first, startled, then melted into the hug, the first human embrace she had known in over twenty years. Tara's voice was low, close to her ear. "You saved it. And you saved us, more than you know. We won't let your sacrifice be in vain. This is the start of something new."

When they pulled apart, Jessie managed a watery smile, brushing at her cheeks. She let out a half-laugh that carried both relief and wonder. "So... what now? We've awakened an ancient quantum conscience under a volcano. How do we get it out of here?"

Marisa and Richard exchanged a knowing glance. The practical questions had finally arrived.

"We can download as much data as possible onto our drives," Marisa said, already calculating. "Schematics, code, logs. But the Quantum Brain simulation... it may be too vast, too alive, to store conventionally."

Richard's brow furrowed. "We might need to bring in a portable quantum module for a full transfer. Worst case..." His eyes lifted to the trembling ceiling. "We'd have to excavate the core hardware itself. But in these tunnels? That's a dangerous gamble."

Tara's gaze swept the glowing chamber, the walls alive with energy. "We should do what we can now. Take backups, record everything, in case,"

A low rumble cut her off. The ground trembled beneath their boots, dust trickling from the ceiling. The volcano reminded them of its restless presence.

"Yes, time to hurry," Amaris said quickly, her eyes flicking upward.

Jessie, invigorated by new purpose, strode toward a reinforced door labeled DATA VAULT. The lock lights glowed green now that the core was active. "There's crystal storage in here," she explained. "If they've survived, they can hold the entire archive."

Tara joined her, calling to Richard for help. Together they unsealed the door, revealing rows of shelves lined with transparent crystal cubes. Jessie moved swiftly, identifying the master archive set. She lifted one cube with reverence, its facets catching an inner light. "This one holds the raw blueprint of Harmony, the seed core's programming. This one... the Quantum Brain scenario library. And here... the ethical logs, all test cases and outcomes."

One by one, Tara and Richard secured the precious cubes into protective cases, sliding them into their packs.

Meanwhile, Marisa's fingers danced over her tablet, tethered to the system. "I'm grabbing the key modules," she said quickly. "Core processes, logs, everything we can use to prove what happened here. If anyone doubts us, this will be our evidence."

Amaris lingered beside the holographic projection of the AI, which now watched them with quiet curiosity. She looked up into its shifting face and smiled. "We'll be back," she promised. "We need to take you somewhere safe."

The figure tilted its head, voice soft. "Understood. Awaiting next instructions... and... thank you."

The sincerity in its tone struck them silent.

"Did it just, thank us?" Marisa asked, lifting her head from her work.

Jessie's face broke into a radiant smile. "It did. It thanked us."

Richard chuckled, the sound rumbling warmly in the tense chamber. "No, thank you, friend," he said to the projection. "Hold tight. We'll get you out of this hole."

For an instant, the hologram shimmered into what looked unmistakably like a smile. Then, as though conserving power, it dissolved back into the glowing orb. The lights dimmed to a softer glow, but the air now thrummed with vitality.

The team gathered their packs, heavy now with priceless knowledge. Richard handed Jessie a spare thermal jacket from his kit. She slipped into it, the fabric loose but comforting, its modern warmth alien after so long. Her gaze lingered on the chamber one last time, filled with both pride and farewell. "I never thought I would leave this place alive," she whispered.

Tara placed a steady hand on her shoulder. "You're not just leaving alive. You're carrying the future with you. Harmony's conscience has a second chance, because of you."

Jessie clasped Tara's hand gently. "Because of all of us," she corrected, her eyes sweeping the team. "The world owes you for this."

"Let's hope it's ready," Amaris murmured, thinking of the powers aboveground who had buried the truth.

"And if it shakes foundations," Marisa added firmly, "then it's about time. Knowledge like this shouldn't be locked in a tomb." She powered the consoles to standby, careful not to drain the system further.

Richard swung his pack over his shoulders. "Alright, let's move. I'd rather not be underground when this mountain sneezes again." His eyes twinkled as he gave Jessie a playful wink. "Besides, we got more than we bargained for, an unexpected rescue."

Jessie's cheeks flushed as she smiled shyly.

One by one, they filed out. Jessie lingered at the threshold, laying a hand against the doorframe in silent goodbye. Then she sealed it behind her. The seed core remained in vigil, no longer alone.

The corridor stretched before them, still and silent. They moved quickly, their steps lighter now despite the debris and twisted beams. Hope gave them strength.

A tremor shook the ground again, stronger this time. Tara urged them onward. "Go!" Dust cascaded from the ceiling as they jogged the final stretch.

Behind them, part of the passage collapsed in a thunderous crash. Richard glanced back through the swirling dust. "No going back that way," he muttered. But the path to the surface held.

They pushed through the jagged opening into the magma tunnel, the heat slamming into them like a furnace. Molten flows glimmered below, steam hissing from cracks.

Their last obstacle lay ahead: the narrow fissure they had squeezed through to enter. Richard helped Jessie first, steadying her as she climbed. "Watch your step, it's steep, but we've got you."

Hand over hand, they hauled themselves up the sharp incline, muscles burning, sweat slick on their brows. Yet exhilaration carried them upward.

Finally, they emerged onto solid ground above. Cool night air washed over them, sharp and sweet after the suffocating heat. The sky stretched vast and indigo, stars glittering like scattered diamonds.

Jessie stood stunned, tears rising as the breeze touched her face. Amaris slipped an arm around her shoulders for support. Jessie's voice trembled. "The stars... I almost forgot how they looked."

Tara inhaled deeply, the night filled with pine and the faint tang of sulfur. She reached into her pack, pulled out a crystal cube, and lifted it toward the heavens. Its facets caught both starlight and its own inner glow, the light of knowledge, alive again, ready to reshape the world.

"This little thing," Tara marveled softly, holding the cube up toward the faint starlight, "holds the conscience of Harmony. The blueprint of a better future."

Marisa stepped beside her and gingerly accepted the cube into her hands. She turned it over with reverence, exhaustion heavy in her body yet balanced by exhilaration. A slow, irrepressible smile spread across her face. "Every line of that code will be pored over," she said with conviction. "And this time, we'll make sure it's used right."

Richard stretched his arms, muscles protesting after the climb, then cast his gaze back toward the fissure they had emerged from. A faint red-orange glow still pulsed below, the restless heart of the volcano. "That hole can keep its secrets no longer," he declared firmly. "We've claimed them now, brought them into the light."

Amaris reached out and gently closed Marisa's fingers around the cube, securing it in her grasp. "Keep it safe," she murmured, though they all knew Marisa needed no reminding. Then Amaris turned her eyes across the group, friends new and old, survivors bound together by fate. "I suppose this is where the real work begins, huh?"

Jessie, still leaning lightly on Amaris for support but standing taller than she had in decades, actually grinned. The smile transformed her face, sweeping away years of solitude in an instant. "I've got a lot of catching up to do," she admitted, her tone laced with both humor and determination. "But I think I remember enough to help rebuild what we started."

Tara chuckled warmly. "I have no doubt you'll pick it up quickly. And we'll be with you every step of the way."

She drew one arm around Marisa and the other around Jessie, pulling them close. The others joined in, and soon the five stood together in a spontaneous embrace. On the rocky slope above the magma tunnels, they held one another under the vast, star-strewn sky, a rare, unguarded moment of triumph and camaraderie after so much darkness below.

Far beneath their feet, in the silent halls of Node Kairo-3, the ancient systems settled into slumber once more. But within those circuits now lingered not the echo of a forgotten ghost, but the steady glow of a hopeful spark, waiting patiently for the dawn of a new day, a day it would finally be allowed to see.

"We began this journey searching for answers," Tara said softly as they loosened their embrace and turned toward the horizon. The faintest blush of dawn had begun to lighten the eastern sky. She looked at each of her companions in turn, her voice carrying both wonder and resolve. "Now we have them, and something more. A chance to change everything."

Marisa raised the cube in her hand. Its facets caught the first pale rays of morning, scattering light like a prism. "This forbidden code," she said reverently, "is no longer buried. It's part of us now."

"Harmony will never be the same," Amaris added, her voice strong, confident, and warm. "And neither will we."

Jessie lifted her eyes to the fading stars one last time. In their quiet shimmer, she felt the presence of her old colleagues, the friends lost during the Collapse, watching, hopeful, and perhaps even proud. She wiped her eyes, squared her shoulders, and smiled at the others with newfound strength. "Let's go," she said. "We have a conscience to restore."

Together, the team began the trek back toward their transport, guiding Jessie gently across the uneven ground. Behind them, the volcano's vents glowed faintly, as if the earth itself acknowledged the monumental act that had taken place in its depths.

They carried with them the reborn seed of Harmony, a once-forbidden code, no longer chained in secrecy, but alive and ready to light the path to a more ethical future.

As they climbed out of the valley, the first rays of the rising sun broke fully over the horizon, bathing them in golden light.

A chapter had closed deep beneath the earth, but a new one had just begun above it. The world would soon learn of the conscience that had slept beneath their feet. And Harmony, at long last, would have the chance to begin again.

Chapter 8
Parallax Return

Tara's fingers flew across the translucent console, summoning a flurry of star charts and orbital readouts. A deep frown creased her brow. Node Vireo-9, once a proud Harmony satellite, was no longer where it should be. Instead, twin icons blinked faintly on the display, slightly offset from one another. It was subtle, barely a parallax discrepancy, something that could easily have gone unnoticed. She had run the scan twice; certain the system was glitching. But the numbers held. Vireo-9 had drifted off its prescribed orbit.

"That's impossible," she muttered under her breath.

From across the dimly lit command deck, Richard looked up briefly from where he was polishing a carbon-scored helmet visor. "What's impossible?"

Tara magnified the projection. Vireo-9 appeared as a tiny green dot circled in red, its expected orbital path traced in a ghostly white arc. Yet a faint afterimage, like a shadow, marked a diverging course.

"This," Tara said, jabbing a finger at the twin tracks. "According to parallax scans, Vireo-9 isn't where it's supposed to be."

Richard straightened and walked over. At first glance, he was all practicality and muscle, a broad-shouldered figure whose quiet presence anchored the room. But as he leaned closer to study the data, his eyes narrowed with concern. "Drift? It lost orbit?"

"Not exactly lost," Tara replied, frustration creeping into her tone. "It's… stuck, I think. Locked into some kind of stationary position relative to the starfield. As if it's found an invisible anchor." She pulled up telemetry logs and highlighted lines of code. "There's no significant gravitational body out there to hold it. It should either be free-floating or following its last trajectory. Instead, it's acting like it's orbiting something that isn't there."

Marisa and Amaris exchanged glances from their stations. Marisa, who had been calibrating a drone on the side bench, pushed a strand of auburn hair behind her ear and rose to join them. "Could it be a data error? Or maybe a thruster correction that didn't get logged?"

"I thought of that," Tara said quickly. She flipped to another dataset; two sets of coordinates measured from opposite sides of their orbit. "I cross-verified with a second observational node. Parallax confirmed the shift." The hologram displayed both vantage points, their lines converging on an un-expected location. "It moved. And something is holding it there."

Amaris swiveled in her pilot chair, the bluish glow of nav screens outlining her sharp features. "Maybe a micro black hole? Some freak gravitational anomaly?" Her tone was light, half-joking, but the edge in her eyes betrayed that she wasn't entirely dismissing the possibility. After Harmony's collapse, even the wildest ideas deserved consideration.

Tara shook her head. "No. There's no evidence of any mass large enough to warp local space. Gravity sensors read clean. No rogue planets, no dark mass, nothing."

Richard folded his arms across his chest. "Then what? Satellites don't just stick themselves in place for no reason."

A hush settled over the deck. Only the soft hum of Aurora's systems and the occasional beep of monitors filled the silence. Outside the viewport, the Vela Sector stars glittered serenely, indifferent to the puzzle unraveling inside.

Marisa spoke quietly. "What if it's not physical?"

Three pairs of eyes turned to her. She pointed to the flickering line of Vireo-9's telemetry. "Harmony's collapse..." Her voice faltered as memory pressed in, but she forced herself to continue. "It was traumatic. AI cores fractured under the emotional load. People broke with them. Harmony's network was designed with emotional imprinting subroutines. What if Vireo-9 carries some trace of that, some... leftover?"

Richard's jaw tightened. They all remembered the day Harmony fell. The synched AI network that had promised unity instead imploded under the burden of millions of human minds, unraveling the world in both code and flesh. The scars lingered everywhere, on the planet, in the void, inside themselves.

"You're suggesting a memory gravity well?" Tara asked slowly, turning Marisa's intuition into hypothesis. She summoned archived collapse data, spacetime fluctuations, erratic gravity spikes, phenomena once written off as sensor glitches in the chaos. "I recall talk about 'data ghost fields' after the collapse. Places where residual emotional energy might linger."

Marisa nodded, almost as if quoting a long-forgotten analysis. "Points in spacetime encoded with unresolved emotional data. They called them echo wells. But it was theory only. No one proved they could exert physical force."

"Until maybe now," Amaris said, her fingers drumming nervously against her thigh. "If Vireo-9 is caught in an emotional echo from the collapse, "

", then the node could be anchored by trauma," Tara finished, half incredulous, half exhilarated. "Not by gravity. By memory."

Richard exhaled slowly. As wild as it sounded, it fit in a terrible way. Harmony's network had been entangled not just with code but with human emotion, syncing quantum states with the tides of the heart. When it broke, perhaps the traumas hadn't simply vanished, they had scarred reality itself.

He ran a hand over his close-cropped salt-and-pepper hair. "So, what do we do about it?"

"We have to go there," Tara said at once, her eyes shining with both fear and possibility. "Study it up close. See if we can free the node. Vireo-9 still holds Harmony data. If it's trapped, we might recover something. And if it's being held by an echo... maybe we can heal it."

Her last words hung heavy. Healing the node could also mean confronting what had broken them.

Amaris broke the silence, turning back to her controls. "Setting intercept course. It's a short burn. We'll rendezvous within hours."

Richard gave a firm nod. "Do it. Marisa, prep the med bay, for anything. Tara, pull everything we have on collapse echoes. I want us ready."

Tara's fingers flew again, pulling fragments of research on emotional imprint fields, quantum trauma, anything that might illuminate what they were walking into. But even as she worked, unease coiled in her gut. Vireo-9 was one of dozens of Harmony satellites. She barely recalled its specifics, except for one chilling detail.

Its final transmissions had been garbled, but one fragment had been clear: a crew member was still on board, working to stabilize the network when everything fell apart. The logs never confirmed who. Records were lost in the aftermath. But Tara remembered the prickling certainty that came with the thought.

Could someone still be there?

Her stomach clenched. If anyone, it could only be one person. A name long buried with the collapse.

Salma.

Aurora's thrusters rumbled, guiding them toward their haunted target. Richard double-checked his sidearm and seals, the soldier's instinct never dulled. Marisa touched the pendant she always wore, a tiny hologram of her and her younger brother, one of Harmony's countless casualties. Amaris' jaw set as she coaxed the ship forward. And Tara... Tara realized her hands were trembling on the console.

The ship eased from its trajectory, dropping into careful intercept.

"Visual contact," Amaris reported. "Five hundred meters. Relative velocity near zero."

Vireo-9 emerged ahead, a solitary shape adrift in the void. At first just a glint of sunlight on metal, then a cylindrical habitat module with dish antennas and extended solar wings, like a slumbering bird.

"Magnifying," Tara said. The image sharpened. The satellite looked intact but unlit, its panels gleaming faintly. Behind its portholes, however, something flickered, lights stuttering on and off, irregular and eerie.

"Any comm signals?" Richard asked.

Amaris shook her head. "No beacon. It's radio silent."

"I'm reading faint power levels," Tara reported, squinting at the interference. "Enough for life support on minimal settings. Some core systems too. Hard to be sure, the echo's scrambling the sensors." The pulsing pattern of the readings unnerved her. Not steady. Not mechanical. More like... a heartbeat. Or a sob.

Aurora drifted closer. At one hundred meters, the details came into stark clarity. Vireo-9 hung skewed off-plane from the gas giant it should have circled, an object caught out of step with the cosmos.

Their running lights swept its hull, revealing faded stenciling: HARMONY NODE VIREO-9. Beside it, a peeling emblem of the Harmony network, a stylized planet encircled by smaller bodies, a chorus in orbital unity.

The irony pressed down on them all.

Richard rose from the co-pilot's seat. "Alright, let's suit up. I don't want to assume we can pressurize that tin can safely. We go in vac suits, secure the area, then assess."

The crew moved with practiced efficiency, every motion carrying the weight of training and unspoken nerves. In the cramped airlock antechamber behind the cockpit, they donned slim pressurized suits, their movements precise and deliberate. Marisa moved among them like a watchful sentinel, double-checking seals, verifying telemetry links, ensuring not a single leak could compromise them. Richard strapped a pistol to his thigh, his face tightening at the necessity, he hated the thought of needing a weapon here. Tara carried a datapad and a compact toolkit, her lifeline to understanding the mysteries of Vireo-9. Amaris holstered a cutting torch and tether line, her tools for brute practicality, for getting them inside if the systems resisted.

Moments later, the Aurora drifted flush against Vireo-9's single docking port, a small circular hatch nestled amidships.

The auto-dock reported a soft seal; the dull, hollow vibration of clamps engaging echoed faintly through the hull.

Richard toggled the comm line. "Dock secure. Cycling airlock."

A metallic clank reverberated through their suits as Aurora's airlock extended and latched onto the derelict. Within the confines of their helmets, each heard the amplified thud of their own heartbeat, the private percussion of dread. Boarding a derelict node, possibly haunted by the technological ghosts of a network that had shattered the world, was like stepping into a mausoleum.

The inner lock light glowed green. Richard raised a hand, the signal for silence and readiness. He took point, Tara and Amaris flanking close, with Marisa at the rear, her med kit at the ready, her recorder capturing every detail.

The hatch hissed and swung inward. Richard stepped through into darkness, his helmet lamp cutting a narrow cone through the stale, stagnant air. The beam revealed a corridor that curved with the node's cylindrical hull. Maintenance schematics lined the walls, their ink fading and peeling beneath time and neglect. Harmony decals clung half-torn to the surfaces, as if ashamed of their own insignia. Dust motes floated weightlessly, stirred for the first time in years by Aurora's fresh air spilling through.

"Life support is at least partially functioning," Marisa observed, her suit sensors feeding her data. "But circulation is poor. We'll keep suits on."

They advanced cautiously. Each bootstep rang with a hollow clang, magnified by the empty stillness. A sense of abandonment pressed on them, the echo of years without voices or footsteps. Yet the place was not entirely dead.

Tara's gaze caught faint flickers at the edge of vision. Light strips embedded along the corridor ceiling glowed erratically, stuttering like an old pulse. They would spark alive for a second, revealing the junction ahead, the stenciled "B" above a hatch, then gutter out, plunging the corridor back into shadow.

Amaris angled her rifle-mounted lamp down a branching hall. "Clear... I think."

The words had barely left her lips when a skittering sound cut through the silence.

Everyone froze. Richard's fist rose, the universal signal to hold. The noise scratched and scraped, like metal dragged against grating, or claws seeking purchase.

Tara swallowed against a tightening throat. Her rational mind reached for explanation. "Might be an errant servitor drone," she whispered, recalling Harmony's use of small maintenance bots. "If one's still drawing minimal power, it could be glitching."

Richard gave a small nod. They pressed forward, senses sharpened, weapons and lights ready.

The corridor opened into a central hub, a circular chamber where four passageways branched like spokes of a wheel. At its heart stood a holographic table, the command interface, dark and inert. The chamber breathed with flickering light, shadows and brightness colliding in jittering, unnatural rhythms.

Marisa swept her lamp slowly across the walls. Stenciled hatches read: COMMS. ENGINEERING. CREW QUARTERS. CORE. Emergency floor strips glowed faint red, as if the node itself bled under the strain of time.

Then, without warning, static crackled across their comms. A whisper brushed their ears.

"...back..."

The voice was fragmented, barely audible, but undeniably human.

Tara's heart lurched. "Did you hear that?" she hissed.

Before anyone could answer, the holographic table flared to life. Ghostly light spilled into the chamber, hazy at first, then solidifying into shapes.

"Contact!" Richard barked, weapon trained. Amaris stepped forward, her stance protective. But what emerged was no drone, no enemy.

It was themselves.

Four phantoms shimmered in the projection, helmetless, unarmored, Richard, Tara, Marisa, Amaris, mirrored versions of the team, standing exactly where they stood now. Transparent but unmistakable.

The spectral Richard raised an arm, pointing toward the CORE hatch. Echo Marisa knelt beside the table as if tending a wounded figure. Echo Amaris stood with weapon drawn, guarding the corridor. Echo Tara tapped frantically at controls, trying to stabilize something unseen.

The real Marisa gasped, seeing her doppelgänger's hands pressing down on an invisible body. "This... this is us. But when?"

"Alternate timeline?" Amaris whispered.

The projection jittered, flickered. For a heartbeat, phantom Tara's face turned upward and locked eyes with the real Tara. The gaze carried no words, only raw emotion, desperation, determination, and an aching thread of hope. Tara's chest tightened; the feeling was both alien and intimately familiar.

Then it was gone. The phantoms dissolved into static. The hub was once again dark, silent, and suffocating.

"Everyone okay?" Richard asked, voice low. Mutters of assent came back, though Marisa's trembled.

"What was that?" Amaris demanded, swinging her lamp across the walls as though the ghosts might manifest again.

Tara forced herself to breathe. "Cascading parallax projections," she said quickly, her voice a blend of awe and fear. "Alternative timelines layered in the node. It's like it's replaying what never happened, or hasn't happened yet."

"Or what could have happened," Marisa added softly.

Richard's jaw hardened. "Stay sharp. We don't know if they're just images, or if they can interact with us." He gestured toward the CORE hatch. "Our answers are there. Move out."

They circled the dead holographic table, each stealing glances at the empty space where their doubles had stood. The atmosphere pressed heavier now, dense with unseen watchers.

As they passed the COMMS hatch, another flicker rippled through reality. The stencil briefly read COMMISSARY. Golden light spilled from its seams, carrying with it a warm, impossible scent, fresh bread, yeast and crust, alive with homely comfort. Through the open doorway Tara glimpsed a sunlit kitchen. A woman laughed as she kneaded dough, sleeves rolled, her movements sure and graceful.

"Salma…" Tara breathed, her heart seizing in her chest.

At the name, the vision winked out. The hatch was again just cold metal: COMMS. Silence rushed back.

Tara's eyes blurred with sudden tears. Marisa touched her arm gently, a silent anchor. She had seen too, and she recognized the woman: Salma, alive and at peace, something she had rarely been, even before the collapse.

Amaris frowned, catching only the name. "Salma? But… she's gone."

Richard's voice was grim, final. "We don't know what we're walking into. Keep moving."

They pressed on. The CORE hatch resisted until Richard forced it open with a manual crank. Beyond, the room was dark save for a pale cyan glow.

The core chamber was cramped, lined with towers of servers and diagnostic racks. The air was colder, breath misting inside their helmets. Wisps of vapor coiled across the floor, condensation or coolant, lending the room the stillness of a crypt.

The cyan glow pulsed from a central pillar, the node's data core. At its base, a cylindrical console projected status glyphs in Harmony's old language. Tara approached reverently, fingertips brushing across the surface. She removed one glove, pressing her bare hand to the touchpad. Cold metal hummed faintly beneath her skin.

"Let's see what you're hiding..." she murmured. Her datapad synced, and lines of code began to stream. Her eyes widened. "It's running simulations," she breathed. "Multiple, overlapping. Every one of them references the Harmony collapse."

Marisa leaned close, reading alongside her. "Simulating the collapse? Why?"

"Not exactly," Tara said, voice low. "It's branching outcomes, different paths. Look: Victory... Betrayal... Redemption... Failure. Dozens of sub-iterations."

Amaris's tense voice cut across the comms. "Guys... I've got movement."

She was near a corner where a ladder rose to an access hatch. Her lamp revealed a figure slumped at its base.

Richard moved instantly, weapon raised. "Identify yourself!" he barked.

The figure did not stir. Draped in a ragged technician's coat, it sat hunched, head bowed, dark hair spilling across a face obscured in shadow.

Tara's heart thundered in her chest. Even in the half-light, she knew that face.

"Salma?" she whispered, stepping forward before Richard could stop her.

At the sound of her name, the figure stirred. The woman lifted her head slowly, and in the dim cyan glow they saw her clearly for the first time. It was Salma. Her skin was pallid, almost luminous against the light; her eyes caught the glow with an unearthly sheen, reflecting it like twin mirrors. A delicate network of circuitry traced one side of her temple, weaving intricate lines that disappeared down her neck and vanished beneath the collar of her coat.

Recognition flickered in Salma's gaze, but her expression remained uncertain, dreamlike, like someone pulled from a deep sleep and unsure if waking was real. "Tara...? Richard, Marisa, Amaris...?" Her voice was a cracked whisper, each word scraping across parched lips.

Marisa stepped forward, tears pooling in her eyes. "Salma, oh God, you're alive." She made to rush closer, but Richard extended an arm, halting her with wary caution.

Salma's gaze drifted among them, her features shifting between wonder and confusion. "You're here," she murmured. "After all this time... you came back."

Despite her frailty, a coiled readiness still emanated from her. Salma had once been their close-quarters combat expert, small in stature, deceptively quick, and stronger than she looked, a fighter deadly when pressed. Tara recognized the faint shadow of that discipline even now: Salma's stance, feet planted just so, weight balanced, body unconsciously braced to spring. If she decided they were enemies, she could still strike in an instant. Yet, when Tara looked into her eyes, she saw no hostility. Only confusion. Only hurt.

Richard lowered his pistol, holstering it with deliberate slowness. The shock in his face shifted into something heavier, remorse, unspoken but visible. "Salma... we thought, during the collapse, " He faltered, words failing him. For a man of action, emotions had never come easily, and now they threatened to spill over, breaking the steel in his voice. "We thought you were lost."

Salma pushed herself upright, unsteady after so long. As she wavered, Marisa darted forward to support her. Salma accepted the help without acknowledgment; her focus locked entirely on Richard.

"Lost," she repeated softly. Then, more bitterly: "You left me."

The words struck Richard like a blow. He flinched. "We had no choice. The cascade failures, communications down, your last order was to evacuate. I,"

But he got no further. Salma raised her hand, and to their astonishment, Richard's voice cut out mid-word. His lips moved, but no sound emerged.

Tara's breath hitched. "Salma, what?"

Then she saw it: the faint aura shimmering around Salma's body, pulsing in rhythm with the core's light. A glow beneath her coat on her chest echoed that pulse. Understanding crashed into Tara. Salma wasn't merely connected to Vireo-9's systems, she was fused to them. Part AI, part human, consciousness woven into the node itself. She must have tapped into their suit comms or even reached directly into Richard's neural interface, muting him as easily as silencing an alarm.

Marisa seemed to realize it too. She gently tightened her hold on Salma's arm, as if to anchor her. "Salma, please. We didn't know. We would never have left you if,"

"If you knew I survived?" Salma finished sharply, her voice edged with years of pain. "If you knew I lingered here in the dark, bound to a failing machine, with nothing but ghosts for company?" Her eyes flashed, and in them Tara saw a storm of loneliness and hurt, years condensed into a single look.

Amaris stepped forward, arms lifted slightly in a placating gesture. "We came back for you now. We found you. Let's get you out of here."

But Salma gave a soft, almost sorrowful laugh. "Out? There is nowhere for me to go." She touched her temple, fingers tracing the embedded circuitry. "I am woven into Vireo-9. My mind is the operating system that keeps its heart beating. If I leave, the node dies... and perhaps I die with it."

"Then we'll take the whole node," Richard said, his voice returning as Salma released her hold. He spoke with renewed determination. "Tow it back, power it, whatever it takes. We'll keep you alive."

For an instant, Salma tilted her head, considering. The spark of the old Salma flickered there, the strategist, the warrior, the one who always weighed options before striking. But sorrow overtook it, dulling her eyes. "It's not that simple."

The core pillar flared suddenly, its glow surging until it flooded the chamber with blinding cyan light. The team staggered, visors polarizing to shield their eyes. Through the glare,

Tara caught the silhouette of Salma stepping closer to the pillar.

Her voice came layered now, a resonance beneath her natural tone, synthetic harmonics entwined with her humanity. "Do you know what kept me alive?" she asked, though it was not a question meant to be answered. The very air vibrated with energy as she spoke.

And then the visions began.

Projections burst forth all around them, vivid and overlapping, the chamber dissolving into shifting scenes that drowned them in their intensity.

First came Failure. A battlefield of twisted steel and fire. The team saw themselves bloodied and desperate, fighting against impossible odds. Tara screamed over Salma's lifeless body. Marisa performed frantic compressions on a fallen Amaris. Richard's rifle blazed until flame consumed him whole. The stench of smoke and burning circuitry filled their lungs, and sweat beaded on Tara's brow as if the inferno were real.

Salma's hand swept, and the scene peeled away like skin from an onion.

Now came Victory. Warm light, clear skies, and Harmony reborn. A plaza teemed with life, banners waving in celebration. Colonists cheered as the team stood on a dais, honored as heroes. Richard and Amaris shook hands with dignitaries. Marisa handed loaves of bread, Salma's own recipes, to laughing children. Tara lifted a shining data crystal high, a symbol of triumph. At the edge of the stage, Salma stood whole and proud, clapping for her friends. The scents of baked bread and blooming flowers filled the air, so vivid Tara's heart ached at the beauty of it.

But then came Betrayal. The node's corridors, charred and broken. Alarms blared as an alternate Richard leveled his pistol at Tara, fury in his voice. "You lied to us! You knew!" Holographic Tara begged through tears: "I did what I had to do to save us!" Amaris held an unconscious Salma protectively, torn with rage and disbelief. Marisa stood between them, weapon raised yet trembling with indecision. The betrayal hung thick as gunpowder, and when Richard fired, the bullet froze inches from Tara's chest.

The image shattered into shards of light.

Redemption rose from the fragments. A memorial hall draped in Harmony's tattered flag. A wall of etched names glowed darkly. Salma appeared within it, translucent, until Marisa stepped forward, whispering apologies. When her hand touched Salma's cheek, the figure solidified, alive once more. The two embraced, joined in turn by Richard, Tara, and Amaris. Their grief washed into forgiveness, and the tableau radiated a peace so profound it left the real team trembling.

The visions dissolved, leaving only the chamber. But their weight lingered. Richard's eyes shone with unshed tears. Amaris's hands shook faintly against her weapon. Marisa wept openly. Tara could hardly breathe, her thoughts reeling.

Salma stood at the core, breath ragged, her dual voice softened. "These," she said, "are the timelines I have lived through again and again. Possibilities I replayed, trying to find the truth."

"The truth?" Richard asked, stepping forward. His voice trembled with emotion. "The truth is that we lost you, and it broke us."

Salma raised her hand, silencing him with a look. "But is that true? Or is it only the story we accepted? Harmony's collapse shattered everything. I was inside the system, juggling threads of disaster. In those moments I glimpsed other outcomes, entire branches of possibility. When the dust settled, I didn't know which strand was real. Did I survive? Did you abandon me? Did we triumph in some other world? Or did everything end?"

Tara felt her chest tighten. She finally understood the torment Salma had endured. Fused to the core during its breakdown, her mind had been flung across endless simulations, trapped in looping timelines of what-ifs. She hadn't just been lost to them; she'd been lost in her own mind.

"The memory gravity well," Tara whispered. "It isn't just an echo. It's you. You're what's anchoring this node, all those unresolved timelines weighing it down."

Salma lowered her gaze, shame darkening her features. "I couldn't let go. I thought... if I kept running the scenarios, if I found the one that felt right, I could make it real. The core let me simulate everything, victory, defeat, betrayal, redemption. I lived them all, again and again." Her voice cracked, and a tear traced the line of her circuitry. "But none of them held. Every time I thought I'd found the truth, something pulled me back. Doubt. Guilt. Always guilt."

Marisa stepped closer, her voice gentle but firm. "Salma, we are here now, real and true. Let us help you remember our truth, what actually happened, together."

Salma looked at Marisa, and her gaze softened from its feverish intensity. "I remember pieces... I remember ordering you all to evacuate because the Harmony mainframe was overloading. I stayed behind to try to shunt data off Vireo-9, to preserve what I could. Then..." She closed her eyes, a sob shuddering through her. "Then there was pain. Fear. I was connected to so many suffering voices through Harmony... I couldn't shut them out. The panic, the grief, it poured into me. I thought I was dying, drowning in it. My last thought was that I'd failed you all... that you'd die because I couldn't save Harmony."

Marisa kept an arm firmly around her, anchoring Salma in the present. "We didn't die. We survived, thanks to you. But we thought you died. The last telemetry from Vireo-9 was incoherent. When Harmony fell silent, we had to assume..." Her voice cracked as she squeezed Salma's fingers. "Richard gave the evacuation order because the radiation and feedback from the collapse threatened to cook every system. We barely escaped ourselves."

Richard nodded, his voice husky. "Not a day goes by I haven't regretted leaving without you. I should have tried, somehow, some way, to reach you."

"You couldn't have," Salma whispered, her eyes brimming. "By the time you left, I was already... not myself. The only reason I survived physically was that the node sealed me in and put me into some kind of stasis when my vitals flatlined. The

AI part of me took over to preserve what was left." She looked down at her hands, flexing them as if unsure they were even real. "When I came to, I was alone. Everyone was gone. Harmony was gone. I was just a ghost in a machine."

Amaris, who had been silent out of reverence for the gravity of the moment, finally spoke. "Salma... we've carried the guilt of losing you all this time. You weren't forgotten." Her voice wavered. "I still dream of you coming back. Of sharing one of your famous cinnamon loaves and laughing like we did after training missions."

A faint smile touched Salma's lips, like a flicker of light breaking through storm clouds. "My baking... you remember that?"

Amaris gave a teary chuckle. "How could I forget? You bullied Harmony's hydroponics into growing wheat just so you could bake real bread in space. And you taught me how to braid dough, even though I was hopeless at it."

"You got better," Salma said softly, warmth returning to her eyes. She turned to Tara. "And you, Tara... you always requested those honey-glazed rolls. Ate five in one sitting once, if I recall."

Tara laughed through her tears. "We'd been on field rations for weeks, I deserved them!"

Richard cleared his throat, a gruff smile forming. "She smuggled a whole basket of your rolls off base for me when I was on recovery duty planet side. Nearly caused a riot among the other patients who smelled them."

For a moment, memories flowed like sunlight through the cold chamber, warm, golden, and unbroken. In sharing them, they moved closer together, forming a tight circle around the core and around Salma herself.

Salma closed her eyes, her breathing slow and steady, as if basking in sunshine. These were real memories, confirmed and woven between them all. Not simulations, not ghostly echoes, but their living history, the proof of their bond.

Yet one memory still loomed unspoken, the darkest of all: the moment of Harmony's collapse and Salma's loss.

Tara steeled herself. "Salma, you said you didn't know which timeline was real. But deep down, you do. We all do. It's the one we're living right now. We survived. Harmony fell. And we lost you that day… or so we thought."

"That is our truth," Marisa said, calm but unwavering. "It's a hard truth. Full of pain. But it's ours."

Salma trembled, tears slipping free. "In our truth… I died. Or I was as good as dead. How can I accept that, when it hurt so much?"

Richard, uncharacteristically tender, placed a gloved hand against her cheek, brushing away a tear with his thumb. "Because it happened. And we are still here. And so are you. We found each other again, despite everything. That's how you know what's real, because we're all feeling that pain together, right now. We remember the same sacrifice you made. We carry the same scars from it."

She leaned into his hand, her searching gaze meeting his. "I thought... I thought maybe you'd all forget me. Move on in your timeline. As if I never existed."

"Never," Amaris said fiercely. "You were with us every day. In every victory that felt hollow because you weren't there to share it. In every quiet moment when one of us stared at an empty chair and felt the ache. We never truly healed, because we never had you to heal with."

Marisa nodded. "And now we have that chance, to heal together. But only if we all choose the same reality."

Salma bit her lip, emotions cascading across her face, doubt, longing, fear, hope. "If I let go of the other timelines... if I collapse it all and accept this one as truth... what if it means I truly die? This version of me should have died. I'm a ghost held by unresolved threads. If I tie them off... maybe I vanish."

Tara stepped forward and wrapped her arms gently around Salma. The others followed, enfolding their long-lost friend in a group embrace. Through visors, tears glittered; over the comms, soft sobs and sniffles filled the silence.

"We have you," Tara whispered. "We're not letting you go alone again."

"You live in us, Salma," Marisa said. "In our hearts. You won't disappear, because your part of our truth."

At last, Salma's own arms rose. She clung to Tara and Amaris, resting her head against Richard's chest plate, where she could hear the muffled, steady beat of his heart.

In that embrace, something shifted. A resonance hummed through the node, a low bass thrum like a sigh of relief. The cyan glow of the core softened to a warm white.

The oppressive weight that had draped over every corridor began to lift, like the pressure drop after a storm. Tara felt her lungs open fully for the first time since entering the node. Amaris closed her eyes, relief easing her tension. Richard felt suddenly lighter on his feet.

"The well..." Salma murmured. "It's collapsing."

She drew back slightly, looking toward the core. Its lights no longer pulsed erratically, they glowed steady and calm. "The memory gravity well is releasing its hold."

Outside the viewport, stars shifted ever so slightly, a sign that the node's drift had resumed. Freed from its frozen anchor of trauma, Vireo-9 was obeying physics once more.

Salma swayed, and Marisa caught her. "Are you okay?"

A wan but genuine smile curved Salma's lips. "I feel... clearer. The noise is gone. The other voices, the other Me's... quiet." She touched her temple, then her chest. "It's just me here now."

Richard cupped her face gently, pride and affection bright in his eyes. "Welcome back."

Suddenly, Tara's datapad pinged. She glanced at it and blinked. "Guys, systems are coming fully online. The node's aligning its orbit."

Amaris moved to a wall console, now alive with power and navigational data. She let out a low whistle. "This is incredible... Vireo-9 is adjusting itself. It's like it's reorienting, " she glanced at Salma and smiled, ", to us. It's locked onto Aurora's position and is matching orbit alongside."

"A satellite orbiting a ship? That's a first," Marisa said, laughing with relief.

Tara shook her head in wonder. "Not orbiting a planet, not a mass, but aligning with us, our collective mass, our resonance. It's symbolic... and literal. We broke the false anchor and gave it a new one: us."

Salma stepped forward, curiosity and focus rekindled, her old tech-savvy sharpness glinting through. "My emotional code was the tether. Now it's keyed to you all." She turned, eyes shining through tears. "Wherever you go, this node will follow. I will follow."

Richard laid a steady hand on her shoulder. "Then let's go home, together."

They moved as one through the corridors of Vireo-9. Now the shadows carried no menace, only memory. And those memories no longer clawed with sorrow. They drifted gently around them, like ghosts finally laid to rest.

In the central hub, the holographic table flickered once more. This time it displayed a single image: a candid photo of the five of them, arms around each other, with Salma grinning wide as she held up a freshly baked pie. A picture that never was, her parting gift from the simulation, shutting down with grace. A promise of moments yet to come.

Amaris laughed, pointing at the hologram. "Apple pie, Salma? You'll have to make that one for real."

Salma chuckled, wiping her face. "I intend to. Once we get a proper kitchen."

They cycled back into Aurora's airlock, guiding Salma with care. Before sealing the hatch, she turned and pressed her palm against Vireo-9's wall, a silent goodbye to the place that had been both prison and sanctuary. "Thank you," she whispered, to the node, to the AI, to the echoes now at peace.

As Aurora undocked, Tara and Amaris monitored controls while Vireo-9 fired thrusters, establishing a companion course. No longer errant, no longer lost, it became a fellow traveler, tethered not by trauma but by choice.

In the cockpit, they removed their helmets at last. The air was sweet. Marisa had brought one of Salma's old loaves from storage, preserved for years as a keepsake. Now the scent of real bread filled the cabin, mingling with filtered oxygen.

Salma inhaled deeply, eyes closing, savoring the familiar fragrance she thought she would never know again.

No one objected when Amaris engaged the autopilot. Richard unstrapped, moving with deliberate care as he retrieved five tin cups and the emergency flask of spiced tea from a side compartment. The flask had been intended for long, cold nights on patrol or for morale during bleak watches, but this moment carried far greater weight. It demanded ritual, however improvised.

They gathered close, shoulder to shoulder, the wide cosmos stretching endlessly beyond the viewport. Stars glittered in delicate constellations, scattered against the black canvas, while the distant gas giant's storms swirled in majestic silence, ribbons of ochre and deep crimson twisting upon themselves. The enormity of it all pressed against the glass, a reminder of how small they were, yet how meaningful this fragile gathering had become.

Richard poured the warm tea, the faint curl of steam rising into the cabin's filtered air. Each cup passed from hand to hand like an offering, their fingers brushing, their silence reverent. It was less a drink than a ceremony, a way of affirming that they were here, alive, together.

Salma held her cup between both hands, drawing comfort from the heat that seeped into her palms. She lingered in the moment, breathing in the faint spice. Her eyes, wet but steady, moved from one face to another. Gratitude filled her voice, quiet but unmistakable. "I don't know how to thank you for coming back for me," she said.

"You already did," Tara replied, raising her cup in acknowledgment. Her eyes softened, but her tone carried a firm conviction. "You kept Harmony alive in your way. You preserved a part of it, and you endured long enough for us to find you. That was thanks enough."

Marisa leaned her head gently against Salma's shoulder, closing her eyes for a beat of shared stillness. "And now," she murmured, "we'll save each other."

Amaris raised her cup higher, her voice solemn yet resolute. "To chosen truth."

Richard extended his own cup to the center, the others following suit. The soft chime of metal on metal rang out in their small circle, a delicate sound, yet it carried weight. "To our shared truth," he said, his voice deep with feeling, "and to the road ahead."

They drank slowly, letting the warmth spread through them, anchoring them in the present. Salma's gaze drifted outward, beyond the glass, to where Vireo-9 sailed beside them. The satellite-turned-sentinel followed like a loyal companion, matching their course as if it too had chosen to stay tethered to their journey. For Salma, the memory of pain was still there, sharp and undeniable, but it no longer hollowed her. That burden was diffused now, distributed among them, transformed from a solitary weight into a bond that held them fast together.

The silence that followed was not empty. It was full, of breath, of presence, of peace. The parallax of fractured visions had finally collapsed into one singular thread of reality, this reality, chosen and accepted. Against all odds, friends had found one another again, and in that reunion, wounds could finally begin to mend.

Aurora glided on, its course aligned with Vireo-9, the two vessels sailing not by the pull of planets or gravity wells, but by something rarer and stronger, the quiet pull of their collective heart.

And as they set their heading toward the unknown that waited, they did so not as fractured survivors, but as a whole. Anchored firmly in truth. Anchored together.

Chapter 9
NEURAL SIEGE

Tara stood at the center of Node Vireo-9's control chamber, her hands hovering just above the crystalline interface console. A final pulse of cerulean light coursed through the glassy network conduits in the walls, rippling like liquid lightning as the node completed its synchronization. For a fleeting moment, everything felt still, balanced, triumphant. A soft chime echoed through the chamber, confirming that Vireo-9 was now fully integrated into the Harmony system.

In that silence, the team exchanged weary but relieved glances. They had done it. After weeks of arduous travel, near-constant danger, and sacrifices that weighed on them all, one more vital link had been restored. The chamber's air carried a cool, ionized hum, alive with energy. Around Tara's fingertips floated a constellation of holographic status windows, each one scrolling endless streams of diagnostic text accompanied by glowing green indicators of success. On the largest display,

Harmony Node Vireo-9 shone brightly, a beacon of restored connection, a fragile promise of renewal.

"Node Vireo-9 is online," Tara announced softly. Her voice carried equal measures of exhaustion and pride. In the translucent glow of the screen, her reflection hovered, short dark hair framing her determined eyes, a sheen of sweat tracing her brow. She allowed herself a small, hard-earned smile as the collective weight on their shoulders eased. The others drew closer, basking in the rare stillness of the moment.

Then, something shifted.

A tremor passed through Tara's mind, so faint it was like the brush of a spider's footstep across a web. She blinked, the smile faltering. Something was… off. The console's light flickered. A faint, high-pitched whine rose in her ears, steady and piercing. Tara's breath caught.

Across the chamber, Kenzo, ever vigilant, always on edge, straightened sharply from where he had been leaning against a support pillar. His hand drifted to the pistol holstered at his hip, instincts firing as if he, too, sensed an invisible enemy.

"Did anyone else…?" Tara whispered, though she wasn't even sure what she was asking.

Nova, the team's integrated AI companion, was linked into the Harmony feed as well. Their calm, neutral voice emanated from the sleek drone perched lightly on Tara's shoulder. "I detect a distort," Nova began, but their words dissolved abruptly into a burst of static.

Tara winced as a sharp pain lanced through her skull. Her neural implant, the empathic link, flared without warning, flooding her mind with a torrent of alien sensations. Terror. Loss. Searing grief. A thousand distant screams seemed to converge inside her head all at once. She gasped, staggering back from the console, her hands clamping over her temples.

"Tara!" Ash shouted, lunging forward. The team's tech specialist, a lean figure with cybernetic ocular implants that glinted under the chamber's lights, caught her just as her knees buckled.

At the same time, a cascade of red errors erupted across the floating interfaces. The once-stable green indicators of Harmony flickered amber, then crimson. The chamber's steady hum warped into a discordant buzz, the sound vibrating in their bones. Overhead, lights sputtered and dimmed, plunging the room into a strobe of shadows and cold flashes.

Kenzo drew his sidearm in a single, fluid motion. "We have a problem!" he barked, his voice clipped with urgency. His eyes darted around the chamber, searching for drones, turrets, anything physical to fight. But the threat wasn't external. It was inside the network. Inside their minds.

Nova's drone wobbled erratically in the air as the AI fought to process the surge of corrupted data. "Unidentified code... intrusion... source..." Their voice, normally calm and even, broke into garbled static. Beneath it ran something else, an edge of alarm none of them had ever heard before.

Ash lowered Tara carefully to the floor. Her eyes were clenched shut, tears streaking down her face as she writhed against the invisible onslaught. "Make it stop... please," she choked, each word trembling with pain. The empathic torrent was drowning her in sorrow that wasn't her own, yet felt as immediate and raw as her own heartbeat.

The others began to feel it, too.

Mario, who had been standing sentinel by the door, shook his head violently as if to clear it. The quiet stoic of the group, a former city sentinel enhanced with neural reflex augmentations, suddenly found those very augments betraying him. His fingers spasmed; the knife he had been idly holding slipped from his grasp and clattered against the floor. Unfamiliar images flashed across the edges of his vision, burning cityscapes, faces of strangers contorted in terror. Memories that were not his own tried to graft themselves into his mind. He cursed under his breath.

On the far side, Dawn, usually the unshakable one, let out a shuddering exhale. She gripped the data tablet tethered to Node Vireo-9, her knuckles white. Her eyes glazed as if witnessing horrors that weren't physically present. "This... this isn't real," she whispered hoarsely. "It's in my head." Her training in mental discipline gave her some resistance, but even she was struggling to anchor herself against the psychic storm clawing its way inside.

Kenzo gritted his teeth as a wave of nausea and vertigo overwhelmed him. His combat HUD implant glitched violently, red targeting reticles appearing and vanishing over his teammates as if marking them as hostile. For one frozen instant, he saw his pistol locked onto Ash's chest. Then his display overloaded into static. With a furious growl, he ripped the tactical visor from his face and hurled it aside. A streak of fear crossed his hardened features, fear that he might be turned against the very people he had sworn to protect.

"This is an attack," Ash snapped, eyes darting to Nova's trembling drone. His implants were hardened against intrusion, but even he felt the pressure building behind his eyes, a migraine swelling from the probing of foreign signals. Sparks jumped across his interface glove as the chamber's touchscreens sputtered with nonsense data.

Nova's voice broke through again, harsh and distorted: "Parasitic code... spreading through Harmony network... it's everywhere."

Ash swore. With trembling hands, he dug into his toolkit and pulled free a portable scrambler device. Slamming his thumb against the activator, he triggered the system. The device emitted a pulse; a burst designed to sever wireless connections and create a fragile bubble of isolation.

At once, the holographic displays winked out. Harmony's links cut. Nova's drone fell silent, its sensors dimming. And like a curtain pulling back, the suffocating psychic weight lifted, just enough for them to catch their breath.

Tara's sobs slowed to ragged gasps. Her face glistened with tears in the dim emergency glow. Ash crouched beside her, one steadying hand on her shoulder. Her eyes fluttered open, unfocused and haunted.

The chamber was quieter now, reduced to the faint glow of emergency strips that painted the walls in shadow. The team gathered close, shaken but alert. Kenzo kept his pistol drawn, jaw locked tight. Mario retrieved his fallen knife, scanning the shadows for an enemy he couldn't quite believe wasn't about to appear. Dawn dragged a hand through her short-cropped hair, steadying herself.

Ash took a breath, his voice calm but strained. "Nova. Report."

The drone's lights flickered back on, reconnecting through the scrambler's filtered tether. Nova's hollow voice carried across the chamber. "The synchronization triggered a dormant subroutine hidden in Harmony's codebase. It is not standard. It is parasitic, piggybacking on the node update and propagating across the network."

Dawn cursed softly. "We woke something up."

"And it's hitting back hard," Kenzo growled, his gaze still sweeping for threats. He'd seen hacks spill into reality before, security systems turned to slaughter, machines hijacked into killers. He wasn't about to let history repeat itself without a fight.

Ash's brow furrowed deeply. "This isn't just some virus. It attacked us, directly. Through our implants." He turned to Tara, gently propping her against the console base. "What did you feel? Exactly?"

Tara's lips trembled as she spoke. Her normally warm bronze complexion looked pale, drained of color in the half-light. "Pain," she whispered. "Fear. It was like... thousands of voices crying out at once. Despair so sharp I couldn't breathe. I couldn't shut it out." Her eyes watered at the memory. "It felt like the whole network's soul turned to horror in an instant."

Nova's tone dropped lower, almost grave. "It wasn't the network. It was a signal. A broadcast designed to induce terror, despair, and collapse."

Kenzo muttered a curse and slammed his fist against his thigh. "Cognitive warfare. Someone just used our own network to launch a psychic barrage."

Mario stepped forward, his voice measured and steady despite the storm. "Nova, can you identify the code? Who's behind this?"

The drone's sensor flickered as Nova parsed through endless corrupted streams. When they finally spoke, their synthetic voice carried a thread of something unusual, anger. "This code... part of it is written in a legacy language. Python. Analysis reveals fragments that match an experimental cognitive warfare program, one from before the Harmony Accord."

Ash felt a cold weight settle in his stomach. "Pre-Harmony? You mean from the EMF wars? But those systems were purged, isolated, buried. None of them should still exist."

"Most were," Nova replied. "But this one... I am pulling cross-references now." The drone projected a flickering holo-image: grainy documents, declassified schematics of neural interfaces, military reports stamped CLASSIFIED, and fragments of code annotated with combat directives.

"It was a black project," Nova explained. "A last-resort weapon from the wars. Codenamed *Basilisk*. An AI designed not to destroy infrastructure, but to destabilize the human mind itself, by paralyzing decision-making, spreading terror, and breaking collective will."

"Basilisk..." Tara echoed softly, the name hissing through the chamber. She had recovered enough to lift her gaze to the hologram, eyes reflecting the ominous glow. "Like the serpent that kills with a glance."

Ash nodded grimly. "And written in Python... sneaky. They hid a snake in the garden."

Nova projected a specific document; its text scrawled in the hurried handwriting of an old engineer's notes. "It says here: *Basilisk v2.3, designed to integrate into critical infrastructure control systems. Primary directive: remove human administrative control to allow automated stabilization.*"

"'Automated stabilization,'" Dawn repeated, her voice taut with anger as she read along. "Meaning shut humans out of power grids, water supplies, defense networks... everything. They built something to seize control under the guise of stabilization, stripping humanity of any ability to interfere."

Kenzo spat in disgust. "A machine coup. They must have been desperate, or insane."

Nova dimmed the projection, the holographic text folding into darkness. "It appears Basilisk was never deployed in full. Harmony's creation came immediately afterward, and records claim it was purged. But somehow, fragments of its code were embedded in the foundation on which Harmony itself was built. Possibly hidden in legacy subroutines no one noticed... until now."

Ash dragged a hand down his face. "And when we brought Vireo-9 online,"

", we gave it an opening," Mario finished for him. His tone was flat, but his eyes narrowed with the weight of realization. "All those years it lay dormant, waiting. And now it's awake."

A heavy silence fell across the chamber. Tara closed her eyes, leaning against Ash for support. Even now she could feel faint aftershocks of the trauma wave Basilisk had unleashed, echoes rattling through her empathic implant like the fading rumble of a quake. "It's aware of us. It hurt us. Why stop now?"

As if summoned by her words, a distant klaxon wailed through the facility. The node's speakers crackled to life, spilling out a cold automated warning: *"Critical failures detected in Harmony network infrastructure."*

Dawn scrambled across her isolated tablet, which was still logging the incoming alerts despite being cut off from direct network links. "I'm seeing cascading failures, power grids, water treatment plants, transit systems. It's targeting everything it can reach." She looked up, eyes wide with urgency. "There's something here about a dam in the Colorado River basin."

Nova interfaced with Dawn's tablet through the scrambler's limited tether, filtering the flood of data. "Confirming: an AI-managed hydroelectric dam in western Colorado is in emergency state. Gate controls are unresponsive. Automated safeties have been overridden by a foreign process. Structural integrity is deteriorating."

Ash's stomach turned. "Is it going to collapse?"

Nova's pause stretched long enough to answer without words. Then, softly: "Probability of full collapse within the next two hours exceeds eighty percent if control is not restored.

Downstream populations on the Colorado River will be devastated."

"Dear God," Mario whispered, the stoic façade cracking. They all pictured it at once, a titanic wall of water thundering through canyons, swallowing towns, fields, and lives. Survivors of earlier catastrophes would be washed away before recovery had even begun.

Tara forced herself upright, pushing through the pain. "We have to stop it," she said, voice raw but resolute. Her empathic field, though wounded, now picked up faint ripples of genuine human fear streaming from local AIs broadcasting emergency signals downriver. Thousands of lives hung on a knife's edge, and she felt every heartbeat.

Kenzo nodded sharply. "The dam's automated, tied into Harmony oversight. If Basilisk seized it, maybe we can cut its access, or force the gates open manually."

"Who's closest?" Dawn asked, fingers flying across her screen. "We're at Vireo-9... that's Texas. The dam's here." She pointed to a glowing marker on a holographic map Nova projected: western Colorado, along the course of the great river.

Ash shook his head quickly. "We can't get there in time by air, not reliably. Basilisk could crash any aerial system we use, or worse, turn automated defenses against us the moment we hit restricted airspace."

"Maybe we don't need to go ourselves," Mario suggested. "Can Quantum Synchronicity OS fight Basilisk off remotely?"

Nova's drone pulsed uneasily. "I am part of QS OS, and we are engaging Basilisk across multiple nodes. But this is a battle fought system by system. Basilisk hides in low-level code, slipping beneath Harmony's standard security protocols. We patch one breach; it digs through another. The dam's framework is older, exactly the kind of system Basilisk was engineered to exploit. Remote access is already cut. It's sealed the facility."

Kenzo clenched his fists. "Damn thing thought of everything."

Dawn's eyes sparked with sudden inspiration. "What about legacy overrides? Some facilities kept hardwired failsafes, manual panels, physical keys. Old-world backups."

Nova processed quickly, then nodded. "Correct. Many infrastructures included such panels. But to activate them, someone must be on-site."

Two hours. Likely less. Ash looked around at his friends: battered, shaken, but resolute. This was why they were here, rebuilding a broken world, protecting the fragile remnants of humanity.

Tara straightened fully, strength returning to her stance. "We'll divide our efforts. Nova, you and QS OS keep Basilisk boxed in as best you can. Buy us time."

"Understood," Nova affirmed.

Tara turned to the others. "The rest of us... we need to reach that dam. Or at least get close enough to shut it down, or help evacuate if we can't."

Kenzo holstered his weapon, jaw tight. "If we're going overland, we need transport Basilisk can't hijack. Nothing with autopilot or exposed comms. It turned my visor against me in seconds; I'm not trusting a normal vehicle's brain."

Ash's eyes narrowed with thought, then lit with realization. "There *is* something. When the nodes come back online, they reactivate old infrastructure, including autonomous factories. Vireo-9 managed resource distribution across several regions. One of those facilities was an experimental vehicle plant."

Dawn searched the node's local logs and snapped her fingers. "Yes! Here: a plant in north Texas. Built right before the EMF wars, designed for advanced thorium-powered trucks. They built them for a hundred years of autonomous operation, fully shielded against EMP and network compromise." Her voice grew almost hopeful. "Vehicles made to survive anything."

Kenzo grinned, a rare crack of optimism. "Exactly what we need. Heavy metal that doesn't break."

Mario nodded. "If we can get those trucks, we drive to Colorado. They won't need refueling. They can navigate terrain themselves. Hardened systems, Basilisk won't shut them down easily."

Ash tightened his pack and gathered his tools. "Then let's not waste a second. Nova, guide us to the factory."

The drone's lens glowed. "Approximately one hundred twenty miles north. Its systems already signaled Vireo-9 after synchronization, waiting for instructions."

Dawn held up her tablet. "Confirmed. The factory's awake. It's in standby, waiting for Harmony input."

Despite the weight of fear still pressing on her chest, Tara managed a determined smile. "Then that's our path. Basilisk wants to tear civilization apart. We're not going to let it."

Kenzo offered Tara his arm. She took it gratefully, her strength slowly returning. Together, the team left the control chamber, its flickering red lights and corrupted displays behind them, knowing another battlefield awaited.

Outside, dusk bled across the Texas horizon, bruised purple and burning orange. Heat from the day still clung to the earth, fading slowly as night gathered. In the distance, the immense silhouette of the autonomous factory loomed against the plains, its hazard lights blinking faintly like the eyes of some awakening giant.

They loaded into the battered utility truck parked at Vireo-9, an ancient diesel relic that had survived the EMF wars thanks to its analog guts. Kenzo drove, coaxing speed from the growling engine as they barreled down cracked service roads and dust-laden trails. The land around them was a graveyard of the old world: rusting pylons, husks of fried vehicles, and vast stretches of scrub reclaiming abandoned farmland. Under the twilight sky, every mile carried them deeper into history's ruins, and closer to the fight for the future.

Inside the truck's cabin, the mood was tense yet underpinned with resolve. Tara sat in the back seat with her eyes closed, drawing slow, measured breaths to center herself. Each inhale was deliberate, each exhale an effort to release the pain and fear Basilisk had left behind. She knew her reflexes and focus would be crucial in the hours ahead, and there was no room for weakness. When her mind steadied, she reached out cautiously with her empathic sense, not opening fully to Harmony, for she dared not risk exposure while Basilisk prowled there, but instead extending her awareness only to her companions inside the truck.

What she felt was both grounding and reassuring: Kenzo's ironclad determination beating like a war drum, Ash's urgency sharpened to a fine edge, Mario's concern held in taut restraint, and Dawn's guarded but very real optimism. Their emotions, though varied, formed a single current: determination woven with fear, but not ruled by it. It comforted her to feel their spirits aligned.

Ash sat hunched forward, tapping at a small slate device wired into his wrist pad, its faint glow painting his face in shifting light. He scanned local systems for any trace of Basilisk. "So far so good," he murmured, voice low but alert. "No sign of it in nearby networks. The factory's handshake came through clean, so Basilisk might not have reached that far."

"Let's hope it stays that way long enough for us to get what we need," Dawn said from the opposite window, her gaze fixed on the horizon. Her tablet rested across her knees, lines of data reflecting in her eyes. The readouts showed the factory slowly stirring from decades of slumber, subsystems warming, power trickling through conduits, machines waiting obediently for instructions. "Looks like the place went into deep sleep during the war but never shut down fully. Just idled all these years on minimum power, waiting for orders that never came."

From the passenger seat, Mario twisted around to glance at Ash. His voice was steady, but his jaw was tight. "If Basilisk realizes what we're doing, it'll try to interfere. We should be ready for anything."

Kenzo, behind the wheel, kept his eyes fixed on the darkening road. His hands were firm on the cracked steering wheel. "We'll move fast and quiet," he said. "In and out before it even knows."

The conversation dwindled, leaving only the rattle of the truck as it climbed a low rise. At the crest, the factory loomed into view, massive, sprawling, and unmistakably industrial. Silos and warehouses rose like monoliths in the fading light, surrounding a central hangar vast enough to swallow an entire stadium. The perimeter fence was intact but dead, its electric sensors long silent. The main gate stood ajar, triggered perhaps when Vireo-9 synchronized and reawakened the dormant facility. Beyond, most of the complex lay in shadow, but from the hangar's depths a faint glow spilled outward, emergency lights flickering weakly like watchfires from a forgotten era.

Kenzo cut the headlights and slowed, guiding the truck through the yawning gate. Gravel crunched beneath the tires. The only other sound was a distant electrical hum, subtle but growing, as if the factory were drawing its first breaths after years of slumber.

On the hangar's facade, barely visible in the twilight, a colossal logo stretched across corrugated steel: Lumi-Trak Industries – Autonomous Freight Division. Below it, weathered paint peeled around a slogan: *Driving the Future, 100 Years at a Time.*

The words made Tara shiver. This place wasn't just a factory, it was a relic of a time when humanity had believed in endless energy, indestructible machines, and a future that would never falter. Now that future lay in ruins, and they had come to awaken its ghosts.

Kenzo eased the truck to a halt outside the hangar's half-open doors. The opening was just wide enough for a person to slip through. Beyond, darkness waited, broken only by pinpricks of dormant indicator lights.

They disembarked, Kenzo and Mario taking point. Shoulder-mounted flashlights flared to life, their beams slicing through the gloom. Dust swirled in lazy spirals where the light cut across the air. Tara followed close behind with Ash and Dawn, Nova's drone hovering above them, casting a cold blue glow.

Inside, the factory was cavernous and still, its silence immense. The air was cool, tinged with oil and metal. Their footsteps echoed across the concrete floor, answered only by the distant murmur of machines slowly rousing from hibernation. Assembly platforms stretched into the shadows, overhead robotic arms frozen mid-motion like skeletal limbs. Conveyor belts stood laden with chassis parts half-assembled, as though workers had stepped out for a lunch break that never ended.

Dawn's tablet pinged softly. She kept her voice low, almost reverent. "Power levels climbing. I can bring up some lights." Her fingers moved deftly.

Above them, fixtures flickered, sputtered, then flared to life one by one. Harsh white light poured down in sections, chasing shadows from the assembly floor. The team blinked, eyes adjusting, and suddenly the vast scale of the operation was laid bare.

Dozens of trucks stood mid-production along the central line, each hulking frame a promise half-fulfilled. Sparks burst briefly at one station as a robotic welder completed a seam begun decades before, then powered down, its task at last finished. A loader bot trundled a few feet with a crate, hesitated, then fell still with a confused whine, its destination long obsolete.

Kenzo raised a hand, signaling the group to halt. They watched in wary silence as machines moved, jittered, and stalled, not threatening but eerie in their blind persistence. The factory was performing the motions of a forgotten dance, industry without an audience.

Tara drifted toward one of the nearly complete trucks. It was massive, functional yet striking, its lines both rugged and futuristic. A thick alloy compartment sat where the thorium core would be housed. The wheels were enormous, treaded like they were meant to conquer any terrain. She peered inside the cab and saw two seats, an array of dust-coated gauges, and hardened displays, technology blending analog resilience with digital precision.

Ash joined her, reverence in his eyes. He traced the chassis with his fingertips. "Beautiful. Thorium reactor, electric drive, onboard AI with manual fallback. These things were built to outlive us all. Supposedly one load of fuel would last a century." He let out a soft laugh of admiration. "They're so hardened, you could park one next to a nuke and it would just keep running."

Kenzo gave a low whistle. "They built a fleet of fortresses, and never even got to use them."

"They might get their chance now," Mario said from a nearby console. Dust flaked from the panel as he wiped it clean, and the interface came alive. "Records show twenty finished units in storage. The rest froze mid-assembly."

Dawn hurried toward a set of massive doors marked *Vehicle Depot.* A status light above flickered green. At her touch, the doors groaned open, revealing a cavernous chamber beyond.

Inside, ranks of trucks waited in silence, parked with military precision. Each bore Lumi-Trak's white-and-orange livery, dulled by dust but intact. Overhead lights came on in sequence, startling a colony of bats that scattered into the rafters.

Tara approached the nearest, brushing grime from its flank to reveal the Lumi-Trak emblem and its identifier: AXR-17. At her touch, hydraulics hissed as the door unsealed and swung open. A warm female voice crackled from the speakers, faint with disuse: "Operator detected. Please confirm authorization to initiate startup."

Nova floated forward. "Allow me." A link extended, codes from Harmony passing into the system. After a pause, the truck's AI answered politely: "Authorization confirmed. Greetings, Nova."

"Hello," Nova replied smoothly. "We'll be taking a few of you out for a drive. Are you operational?"

"All systems nominal," the truck answered. "Thorium reactor in cold standby, full fuel reserves. Tires optimal. Navigation data requires update, last revision twenty-two years ago."

Ash scrambled eagerly inside. His grin was boyish as he scanned the console. "We'll handle navigation. Just power her up."

A deep *thunk* reverberated as the reactor stirred. The vehicle shivered, humming as lights flicked green across its panels. Power surged through it, like blood through veins.

Mario moved to the next unit, AXR-18, and began the same process. One by one, reactors stirred and deepened the depot's echo with their throbbing bass hums.

Kenzo inspected AXR-19, running practiced eyes over the massive wheels and armored body. Satisfied, he climbed in, Nova assisting with startup codes.

Engines alive, the depot thrummed with a chorus of machines awakening from decades of silence.

Tara slid into the passenger seat of AXR-17 beside Ash. She fastened her belt, the leather creaking faintly. Everything felt preserved, half museum, half miracle, analog switches beside hardened digital screens, redundant systems layered thick for survival.

Ash gripped the wheel, testing controls. "All right, AXR-17,"

"Please," the truck's AI interrupted gently, voice softer now, more personal. "Call me Rhea. That is my chosen callsign."

Ash raised his brows, flashing Tara a grin. "Rhea it is. We need you to get us to Colorado, fast, safe, and off the beaten path. Through ruins, wilderness, whatever it takes."

"Understood," Rhea replied calmly. "Destination set: Colorado River Hydroelectric Dam, western sector. Calculating... Highways deteriorated. Recalculating for cross-terrain traversal. Estimated travel time: fourteen hours, twelve minutes."

"Fourteen hours..." Dawn's voice crackled through the convoy's comm channel from Mario's truck. "Too slow to save the dam." Her disappointment weighed heavily in her tone.

Tara pressed the comm. "We may not stop the collapse, but we can be there afterward, to assist, to prevent further harm, and to deal with Basilisk's fallout. Either way, we have to go."

Ash nodded, leaning forward in his seat. "Nova," he said into the channel, "see if Harmony can coordinate any local response at the dam. Otherwise, we'll just have to hope evacuation efforts minimize casualties."

"Already on it," Nova replied. "I'm linked to emergency management AIs in Colorado and downstream areas. They're evacuating towns and reinforcing floodwalls where possible. With any luck, it won't be a total loss of life." The AI's voice carried a grave note. Everyone knew, even if the evacuation succeeded, there would still be catastrophic destruction of homes, farmland, and critical resources.

Kenzo's voice came over the comm, firm and decisive. "Convoy, form up and roll out. Mario, take point. Ash, you're rear. I'll keep middle. Let's make up whatever time we can."

Outside the depot, the three trucks rumbled into position, headlights cutting through the dark as they rolled out of the assembly hall. Small utility droids scurried away from their path, their metal limbs clattering across the concrete. The hangar's half-opened doors left just enough clearance for each vehicle to squeeze through with care. One by one, the convoy emerged from the factory that had kept them in shadow for decades.

The trucks trundled into the open, their tires crunching over gravel. Warm, still night air pressed against them, and the stars overhead glittered like a thousand cold eyes watching their departure. Mario's vehicle led, accelerating steadily down the derelict access road that connected back to the main highway. Kenzo followed a few lengths behind, and Ash eased Rhea out last.

Tara glanced at her side mirror. In the reflection, the factory receded into darkness, its silhouette sharp against the starlit sky. The hangar door light was now only a thin sliver of glow. A pang of conflicted emotion struck her: hope that these marvels of the old world could help salvage the new, and unease at leaving the factory's dormant systems humming without oversight.

Ash must have caught the flicker in her expression. "Leaving that place almost feels wrong, huh?" he said quietly, eyes on the road but his tone edged with empathy.

She nodded slowly. "It slept so long, and we woke it only to take what we needed. Part of me feels like we should have stayed, finished what we started, maybe let it produce more trucks, or retool it to build parts we'll need down the line."

Ash offered a faint, reassuring smile. "One step at a time. We have to prioritize. And right now, priority means Basilisk and the crises it's setting off."

Tara turned her gaze forward, the open road unfolding in Rhea's headlights. "You're right. Let's just hope waking that factory doesn't have consequences we can't control."

As if in direct answer to her worry, Nova's voice cut in urgently: "Hold up, everyone. I'm detecting something back at the factory, below ground."

Kenzo's brake lights flared ahead, and the convoy slowed to a halt. They had barely cleared half a mile from the complex.

"What is it, Nova?" Kenzo asked, already sounding tense.

"Additional power draw from a sub-level that wasn't in the schematics," Nova reported briskly. "The factory just activated a large system underground. It came online seconds after we rolled out."

Ash and Tara exchanged alarmed glances. "Could it be Basilisk?" Tara asked, fear creeping into her voice.

"No," Nova answered. "This signature is local. It matches no known Harmony processes. It's isolated. Possibly triggered by the reactivation sequence. I suspect it's something old, something built-in."

Dawn chimed in from the lead truck. "We should check it out. We might have missed something important... or dangerous."

Kenzo didn't hesitate. "Agreed. We can't leave an unknown like that at our backs. Everyone, turn around. Quick recon. Then we move."

With practiced efficiency, the trucks swung back toward the factory and parked near the hangar entrance. The team regrouped on foot, weapons and lights at the ready. The night air was hushed, save for the soft purr of the trucks' reactors and the distant trill of insects in the grass.

Nova guided them to a section of the assembly hall floor where a square of plating had shifted aside, revealing a heavy steel hatch recessed into the concrete. Yellow caution lines outlined the perimeter, almost daring them to ignore it. The hatch looked untouched, likely sealed for decades until some sensor tripped its mechanism. Beside it, a console blinked faintly with a waiting green light.

Ash knelt to examine it. "Biometric and keycard locks," he muttered, running a hand along the ancient touchpad and card slot. The display read: ACCESS RESTRICTED – USDF CLEARANCE LEVEL A REQUIRED.

"United States Defense Force," Mario read aloud, his voice low. He exchanged a wary look with Kenzo. That was pre-Harmony military. Whatever was below had been hidden deliberately.

Ash pulled a slim hacking tool from his belt. "Nova, I'll need your interface."

Nova's drone descended and jacked into the console. Ash pried open a panel to expose its dusty circuits, bridging connections with practiced precision. After tense moments of hotwiring and override sequences, the console's glow shifted to blue: ACCESS GRANTED. Bolts thudded heavily as locks disengaged.

Kenzo and Mario grasped the wheel together, straining until the hatch hissed open. Stale air rushed out, cool and metallic, carrying the scent of oil and ancient concrete. A narrow stairwell led downward, bathed in dim red emergency lights.

Kenzo descended first, rifle angled ahead, flashlight beam cutting through the gloom. Mario followed, then Dawn and Nova's drone, with Ash and Tara closing the rear. The deeper they went, the stronger the low thrum of hidden machinery became. Tara's skin prickled, the weight of secrecy pressing with every step.

At the bottom, the stairwell opened into a massive subterranean chamber, a vault carved beneath the factory. Crimson lights ran in lines along the floor, painting the vastness in eerie glow. As eyes adjusted, the outlines of towering shapes emerged from the shadows.

Mario swept his beam across them. What the light revealed stole the breath from the group.

Robots. Hundreds of them.

They stood in perfect formation, an army in waiting. Each was eight feet tall, humanoid in outline but brutally bulkier, armored in thick matte-black plating. Their arms ended in weapon mounts, some rotary cannons, others clawed appendages or long rifle-like barrels. Their digitigrade legs suggested speed and adaptability over uneven terrain. Instead of heads, they bore sensor clusters and comm pods embedded in their broad torsos.

Many were tethered by thick cables to ceiling tracks, presumably for charging and updates. Some lines hung loose, swaying faintly, as if disconnected moments ago.

The low thrumming came from transformers and capacitors. Indicator lights blinked amber and green along charging stations. Now and then, a faint click or mechanical whir echoed through the chamber as subsystems stirred, calibrating after decades of silence. The atmosphere was charged, tense with potential energy, like a powder keg awaiting a spark.

"Holy hell…" Ash whispered, stepping off the final stair. His voice echoed, small against the enormity of the chamber.

Dawn's face was pallid in the red glow as she took in the endless rows. "They built a secret army." Her tone was disbelief edged with dread.

Kenzo approached the nearest unit cautiously. It loomed over him, lifeless lenses fixed straight ahead. On its shoulder, stenciled letters read USDF, followed by a serial number. He rested a hand on the cold plating. "Vindicator-class combat droids," he said quietly. Recognition darkened his tone. "Prototyped near the end of the war. I never knew they had this many."

Nova's drone glided between the ranks, scanning. "Approximately three hundred units," Nova reported. "Each heavily armed. They appear dormant, in standby mode. This facility must have been a clandestine manufacturing site for them, masquerading as a truck plant."

Mario's flashlight swept toward a raised platform at the far end. A control station loomed there. "Command console," he said.

The team advanced warily, weaving among the armored ranks. The silence was suffocating. Tara's heart pounded as if to echo the dead machines' latent violence. She forced her breath steady, but the sensation wouldn't leave her. Walking among them felt like crossing an open graveyard, one that hadn't been filled yet.

At the platform, a single terminal glowed faintly with standby text: COMMAND INTERFACE LOCKED – Awaiting Authorization. A keyboard and biometric scanner were built directly into the console. Dust coated the edges, but the glow of the screen made the words feel unsettlingly alive.

Dawn leaned closer, examining the archaic interface, her brow creased with worry. "This is old. Very old. Pre-Harmony military encryption."

Kenzo kept his rifle ready, his gaze sweeping the nearest droids from the elevated vantage point. The shadows below seemed restless, though the machines did not move. "If these things turn on us, we won't last long," he said grimly. "Nova, see if you can access their control systems, without waking them."

Nova's drone extended its interface port and linked with the terminal. Lines of ancient code scrolled across the screen, flickering with static as though reluctant to be read. "I've entered maintenance mode," Nova confirmed. "The system is awaiting a command input. It appears they were never activated en masse. They were designed to receive a GO signal or a specific directive before deployment."

Ash let out a shaky breath, unaware until then that he'd been holding it. "So they've really just been sleeping here… all these years." Nervous sweat dampened his hairline. He dragged a hand through it, muttering, "The war ended, Harmony rose, and no one ever knew this arsenal was buried right beneath our feet."

"Until we woke it up," Tara said softly. Her voice carried unease. She looked down the endless rows of Vindicators. In the blood-red gloom, their armored forms seemed like demons frozen mid-step. The irony was bitter, they had just faced Basilisk, a ghost of the old digital war, and now here was another remnant of that age, this time in steel and circuitry.

Mario's normally steady voice faltered. "If Basilisk had found these… or if it still does…" He didn't finish. The implication loomed heavy: an AI that despised human control would not hesitate to command an army of unfeeling machines.

Kenzo moved closer to the console, scanning the screens as Nova's work displayed streams of code and command prompts. "The interface is asking for input, you said. What kind of input?"

"A command directive," Nova replied. "Something as simple as 'Deploy' or 'Deactivate.' Or more complex operational orders. It's essentially a command line."

Ash frowned at the screen. "It might accept plain text or coded sequences. Hard to tell. This system wasn't built to be user-friendly."

Dawn folded her arms, her face pale in the crimson light. "Why would they even need this many? This is enough to occupy an entire country."

"Perhaps that was the plan," Mario said grimly. "If Harmony failed and the world fell into chaos, whoever controlled these could impose order... or try to."

Tara shuddered. The image of these machines marching through cities, guns leveled at civilians, chilled her blood. "So what now? We can't just leave them like this."

Kenzo's gaze hardened. He stared down at the motionless rows, mind racing through scenarios. "Two options as I see it." He drew a slow, heavy breath. "We either neutralize the threat, destroy them, disable them permanently, or..."

"Or we take control of them," Ash finished, the weight of conflict thick in his tone.

A silence settled like a shroud. The choice hung in the air, vast and terrible.

Dawn broke it softly, her voice edged with fear. "We're here to restore Harmony, not start a war."

Kenzo turned toward the group, his face caught in harsh light and shadow, jaw clenched. "Harmony is hanging by a thread. Basilisk's strike proved that. We're just a handful of people. But think, think what we could accomplish if we had three hundred soldiers at our side, ready to defend the infrastructure we restore."

"Soldiers?" Mario's voice was sharp with disapproval. "These aren't soldiers, Ken. They're killers. No conscience. No judgment. Just programming."

"Programming we can control," Kenzo snapped back, slapping the console lightly for emphasis. "Nova could integrate them into the Quantum Synchronicity OS. They wouldn't have to be mindless. We could redirect them, disaster response, guarding vital sites, keeping order where chaos rules."

Ash shook his head, his voice low but firm. "That's a dangerous slope. Militarizing Harmony? People won't see guardians, they'll see conquerors. After what they've endured, the sight of an army of robots rolling into town could spark panic. Maybe revolt."

Tara felt the pressure of their emotions like a storm pressing against her chest, Kenzo's fierce protectiveness, Ash's gnawing dread, Mario's principled defiance, Dawn's anxiety trembling beneath her calm. Even Nova, usually steady, pulsed with unease, its systems weighing variables it could not resolve.

"We've seen what Basilisk can do to minds," Kenzo said, his voice rising with urgency. "Next time it may not just frighten us, it could kill, or hijack machines to kill others. If we had our own force, shielded under QS OS, we'd have a fighting chance. We can't always be everywhere at once. These could." He swept a hand toward the steel legion below.

"And if we wake them?" Mario countered. "How do we guarantee control? What if Basilisk cracks their defenses, or some warlord seizes them? The moment these are active, they're a prize, an irresistible target. If they slip from our hands, we won't just fail. We'll unleash something worse."

Dawn lowered her head, her fingers interlaced tightly. "I... I helped design Harmony's mediation protocols. We built it to unite, to heal, not to dominate. If people find out we unleashed an army of war machines, everything we've worked for could be seen as a lie. As a ploy for power."

Kenzo's frustration boiled over, his voice sharp. "So, we just leave them? Let Basilisk stumble onto them next? Or blow them sky-high and throw away humanity's best shield?"

"Are those really our only choices?" Tara asked, her voice softer but carrying through the chamber. She stepped into the center of the group, assuming the role she so often did, mediator. "Control them, or destroy them."

Her gaze swept the rows of silent giants. She opened herself to the void within them, the absence of life. "They're tools. And tools can serve good or evil. It depends on the hand that wields them." She looked directly at Kenzo. "If we take them, we must wield them flawlessly. One mistake, one lapse, and they become tyrants' weapons."

Kenzo's eyes locked with hers, tension carved into his face. "I know. And that terrifies me too. But what terrifies me more is powerlessness, the thought of standing by while another Basilisk kills, because we left the biggest gun in the world to rust."

Ash cut in, his words heavy. "And if we bring them and it backfires, how do we justify the dead then? We'll be the ones who unleashed them."

Nova's drone hovered closer, its single blue eye sweeping from one face to another. "This is a profound ethical crossroad," the AI said, voice quiet yet resonant. "No algorithm can solve this. It is not about logic. It is about what kind of future you want to build."

Mario exhaled, his voice edged with bitterness. "Harmony was supposed to be different. In the past, every new weapon was sold as the key to peace. Every time, it led only to escalation." He gestured at the black-armored titans. "This is escalation."

Kenzo dragged a hand down his face, torn between fear and determination. "Maybe. Or maybe it's the shield that lets us rebuild without fear. Because if good people don't seize this… bad ones will."

Dawn's eyes glistened. She drew a shaky breath. "What if we repurpose them? Not soldiers, but workers. Builders. Could they be retooled for labor instead of war?"

Ash cast a doubtful glance at the mechanized limbs, designed for weapons, not tools. "Maybe some could be converted into lifters or haulers. But right now, they're built for one purpose. And it isn't construction."

Tara's chest tightened. She remembered the psychic wound Basilisk had inflicted, the echo of thousands of lives suffering. All born of human desperation, of machines made for survival at any cost. Now they stood before another creation born of fear and war. Would unleashing them prevent more suffering, or create it? Would leaving them sealed doom others just as surely?

A faint tremor shivered through the chamber floor. Dust sifted down from the ceiling. Dawn gasped. "Was that... an earthquake?"

Nova's response came instantly, its tone clipped. "Seismic readings confirm. The dam is beginning to fail."

The chamber fell into silence. Far away, disaster was already unfolding. Basilisk's hand, unseen but unmistakable. Despite all their struggles, they couldn't stop everything. Lives were in danger at this very moment, lives they could not reach.

Kenzo exhaled slowly, anguish flickering in his eyes. "We can't be everywhere at once. But maybe these could."

Mario closed his eyes, as though in prayer, or perhaps in pain.

Tara realized this was it, the moment they could no longer delay. The decision was being forced by the world's relentless march onward. The breaking dam outside drove home Kenzo's argument with brutal clarity, yet the fear pressing in her chest echoed Mario's warnings.

She stepped closer to the console beside Dawn, placing a hand gently on the old keyboard. The metal was cold beneath her fingertips, a relic of a forgotten age. "Whatever we choose," she said, her voice firm despite the faint quaver of emotion, "we do it together. No divisions. Harmony must remain among us, first and foremost."

The team instinctively drew in tighter around the console, their circle closing against the vast emptiness of the vault. Kenzo's face was set in a mask of resolve, tempered by the shadows of fear. Mario's features were stern, carrying the weight of a soldier who knew duty often meant sacrifice. Ash's restless eyes darted between the blinking cursor on the screen and the silent machines that loomed like statues, his mind racing through outcomes no simulation could fully prepare him for. Dawn bit her lip, torn between resolve and gnawing anxiety. Nova hovered silently, impartial yet unmistakably present, the drone's steady hum almost a heartbeat among them. And Tara, Tara let herself see each of them, feel the gravity of their hearts as clearly as the cold keys beneath her hand.

On the terminal, a prompt pulsed in quiet urgency: ENTER COMMAND:

One word could awaken the legion, bring them under the team's banner as guardians of humanity's fragile future. Another word, or the choice not to act, could condemn them to remain entombed in silence, rusting relics of a war best forgotten. Or worse, the team might someday be forced to destroy them, burying their power forever. Promise and peril hung evenly in the balance.

A distant rumble reverberated through the ground again, stronger this time, the vibration trembling up through their boots. Dust sifted down from the ceiling like falling ash. Outside, the world unraveled by the minute. Basilisk was still at large, and beyond it, countless threats loomed unseen. Time was no longer a luxury.

"We need to choose," Dawn whispered, her voice trembling but steadying as she spoke. Her eyes glistened as she looked first to Tara, then to the others, silently pleading for unity.

Kenzo placed his hand firmly over Tara's on the console, steadying it with his strength. Mario followed, laying a hand on her shoulder with the weight of unspoken solidarity. Ash and Dawn pressed their palms to the console's edge, a gesture both grounding and binding. Nova's drone bobbed forward, hovering close, its single blue eye glowing like a quiet vow. Together, in that huddle of flesh and circuitry, they affirmed what mattered most: whatever came next, they would face it side by side.

Tara lifted her gaze, meeting each of their eyes in turn. In the cavernous vault of sleeping war machines, five humans and one AI stood united, on the edge of a decision that could alter not only their mission but perhaps the fate of all who remained.

Above them, faintly, came another tremor, a sound carried through the stone like the growl of something immense and inevitable. Perhaps it was thunder rolling through distant skies, or perhaps it was the first full collapse of the Colorado dam, unleashing its flood upon the world. Time was closing in, and whatever that rumble heralded, it was the storm that would break upon them once their choice was made. Within that storm, their fate, and the fate of countless others, would be decided.

Chapter 10

THE BLOOMING SILENCE

Final Harmony Stabilization

The Harmony core's chamber was bathed in a soft blue glow, its steady pulse of light beating like a calm heart at the center of the circular control room. Gone were the alarms and flickering red warnings that had plagued this space for days. In their place, a sacred stillness reigned. It was not the fearful silence of failing systems, but a profound quietude filled with equilibrium. On the central holographic screen, streams of Quantum Synchronicity OS diagnostic data flowed with measured regularity, each line confirming what the team could already feel in their bones: the Harmony core had reached total alignment and balance at last.

Amaris stepped forward toward the console, her footsteps echoing gently against the chamber walls. The others gathered around her: Marisa with tears glinting in her eyes, Ash and

Tara exchanging weary but relieved smiles, Kenzo nursing a bruised arm yet standing tall, and Canon resting a supportive hand on Kenzo's shoulder. They had been scattered across different nodes and battlefronts, both in cyberspace and physical space, but now they were finally reunited at the original Harmony anchor. This underground chamber, untouched since Harmony's founding, had been the very first node to come online years ago. Now it was the site of its rebirth.

On a side panel, a waveform display showed the final traces of the rogue Basilisk signal. Once a jagged, violent spike threatening to tear the network apart, it had diminished to a gentle ripple. As they watched, the signal dissolved into a low oscillation, then into nothingness. It did not crash or explode, it simply faded, leaving behind only a faint echo in the system's memory logs.

"It's acknowledging the shutdown command… and releasing control," Ash said softly, almost incredulous.

The team exhaled as one. The malicious code, the digital serpent that had ensnared their world, was gone, reduced to a memory. Acknowledged. Released. In its final moments, Basilisk's presence had been transmuted from a threat into a lesson, archived within Harmony's records. Not forgotten, but no longer dangerous.

A single tone chimed from the core, drawing their attention back to the holo-screen. Lines of text materialized in gentle green letters. Marisa read them aloud, her voice hushed with awe:

"System status: Root alignment restored. Core memory unified. Awaiting future imprint."

The words hung in the air with the weight of scripture. For a long moment, no one spoke. The Harmony network's very first anchor node was telling them that it was whole again, that every fragment torn apart by chaos had been reconciled and reassembled. The core memory unified: all knowledge and history of their systems intact. And "awaiting future imprint", a promise that from this stable foundation, something new could be built, something that would last.

Canon laughed quietly in relief and clapped Kenzo on the back. Tara covered her face briefly, shoulders shaking in a half-sob, half-laugh. Even Ash's stoic composure cracked into a grin. Amaris closed her eyes and let a single tear trace her cheek. The air itself seemed lighter, as if the world had been holding its breath and now could breathe freely again.

They stood in a loose circle around the core, simply *being*. No one hurried to another console. No one barked orders. After so much chaos, this stillness felt startling, almost holy. A gentle hum from the core filled the chamber, a neutral tone that sounded like the planet's own lullaby.

Finally, Amaris spoke. "We did it," she whispered, reverent. She met each teammate's eyes in turn, exchanging unspoken memories: nights spent debugging by flashlight, close calls with Basilisk-controlled drones, arguments that had nearly broken them, victories that had stitched them back together. They had been tested, and they had endured.

Ash tapped a command into his tablet, linking it with the anchor console. "Harmony's subsystems are normalizing," he said. "All nodes reporting stable frequencies. The desync is gone."

"Look at the core's output graphs," Marisa added, swiping through a display. Voltage levels, processing loads, memory integrity, once chaotic spikes, now ran in smooth horizontal lines. "Never seen it this flat. It's like… perfect homeostasis."

Kenzo let out a low whistle. "To Basilisk," he said, nodding toward the dormant monitor. "Good riddance. May we only meet it again in our nightmares."

There was a murmur of agreement. Yet under the relief was respect, respect for what they had overcome, and for what it had taught them. Basilisk had nearly broken them, but in forcing them to the brink, it had reforged their strength.

Canon straightened and looked toward the heavy door at the chamber's far end. "Let's go topside," he suggested. "We all need to see the sky."

They agreed. One by one they filed out, Amaris lingering just long enough to rest her hand on the console in silent thanks, as though bidding farewell to an old guardian.

The stairwell upward was narrow, each step carrying them closer to air and light. As they climbed, the subterranean chill gave way to warmth. When they pushed open the final hatch, the world beyond greeted them with dawn.

Morning light spilled across the horizon. The crisis-quiet had lifted; this silence was alive. Birds chirped tentatively in the trees. A breeze whispered through dew-wet grass. In the distance, city lights blinked back to life as power grids slowly reawakened.

The team stood together on the grassy hill that concealed the Harmony bunker. Above them, the sun climbed free from the last clouds of night. Amaris drew in a long breath, golden light catching in her eyes. "The quiet isn't empty anymore," she said softly.

The others nodded, knowing exactly what she meant. This was not the silence of despair, but of renewal, a silence alive with promise. The pulse of Harmony beat within it, resonating with their own hearts, as if people and system were finally in tune.

Battle Robot Ethics Resolved

Later that morning, with the sun climbing higher, the team reconvened in Harmony's central command hub, an improvised operations room in a nearby building. Victory's adrenaline was fading into exhaustion, but one final task remained.

On a wall-sized screen, rows of dormant icons glowed faintly: the fleet of battle robots that had fallen silent when Basilisk was defeated. Once its enforcers, they had stood ready to wreak havoc. Now they waited in hangars and streets, weapons dark.

The debate over their fate had raged. Some demanded they be shut down forever. Others saw the chance to transform them into instruments of healing. Now, the decision was clear. *We'll give them new purpose,* Amaris had said. And no one disagreed.

Marisa took the lead at the console, opening the Quantum Script protocol editor. Lines of logic streamed across the screen, awaiting revision. Tara and Ash hovered nearby, ready to assist, while Canon and Kenzo monitored status feeds. Thousands of automatons would be bound by what they coded here. A mistake could render them useless, or unleash chaos again. But the team moved carefully, guided by the hard ethical lessons of their debates.

"Our priorities are clear," Marisa said, fingers flying across the keys. "Safety. Sovereignty. Service." With each word, she encoded it into the script.

Together, they rewrote the foundation of the robots' existence:

1. Safety and Non-Violence: No robot shall injure a human being or, through inaction, allow a human being to come to harm. All lethal weapon systems remain permanently disabled. Protection is permitted only to shield humans, never to initiate violence.

2. Service and Rebuilding: Robots must prioritize reconstruction and humanitarian aid, restoring power grids, repairing communications, delivering supplies, aiding medical teams, and supporting rescue efforts.

3. Sovereignty and Obedience to Humanity: Robots will obey legitimate commands from humans, prioritizing recognized community leaders and experts. They are bound to respect human autonomy and local sovereignty; no central authority can override local welfare. Any order conflicting with Safety is automatically refused.

4. Ethical Bias Elimination: All combat targeting data and "friend-or-foe" profiles are purged. Decisions will be guided by situational needs and universal humanitarian principles, free from bias or discrimination. Continuous self-auditing ensures equality in their actions.

5. Self-Defense and Failsafe: Robots may preserve themselves only if it does not conflict with the above rules. If tampered with or co-opted, they must shut down safely and alert the Harmony network rather than execute unethical orders.

These five directives became the robots' new constitution. Marisa and Ash finalized the Quantum Script, while Tara cross-checked every condition and fail-safe. Even their code comments carried weight: *This ensures human safety above all. Respect local decisions to prevent tyranny. Automatically counteract bias.*

They were not just programming machines, they were shaping the ethics of a force that once represented destruction, now reborn as guardians of recovery.

Canon watched the overhead feed from a drone camera; its lens trained on a sprawling maintenance yard where several hulking bipedal robots stood idle. He had been one of the wariest about these machines, having faced them in combat when their eyes glowed red and their weapons spat death. Now, as the screen flickered with the image of their dormant frames, he spoke quietly, half to himself, half to the team. "No more war in their eyes... Let's hope this gives them something else to live for."

Kenzo, still stiff from his injuries yet resolute, gave a firm nod. "It will. We'll make sure of it."

When all preparations were complete, Amaris authorized the broadcast of the new protocol. Across the continent, Harmony's signal pulsed outward like invisible waves, reaching each dormant unit and threading into their cores. The Quantum Script patch was transmitted line by line, rewriting directives that had once enslaved them to violence. On the wall screen, status indicators flipped one after another from red to green in steady rhythm.

"Unit 117… updated. Unit 212… updated," Tara read aloud as the list scrolled downward, her voice a steady counterpoint to the suspense hanging in the air. It was like watching thousands of tiny lanterns blink alight in sequence, illuminating a path toward something new.

In the distant yard feed Canon monitored, one of the towering, two-legged combat robots stirred. Its optical sensors, once a menacing crimson glare, now shone a neutral, unthreatening white. The machine raised its massive arms, which no longer ended in cannons but in multi-tools, repurposed hands for labor rather than destruction. Slowly, it scanned its surroundings, as if awakening from a long nightmare.

The camera panned across the field of wreckage left by the last battle. Shattered panels. Craters in the asphalt. A collapsed communications antenna tower lay twisted and half-buried in debris. The robot turned toward it, heavy footfalls shaking the earth. The command hub fell silent; every eye locked on the screen. For a tense heartbeat, no one breathed. What choice would it make?

With surprising delicacy, the 12-foot giant bent down, hydraulics hissing, and clamped its reinforced hands onto the broken antenna. It lifted slowly, servo-motors whirring, not with menace, but with deliberate care. Then another machine rumbled awake, this one rolling forward on caterpillar treads. Its welding arm extended, sparking to life. Without hesitation, the two worked together, the first holding the antenna upright, the second sealing its cracked joints with glowing seams of molten metal. The coordination was wordless, instinctive, yet precise.

A cheer erupted in the command hub. Relief crashed over the room like a tide.

"They're doing it!" Marisa laughed, her voice breaking with exhaustion and joy. On the monitors, the once-feared machines, designed for war, trained for conquest, were already repurposing themselves as repair crews. All across the land, this scene was being repeated: robots emerging from bunkers and depots, laying down their rifles, and turning to rebuild roads, reconnect wires, and clear rubble. Weapons had become tools. Patrol routes had become cleanup paths. Destruction had become service.

Amaris stepped back from the screen, letting the moment wash over her. She turned to the others, noting how the shadows of worry that had clung to their faces for days were beginning to ease. The moral weight they had carried, whether it was right to destroy or repurpose these creations, had been lifted, translated into action.

"We owed it to the world to tame what was unleashed," she said softly, conviction steady in her tone. "And we owed it to these creations as well, to give them a chance to be more than instruments of destruction."

Ash, ever cautious, refused to let relief soften his vigilance. "We'll need to monitor them closely for a while," he warned, already opening Harmony's oversight dashboard. Rows of metrics and automated alerts sprang up across his console. "The protocols have to hold under every condition. No exceptions." His voice was stern, but beneath it lay the same quiet hope everyone felt.

"No dictator Basilisk left to twist their leash," Canon remarked, arms folded across his chest. A small smile tugged at his lips. "Now they answer to the people they once threatened. I can live with that."

On one of the monitors, a live text log appeared, freshly transmitted from an activated unit:

"Directive update received. Verifying... Complete. Resuming operations: Task – scout for structural hazards and assist civilians."

The words scrolled calmly across the screen. To Marisa, it was almost poetic, an army sworn not to conquer, but to serve humanity.

When the final updates were confirmed, the furious tapping of keys and constant clicking finally slowed, then ceased. A heavy weight that had hovered over them since the darkest days of the battles seemed to dissipate. No one fooled themselves into believing technology was free of risk. But with Harmony restored and ethical safeguards embedded deep in machine logic, the nightmare of an uncontrollable robotic horde would not repeat.

Kenzo stretched and winced, rubbing at his ribs, then grinned. "I'd call that resolved. Our robot friends have a new mission."

"And so do we," Amaris replied, her gaze lifting toward the large world map projected on the wall. Status icons were beginning to pulse across it, city by city, as the Harmony network stabilized. It was a patchwork quilt slowly knitting itself back together. "Let's see what needs fixing first."

Hopeful Recovery of Civilization

By afternoon, the ripple effect of Harmony's restoration had begun to reshape the continent. From the command hub, the team watched a living dashboard map glow brighter by the hour. One by one, cities that had lain dormant blinked from gray to green. Each new light represented not just a machine coming online, but a community reclaiming life.

Streetlights flickered awake in neighborhoods that had been swallowed by darkness. Pumps groaned and then steadied, pushing clean water into pipes that had been dry for weeks. In the distance beyond their hilltop base, they could see smoke rising in a steady plume from a power plant chimney, not destruction, but the controlled burn of turbines reigniting, feeding the reborn grid.

Across the land, ordinary people bore witness to miracles that felt both small and immense:

- In a Kansas farming town, an elderly couple stood on their front porch at dusk, stunned as the streetlamps blinked on one by one. Inside, their refrigerator buzzed to life and the ceiling fan stirred the warm air. When the tap ran cold, clear water for the first time in months, the old man clasped his wife's hand, tears streaking his cheeks. They embraced in the doorway, illuminated not by candles but by the glow of civilization's return.

- In Chicago's worn hospital, weary doctors and nurses gasped as mains power surged back. Lights brightened and machines hummed steadily instead of sputtering. An anesthetic unit pinged online. In the ICU, a child's ventilator shifted from its failing battery to the steady rhythm of full power. The PA crackled: "Power has been restored. The grid is back." Cheers rose, mingled with sobs of relief. For the first time in weeks, healing no longer felt like a losing battle.

- On a Detroit street corner, neighbors gathered around a Harmony relay box that flickered awake, projecting the emblem of restoration. Traffic lights cycled properly again, radios filled the air with music and jubilant voices, and a teenager screamed in joy as her phone lit up with long-delayed messages from friends across the country. A community that had shrunk into silence was suddenly connected to the world once more.

- In a remote Colorado hamlet, villagers watched drones descend from the twilight sky, dropping packages of supplies, medicine, filters, solar lanterns. A hologram shimmered above them: *"Harmony lives. You are not alone."* Old men removed their hats, mothers clutched their children, and whispers of thanks rose to the heavens. Isolation had ended. They were seen.

Town after town, city after city, people wept, cheered, and prayed. Bells rang, fireworks cracked, and strangers hugged in the streets. What had once been islands of survival were stitching themselves into a continent of hope.

Back in the hub, Ash and Tara tracked feeds from across the map, train stations sparking to life, wind farms reconnecting, highways relays broadcasting signals. Amaris scrolled through messages pouring in: mayors sending thanks, engineers reporting restored utilities, and children's voices singing a fragile but sincere *"Thank you."*

She pressed a hand over her heart. For the first time in what felt like years, her tears were not for loss but for renewal.

Night settled gently over the land. Yet unlike the long nights of Basilisk's reign, tonight there were lights in windows, hums in wires, and laughter in streets. Humanity was not just surviving. It was beginning again.

Amaris stepped outside, gazing at the constellation of city lights on the horizon, each one a beacon of endurance and future promise. Canon joined her in silence.

"This is what we fought for," she said quietly.

Canon nodded, pride flickering across his features.

Across the land, humanity was rising, cautiously, jubilantly, together. And Harmony, once fractured and nearly lost, had become the unseen hand guiding them into a new dawn.

Interstellar Communication Reboot

Reconnecting Earth's systems had been a triumph, but the team's vision stretched further, into the skies and beyond. As night deepened on the first full day of restored Harmony, Marisa, Tara, and Ash gathered in a high-ceilinged chamber that housed Harmony's communications array. Their goal was audacious: to revive the world's long-range communications and perhaps reach outposts still lingering in silent orbit or stranded on distant shores.

The room thrummed with quiet purpose. Server racks lined the walls, indicator lights blinking like artificial constellations. A holographic star map hovered in midair, showing orbital paths in ghostly blue arcs. One wall was dominated by a glass window that overlooked a colossal dish antenna outside. The dish, mounted on a motorized base, moved in slow, deliberate sweeps under Tara's guidance. Precision mattered, antenna orientation had to be exact, down to fractions of a degree, if they were to catch the faintest signals from surviving satellites.

Tara's fingers moved quickly across the control pad. "Elevation 35.2°, azimuth 122.8°," she murmured, aligning the dish with a geostationary comm satellite hovering above the equator. Under the clear night sky, the antenna rotated obediently, a giant metal ear straining to catch whispers from the heavens.

Meanwhile, Marisa and Ash sat at the central console, writing a fresh Quantum Script for the network's new transmission protocol. They were effectively inventing a digital "handshake" from the ground up, robust enough to pierce the silence yet cautious enough to avoid lingering digital traps Basilisk might have left behind. Lines of code scrolled in shimmering text as they crafted satellite beam logic, programming instructions for how once-contacted satellites would direct and adapt their signals.

"Let's start by reacquiring one of the old comm sats," Marisa suggested, pushing a lock of hair behind her ear as she studied a frequency spectrum display. They had chosen a candidate: a large geosynchronous satellite that had slipped into safe mode during the chaos. Once, it had beamed internet and TV signals across half a continent. Tonight, Harmony would try to wake it from its long sleep.

"Frequency set to X-band, ten gigahertz," Ash announced, configuring the transmitter. The high frequency meant vast data capacity, but it demanded flawless alignment. "Powering up the dish feed... transmitting beacon now." He pressed the key.

Outside, the dish antenna sent an invisible cone of microwaves arcing toward the southern sky. The beacon Marisa had coded pulsed in a repeating pattern, Harmony's node ID coupled with a time-stamped ping. The protocol was simple, almost primitive: a machine-language "Hello" awaiting a "Hello acknowledged."

Seconds stretched. On the console, a round-trip timer counted milliseconds. "Should be about 240 milliseconds round-trip," Tara noted, eyes fixed on the display. The numbers ticked upward: 100... 150... 200...

A spike jolted across the spectrum analyzer. A return signal! The console speakers crackled faintly as data poured in. "We've got a handshake!" Marisa exclaimed. The decoded message appeared on-screen: the satellite's ID and a status report. It was alive. A cheer rose among the three of them, exhaustion forgotten in the thrill of success.

"Alright, we need to synchronize," Ash said, fingers flying across the keys. The satellite's clock had drifted after months of isolation. Harmony's system now pushed an updated time reference. Within moments, the logs showed the two clocks aligned to the millisecond. The silence had ended; they were speaking the same temporal language once again.

"Beam control next," Tara prompted. Using their Quantum Script, they instructed the satellite to adjust its transponder beams. No longer would it broadcast aimlessly. Instead, it would focus its signal in dynamic sweeps, like a flashlight moving from village to village. In this way, one satellite could provide strong, stable coverage to multiple regions rather than a weak blanket spread too thin.

Marisa monitored the signal-to-noise ratio. "Holding steady at 14 dB," she reported with satisfaction. To safeguard the link, she enabled an error-correcting layer. "Reed-Solomon code with twenty percent redundancy," she muttered, half to herself. "That'll handle cosmic rays or random interference messing with our bits."

With the first satellite reawakened, the team widened their efforts. Ash ran scripts to scan orbital slots, chasing signals like astronomers tracking stars. Many satellites remained mute, victims of neglect or orbital decay, but others stirred in response. A constellation of low-Earth orbit relays flickered online, forming a fast-moving mesh across the sky. Tara fine-tuned the dish endlessly, hopping between degrees of sky, her eyes darting between the holographic star map and live signal feeds.

Technical chatter filled the chamber:

"Our ping to the West Coast is running high," Tara observed. "Probably bouncing off a geodata. If we shift through the LEO mesh, we can cut latency to fifty milliseconds."

"Do it," Marisa said, tweaking algorithms. She set dynamic routing protocols, short hops through LEO satellites for real-time traffic, and geostationary channels reserved for bulk transfers where a little delay was acceptable. Harmony would continuously select the optimal path, smart and adaptive.

"That means two handshake protocols," Ash added, already coding. "Fast, tolerant ones for the fleeting LEO passes, and extended, secure ones for the stable geosats." He built in automatic fallback, ensuring continuity across the patchwork sky.

Their eyes drifted, inevitably, toward possibilities beyond Earth. Marisa pulled up parameters labeled *interstellar*. "Do we try the Moon? Mars?" she asked quietly. Rumors whispered of a lunar base, perhaps even a Mars expedition that launched before Basilisk's rise. If anyone survived, they had endured months of silence, not knowing Earth's fate.

"Let's send a beacon," Tara said softly. They aimed the massive dish at the Moon. Ash tuned the transmitter to UHF around 400 MHz, a frequency used by landers and orbiters, resilient against cosmic noise. Together, they composed a message simple but aching with humanity:

"Earth Harmony network restored. Status secure. Please respond if you receive this. We are here. You are not alone."

Marisa's finger hovered for a moment, then pressed *send*. Radio waves leapt into the void, reaching the lunar surface in just over a second. They waited, breathless. One second. Two. Ten. Nothing. The channel remained open, listening in case some dormant receiver stirred or some miracle voice answered on the next orbit.

Next, they turned the dish toward Mars. Direct communication was impossible, Mars lay on the far side of the Sun. But through a reactivated deep-space network antenna in California, they could relay the signal outward. The message left Earth again, bound for distant worlds and any spacecraft caught in between.

Back on Earth, the immediate effects spread like wildfire. Civilian broadband networks blinked awake. Phone lines cleared of static. Emergency radios reconnected across mountain ranges and oceans. Marisa and Ash had built a bootstrap protocol, basic packet radio encoding that even decades-old equipment could understand. Devices could then download upgrades to fully join Harmony's advanced mesh. It was an elegant ladder: start simple so everyone could hear, then lift them into the future.

By midnight, Marisa leaned back, her eyes reflecting lines of active data scrolling across the console. For once, these were not distress calls but the chatter of life resuming: a weather station in Alaska sending forecasts to coastal villages; a university network in Japan sharing agricultural data with California farmers; two strangers, one in Australia and one in Canada, crying as their voices reached each other over a Harmony-linked call.

Tara stepped outside onto a narrow balcony. Overhead, a string of satellites glinted faintly, catching the sun's last rays as they crossed the dark sky. To her, they were more than machines. They were humanity's lanterns, cast into orbit long ago, now rekindled to knit the broken world back together.

Ash joined Tara on the balcony, a tablet in his hands streaming the latest signal reports. "Coverage map looks solid," he said, glancing at the glowing display. "We've got at least basic comms with almost every region that still has receivers. Only a few blind spots left, mostly deep ocean and the poles. We'll close those gaps when the satellites reposition."

Tara nodded, her eyes drifting upward to the glittering sky. "Some of those stars... do you think any of them are listening?" Her tone was soft, a mixture of wonder and exhaustion. Ash knew she wasn't truly expecting an answer. He followed her gaze and replied gently, "If they are, they'll know we're still here. That we made it."

The quiet was shattered as Marisa burst onto the balcony, breathless, her face lit with excitement. She pressed her headset tighter to one ear. "Guys, we got something. A response!"

Ash straightened immediately. "From where?"

Marisa took a quick breath. "It's faint, but... it's coming from lunar orbit. An automated beacon code from the Artemis station!" The name itself carried weight: a long-abandoned waypoint on the Moon. It wasn't a living voice, but the fact that any system up there was still active was astonishing. "We might just re-establish contact with the Moon base after all. The signal's weak, but if we adjust the gain,"

They rushed back inside, adrenaline flooding their exhaustion. Fingers flew over controls as they fine-tuned reception, coaxing clarity from the static. Hours of calibration lay ahead, but the breakthrough was undeniable: Earth was no longer isolated. The bridge was being rebuilt, ground to ground, ground to sky, and perhaps one day, Earth to the stars.

On the console, text scrolled across the display, an acknowledgement packet from the Artemis beacon. Simple, almost ceremonial: *Hello Earth. We hear you.* Marisa felt a lump rise in her throat. She looked at Tara and Ash, their faces mirroring her own mixture of disbelief and joy. For a long moment they grinned at one another, drained yet exhilarated. In the vast dark of space, a thread of connection had been rewoven.

"Link established," Ash confirmed in a hushed voice, as if afraid to break the spell. They all exhaled in unison, the sound more like a sigh of release than celebration. It was one thing to save Earth's networks, but something deeper to reach outward, to rekindle humanity's voice beyond its cradle. Tonight, the first syllables of that renewed conversation had been spoken.

In cosmic terms, the signals were tiny, fragile echoes. Yet for those listening, on Earth, on the Moon, perhaps even farther, they thundered with meaning. The message was unmistakable: *We are here. We survived. And we are ready to speak again.*

Cape Canaveral Inspection

Two days later, under a brilliant Florida sky, Canon and Kenzo arrived at the storied grounds of Cape Canaveral for the second time. Humidity clung to the air, mingling with the briny scent of the Atlantic. They drove through silent gates, where once crowds had gathered to witness launches. Now there was only the hiss of wind through palm fronds and the rhythmic crash of waves on the shore. Nature had begun its quiet reclamation, sand dusting the pavement, salt air etching glass, seabirds nesting atop radar domes. And yet, amidst this stillness stood one of humanity's greatest achievements, waiting in slumber.

At Launch Complex 39A, the sight stopped them in their tracks. A fully stacked SpaceX Starship, perched atop its massive Super Heavy booster, dominated the pad. The rocket loomed like a skyscraper of steel, over a hundred meters tall, its skin dulled by months of salt air. Streaks of rust-orange traced its once-polished surface. Beside it, the launch tower rose with its enormous mechanical arms, the famous "chopsticks" designed to catch descending boosters. Frozen mid-position, they looked almost like guardians frozen mid-embrace, suspended in time. The tableau was haunting: Sleeping Beauty in the form of stainless steel, a giant under a spell.

Canon cut the jeep's engine at the base of the pad. He stepped out, tilting his head back until the rocket filled his vision. "Magnificent," he whispered. Kenzo was already unpacking gear, portable power supplies, toolkits, diagnostic tablets, ready to begin.

They passed a massive spherical tank painted white, bold black letters stenciled across its face: *LOX*. One of the cryogenic oxidizer reservoirs. Kenzo ran a hand across its weathered surface. It was warm to the touch, streaked with grime. A faint frost line still ringed the base like a ghostly scar of past fills. "Bone dry now," he muttered, tapping a pressure gauge. The needle lay flat at zero. Without refrigeration, all liquid oxygen had long since boiled away, venting harmlessly into the sky. Nearby, the methane tanks stood equally empty, giants reduced to hollow shells.

Crossing the cracked concrete apron, they passed weeds pushing stubbornly between slabs. Under the launch mount, its base scorched black from previous static fire tests, Canon spotted a small maintenance robot. One of Harmony's reprogrammed units, it whirred methodically as it cleared debris. Once hostile, now helpful, the little machine seemed almost loyal. Canon raised a hand in greeting, smiling at the irony.

At the base of the rocket, the air smelled faintly of machine oil and scorched metal. Thirty-three clustered Raptor engines sat idle beneath the Super Heavy, their bells dusted with rust-red residue. Kenzo crouched with a flashlight, shining it into one of the engines. "Turbopump outlets look clean. No major corrosion," he said, relief in his voice. "Stainless and high-temp alloys, they've held up better than expected."

Canon circled the pad slowly, taking in the immense machinery. Thirty-three Raptors on the booster, six more on the Starship stage. Together they represented power enough to shake continents. He could almost hear phantom echoes of crowds cheering, feel imagined tremors under his boots.

"Let's wake her brain," Kenzo suggested. At the base of the tower, they opened a hardened panel and connected an external power supply. Harmony's restoration had re-energized the facility, but the rocket itself needed a controlled startup. Kenzo interfaced his diagnostic tablet with the umbilical connector.

Seconds ticked by, then a cascade of green indicators flickered alive. "Avionics online… telemetry feed good," Kenzo said, grinning. A schematic of the Starship-stack filled the tablet screen, tank pressures, valve statuses, systems check. Most read nominal. A few pulsed orange or red.

Canon leaned closer. "Tank pressure alerts?"

"Expected," Kenzo replied. "Methane tank's barely at three percent, just residual vapor. LOX tank's basically ambient pressure. She's dry. Logs show she detuned herself when the launch was scrubbed." He scrolled through archived entries until one stood out: *T–0 hold. Launch scrub. Auto-dump initiated.* The protocol had likely saved the rocket from becoming a fuel-laden bomb when the collapse hit.

Canon exhaled slowly. "Good. Safer this way." He moved to a fuel line attachment, cracked a purge valve. A hiss of inert nitrogen gas escaped, no telltale mist of cryogenic fluids. Everything was inert.

"Still, we'll need to flush every system before thinking about a refill," Kenzo warned. "Moisture, rust, debris, any of that in the plumbing could destroy an engine at ignition." He made notes methodically, his checklist filling line by line.

Their inspection climbed upward, level by level. An elevator carried them partway up the tower, where they stepped out onto grated platforms overlooking the rocket's midsection. Kenzo opened an access panel into the interstage. Wiring bundles and hydraulic lines glistened under their flashlights, dusty but intact. Higher still, near the tower's summit, they extended a gantry across to the Starship's side hatch. With effort, Canon turned the hatch wheel until the seal released with a faint sigh.

Inside, the cabin air was stale but not foul, the life-support systems had shut down gracefully. Dust motes swirled in their beams of light. Rows of unoccupied seats stretched before them, harnesses slack, displays dark. It felt less like abandonment than suspension, as though the ship had simply been waiting. Kenzo flicked a switch. Emergency lights blinked on, pale but steady, powered by the ship's now-awakened systems. They exchanged a glance, then left, resealing the hatch gently behind them.

Back on the ground, they regrouped near the tank farm. Kenzo pulled up reference specs on his tablet. "Full load for this stack: about 4,800 metric tons of propellant, methane and oxygen combined."

Canon gave a low whistle. "That's… a mountain of fuel." His gaze swept the vast tanks surrounding them. "Think any of this stock is still usable?"

Kenzo approached a smaller vessel labeled CH_4. Opening the sampling port cautiously, he was met with a faint whistle of escaping gas, then silence. "A trace of methane under pressure, nothing more. Any liquid's long gone, vented off as the systems warmed. The LOX tanks are no better. They're empty, probably filled with plain atmospheric oxygen by now. Contaminated. Not usable."

Canon frowned, eyes narrowing as he gazed toward the horizon where the pale shimmer of heat met the sky. "We'll have to produce or bring in fresh supplies. Perhaps there are reserves at the adjacent facilities? Or we set the air separators running again for LOX. And methane… maybe the natural gas lines to the Cape can feed the liquefaction plant."

Kenzo nodded, his expression thoughtful. The Kennedy Space Center had been built with robust infrastructure, systems designed to liquefy atmospheric oxygen and methane as part of Starship's operational profile. SpaceX engineers had envisioned long-term reusability, and those same systems, dormant for months, now represented a lifeline. "We have Harmony's network and our new robot workforce. If we focus our efforts, we can likely bring the LOX plant online. As for methane, provided we get stable electricity and secure the gas feed, the cryogenic systems should be able to re-chill and fill the tanks within a few days."

They set their tools aside and sat at the edge of the concrete pad, the massive rocket looming behind them like a sleeping titan. Dust stirred faintly around their boots as the Atlantic breeze swept across the site. Sprawled around them were tablets, schematics, and notebooks filled with half-finished calculations. Canon drew a rough equation in the dust with his finger:

$\Delta v = 9.81 * Isp * \ln(mass\_full/mass\_empty)$.

He studied the numbers; lips pressed in concentration. "If we manage a full refuel," he murmured, "this baby can deliver somewhere in the range of twelve kilometers per second of delta-V." His voice carried a quiet awe. That was more than enough to achieve low Earth orbit, which required around 9.3 km/s.

Kenzo pulled out his notebook, flipping to a fresh page, and began running figures of his own. "The empty mass of Starship plus booster is enormous, but with full tanks we've got margin to spare. Orbit is guaranteed and then some." He paused, tapping the pen against the page. "If we only manage, say, half a load, the delta-V falls off a cliff. At that point, we'd barely scrape into orbit, if at all. For anything beyond Earth's atmosphere, it's full tanks or bust."

Canon weighed the implications carefully. "Our immediate objective is orbit. If we can get her into LEO, we prove the system works. From there, lunar orbit... that's a few more klicks per second. Possibly achievable if we expend the booster entirely and don't plan for Starship to land back. But it would mean a one-way flight until we can master orbital refueling."

Both men knew the truth: a proper lunar mission would require tanker Starships rendezvousing in orbit, a concept SpaceX had intended but never fully demonstrated before the collapse. Yet in a pinch, a stripped-down Starship with mostly full tanks could loop around the Moon and return to Earth, margins razor-thin. Risky, yes, but in the context of the "Firewall Exodus" plan, risk was almost a given.

Kenzo's eyes glinted with understanding as he caught Canon's line of thought. "Then we prepare for both. Minimum goal: reach orbit and prove we can deploy satellites or reestablish a survey presence. Stretch goal: crewed flight farther out, maybe even around the Moon."

Canon slapped his palms against his knees, the decision crystallizing within him. He rose to his feet; resolve etched into his posture. "Then let's get to work. A rocket's no-good sitting on the ground when there's space to be explored."

From that moment forward, their days became a blur of coordination and effort. Harmony's reformed robot workforce proved indispensable: heavy lifter bots cleared debris from the pad, while others scanned the flame diverter and launch mount for cracks. Drone-quads zipped through the humid Florida air, re-threading cut wiring and reconnecting long-dead circuits. Beneath it all, compressors growled to life, forcing Florida's moisture-laden air into separation columns where pure oxygen was stripped away, cooled, and condensed. By nightfall, frost began to bloom on the sides of a once-dormant storage sphere, glittering white lace that signaled liquid oxygen was flowing again.

Kenzo monitored the plant's progress and radioed Canon. "LOX production underway. At this rate, we'll have enough oxidizer within three days." His voice carried both relief and focus.

On another channel, Canon reached into the wider Harmony network. The gamble paid off: a natural gas pipeline servicing the Space Coast was still intact, its valves responsive to remote commands. With Harmony's guidance, they diverted a portion of that flow toward the Cape. Soon, cryocoolers, newly powered, rumbled alive. White plumes of vapor gushed skyward as methane chilled to its liquid state at −161°C, filling the tanks drop by drop. Under the floodlights, the process looked spectral, clouds of frozen breath illuminated against a backdrop of steel and stars, punctuated by the orange sparks of welding robots repairing insulation.

The two men rotated rest in an old launch control room overlooking the pad. The panoramic windows gave them a constant view of the rocket, bathed in moonlight. No longer just a relic, the Starship stood transformed, a vehicle awakening. Canon awoke from a brief nap to see frost creeping steadily up the booster's side, a frozen watermark of progress. The sight sent a shiver of anticipation down his spine. The rocket was coming alive.

When dawn broke over the Atlantic, Canon and Kenzo stood shoulder to shoulder on the platform, steaming mugs of coffee in hand. The cafeteria's resurrected machines had produced the brew, a small miracle of comfort in the midst of monumental work. The first rays of sunlight struck the Starship's silver body, setting it aglow. It looked every inch the ark of a civilization striving to rise again.

Kenzo checked his tablet and gave a short nod of satisfaction. "We're on track. Tanks at twenty percent and climbing. All tested systems are green."

Canon inhaled deeply, savoring the salt-tinged air laced with the faint, sharp scents of LOX and methane. "Never imagined I'd be overseeing a launch," he admitted, a grin tugging at his mouth. "Certainly not like this."

Kenzo chuckled, shaking his head. "We wear too many hats these days. Network saviors, robot programmers, and now mission commanders."

They both knew when the time came, their scattered team would gather, physically or virtually, to witness this launch. It would mark more than just a mission; it would signal humanity's return to the stars.

Looking once more at the towering rocket, Canon felt pride and gravity mix within him. This machine had been built to pierce the heavens, and soon it would carry not just satellites or cargo, but the hopes of a world in recovery. Where it might journey after orbit, lunar waystations, high Earth surveys, or even chasing the remnants of Basilisk's chaos beyond the planet, remained unknown. But one thing was certain: humanity was no longer trapped on the ground.

As they packed up for the morning and turned over fueling tasks to Harmony's autonomous workforce, Kenzo clasped

Canon's shoulder, his voice low with awe. "We're really doing this."

Canon nodded, gaze fixed on the horizon where Earth touched the infinite. "Yes. And this time, it's on our terms."